COUNTED IN BLOOD

MAGGIE SLOAN THRILLER, Book 7

JUDITH A. BARRETT

WOBBLY CREEK, LLC

COUNTED IN BLOOD

Maggie Sloan Thriller, Book 7

Published in the United States of America by Wobbly Creek, LLC

2023 Georgia

wobblycreek.com

COUNTED IN BLOOD is a work of fiction. Names, characters, businesses, places, events, locales, and incidents either are the products of the author's imagination or used in a fictitious manner. Any resemblance to actual persons, living or dead, or actual events is purely coincidental.

Cover by Wobbly Creek, LLC

ISBN 978-1-953-87036-0 ebook

ISBN 978-1-953-87037-7 paperback

DEDICATION

Counted in Blood is dedicated to the colors calico and pearl and to the wonderful people who are kind.

Previously...

My name is Maggie Sloan Ewing; my tall, blue-eyed husband is Larry Ewing; his original name was Kevin, but he's become so accustomed to being called Larry that he claims Kevin is his undercover name.

Lucy, our sweet, old, brown German short-haired pointer and my imaginary men, Palace Guard and Spike, live with Larry and me near Savannah, Georgia. Larry completed his crime scene specialist training for his new Georgia Bureau of Investigation position as an agent who investigates the technical aspects of crime scenes.

You might have noticed I mentioned "imaginary men." There's a long story behind that, but the short version is I was severely injured several years ago by a massive explosion in the library where I worked. Palace Guard and Spike helped me when I struggled with physical therapy then stayed with me after I left the hospital. Palace Guard ran with me to build up my strength and taught me how to throw a knife; Spike toughened me up and taught me how to cheat.

Lucy and Larry can see Palace Guard and Spike; I think all animals and small children can see the imaginary men. Larry and I are in good company.

My severe injury days weren't quite behind me, though; a jewel thief sprayed my face with a powerful alkaline cleaning solution, and the surgeon couldn't save my left eye. The sight in my right eye isn't all that great; I see people as blobs with my right eye except for Larry, Palace Guard, Spike, and Lucy. I wasn't slowed down, though, because Palace Guard and I worked out some signals for him to guide me when I walk or run, and he became my shooting instructor and trained me to aim and shoot with his help.

Paul Vargas, a private investigator, came to Savannah to protect me from a killer; his wife, Julie came with him. They fell in love with Savannah and stayed. The three of us created a new detective agency, Gray Flanagan Agency, named for me because I've always been the Gray Lady, and for my great-grandmother, Maggie Flanagan, who was a force back in the day. Larry and I are co-owners of the business: he's the silent partner, and I'm the advisor or maybe meddler; I'll have to check with Paul on that.

Paul's first act as Operations Director of Gray Flanagan Agency was to hire Heather, who brings her amazing talents as a former undercover detective and a technical whiz. Heather gave me a super cool walking stick that doubles as my cane and records audio and video; she told me it's modeled after the jo, which was a Japanese fighting stick, except it's my size: a petite. Palace Guard taught me some really cool moves with it.

Spike has a huge crush on Heather and is really obnoxious about it; Heather can't see Spike, but he still gets on her nerves.

CHAPTER ONE

"You're late for work, Chief," Julie said when Lucy, Palace Guard, Spike, and I strolled into the office at eight o'clock after Larry dropped us off.

"I am not, and don't call me Chief. Do we have coffee?"

"Coming right up; did you get settled in over the weekend at the old house you bought? I was surprised that you considered a four-bedroom, but I knew you and Larry wanted to be surrounded by woods out in the country, and you certainly got a great price and will have room for company. A middle-aged couple is in your office; they were parked in front of the building when I arrived this morning. I'll bring you a cup; they already have theirs."

"Is anybody else here?"

"Just us; do you want me to sit in and take notes?"

"What about the phone?" I asked.

"Nobody calls this early," Julie said as she hurried for the coffee while Spike and Lucy settled into their usual positions to guard the front door.

When Palace Guard and I went into my office, the man-blob rose from his seat. "Nice to meet you, Miss Flanagan; I'm Bob Collins, and this is my wife, Becky."

I assumed he had his hand out, so I reached in front of me with my right hand, and he shook it.

"Did you see his hand or guess, Miss Flanagan?" Becky asked.

"I guessed, Miz Collins, and please call me Maggie."

"If you'll call us Becky and Bob, I will." I heard the smile in her voice mixed with sadness.

Julie came into the office. "I'll put your coffee on your desk in front of your chair, Chief."

I glanced toward the front door, and Spike waved; he and Lucy were on guard there.

After I sat and pushed the record button on my jo, I set it on the floor next to me then held my hot cup with two hands while I waited for it to cool.

"What brings you here?" I asked.

Bob cleared his throat. "Our daughter, Vanessa, was murdered last month. The police told us..." his voice broke, then he continued, "Sorry; the senior investigator said that her torso had been mutilated and recommended that we remember her as she had been, so we identified her as our daughter when he uncovered her face in the morgue. Our local funeral director has been a good friend of mine for years, and he invited me to say goodbye before her body was cremated. He warned me in advance that her abdomen had been carved like a tree trunk; it looked like the number twelve to me."

"This weekend, I was going through Nessie's things, and I found this," Becky said.

"Becky gave me a slip of paper, Chief; it has the number twelve written in a childish style of printing," Julie said. "The other side of the paper is blank."

"I didn't say anything about what I saw to Becky until she showed me that piece of paper; I told her we had to come to the Gray Flanagan Agency with what we knew," Bob said.

"Our neighbor is good friends with the real estate agent who helped Miz Julie find your building, so we were already acquainted with you, in a way," Becky added.

"Please call me Julie."

"We're newly retired teachers; I taught biology, and Becky taught English literature," Bob said.

"I heard about another girl who was murdered, so I did a little research; I couldn't find anything that suggested the murders were related, but I think they were," Becky said.

Bob added, "Her women's intuition has been finely honed from years of teaching; sometimes I think she goes a little overboard because she's also a frustrated amateur detective."

"What was Vanessa like?" I asked.

Becky's voice brightened as she spoke. "Nessie was smart and loved the outdoors, animals, and children. She was working as a teacher's aide while she was enrolled in online education classes. She would have completed her degree at the end of this year."

"She went to work then studied in the evenings and most weekends," Bob said.

"Did she live with you?" Julie asked.

"It was the one thing we could do to help her," Becky said. "When she was twelve, she asked if she could take over the cooking on Friday nights."

Bob chuckled. "We ate box macaroni and cheese casserole with slices of hot dogs every Friday for almost a year, then she found a cookbook she liked, and our Friday dinners finally had a little more variety."

"Did she have any friends?" Julie asked.

"She never was much for large groups or parties, but she, her boyfriend Fred, and a few of their friends hiked and camped in the Georgia and Tennessee mountains two or three times a year. I'll get you their names, addresses, and phone numbers," Becky said. "Fred joined Nessie in cooking our Friday dinners last year."

"Their food wasn't too bad," Bob said.

"Their meals were delicious," Becky said.

"Were they engaged?" Julie asked.

"Not formally," Becky said, "but we all knew they were saving money so they could marry after Nessie graduated."

"What else do you have for us?" I asked.

I waited for them to speak then glanced at Palace Guard who narrowed his eyes at Bob and Becky.

"That's about it," Becky said. *She's hiding something.*

"We have a staff meeting every Monday morning to discuss our workload; I'll get back to you," Julie said.

After Bob and Becky left, Julie said, "If Paul and Heather are too busy, can this be my case? I want to find the killer and hack his heart right out of his chest."

Palace Guard nodded.

"We'll have to get you a nice knife to keep in your desk drawer in case the killer drops by."

"I'd love that; there's room for one in my bottom desk drawer where I keep my sunhat. I'll research knives after I research murders of young women over the past two years. Did you notice how Bob stared at you, Chief? I wonder if he was trying to decide whether you were really blind."

Paul rushed into the office and went straight to our meeting room; when he came out with a cup of coffee, he said, "Morning, everyone. Heather's on her way, Chief."

"We'll have a staff meeting this morning as soon as Heather gets here," Julie said.

"If we're talking about a new case, I'm ready for something more interesting than our usual embezzlers who have no imagination and are no challenge at all. I appreciate we don't accept any divorce cases, Chief, except sometimes I wouldn't mind the hectic pace of juggling several cases at once," Paul said.

Heather carried a white sack when she came into the office. "I picked up breakfast burritos for us. There were several food trucks at the hardware store, of all places. We'll have to go back for lunch."

"Staff meeting," Julie said. "I've already made coffee."

After everyone was seated around the large table that seated six comfortably, Heather passed around the sack.

"I'll unwrap yours for you, Chief," Heather said.

While we ate, Julie told Paul and Heather about Bob and Becky Collins and their daughter, Vanessa.

"This is definitely something Heather and I could work on together," Paul said. "What do you think?"

"If we can identify any of the other victims, I could profile them and go undercover," Heather said.

"There's always something that a client doesn't tell at the first meeting. Maybe I can arrange for Bob and I to have lunch or coffee together tomorrow," Paul said.

"I can ask Becky for help with something or other," Julie said. "Becky's going to send me the names and numbers of Vanessa's friends. As soon as I get those, I'll share them."

"I'd like to know who the investigator was and where Vanessa's body was found," Heather said.

"I'm keeping a list; I'll call Becky after our meeting," Julie said.

"I wonder if the Coyle Agency has heard of anything like this. I'll give Glenn a call when we're done here," Paul said.

After the meeting, I went into my office; before I closed the door, Palace Guard, Spike, and Lucy joined me.

"The three of them are perfectly capable of handling any case; I hate being the figurehead boss. Is it just me, or have I become invisible too?"

Palace Guard nodded, and Spike grinned.

"It's been ages since we've gone for a run, and the weather's perfect: not too hot or too cold; I have my running clothes in my backpack for emergencies, and this is definitely one. It shouldn't be a problem since I'm invisible, right?"

I took my backpack into my office and changed clothes. When I stepped out, Julie was on the phone, Paul and Heather were in Paul's office debating the best approach, and Palace Guard waited at the front door.

Spike and Lucy followed us when we strolled out of the office, then after I stretched, I set the pace for our warmup. Spike stayed behind with Lucy when she stretched out on the warm sidewalk.

When Palace Guard ran past me, I grumbled, "I wasn't ready, your legs are longer than mine, and it's awkward to run with my jo."

After I caught up with Palace Guard, we ran past the upscale boutiques and coffee shops then continued to the seedier neighborhood of warehouses and abandoned buildings.

"Hey, Gray Lady," a blob who sat on the sidewalk next to a building called out then coughed, and I waved.

"You got a minute?" he asked in a weak voice.

Palace Guard and I made a large circle in the street then returned to the man.

"You have to be safe," the man said.

I resisted wrinkling my nose or gagging at the sour odor that floated around the man and the foul smell from his mouth.

The man lowered his voice, and I steeled myself against the reeking odor as I knelt next to him.

"I saw this guy that lives in an apartment over one of the vacant stores take another girl up the fire escape. He was dragging her like she was dead, you know? I've seen him around here before and always get a bad vibe from him, so I stayed in the shadows. It was just like the other two girls. You just stay away from that next street. Ya hear?"

I nodded. "Okay, I will; thank you. You need anything?"

The man shivered. "If ya see a nice blanket, I wouldn't mind havin' one."

"I'll work on it. What's your name?"

"They call me Doc, but my name is Henry."

"I understand; they call me Gray Lady, but my name is Maggie." I rose, then Palace Guard and I raced back to the office.

When we went inside, I asked, "Julie, is there a thrift store nearby? I need a blanket for a friend."

"I'll be right back," Julie said.

After she left, Spike raised his eyebrows.

"She surprised me too; I guess we're in charge of the phone."

I sat in Julie's chair then propped my elbows on the desk and cupped my face while I pretended to stare at the phone. "What do I do if it rings? Just pick it up?"

Spike shook his head and pointed to the phone.

"Does it light up or something?"

Spike nodded.

"Maybe Julie will get back before it..."

Spike interrupted me with a poke then pointed at the phone.

"I didn't hear anything, Spike."

He pointed again, and I picked up the handset then pushed on the phone with my index finger where he pointed. *It must flash a light when someone calls. This is not the right phone for our office.*

"Gray Flanagan Agency." I tried to emulate Julie's calm tone.

"Is that you, Maggie?" Glenn Coyle asked. "Paul left a message for me to call. Are you doing okay?"

Glenn was my best friend's dad, and mine too, as far as I was concerned.

"Other than bored to tears, I'm fine; these people are really efficient," I said.

"I'll speak to Paul and tell him he's ignoring his slacker duties. Would that help?" Glenn asked.

I giggled. "You know it wouldn't; he'd be cranky the rest of the day."

Glenn chuckled. "Nothing throws a perfectionist into a bad mood quicker than calling them on it."

"I think our new phones have an intercom system, but I don't know how to work it."

"You'll figure it out," Glenn said.

I shouted, "Hey, Paul. Glenn's on the phone."

"Put him on hold, so we can pick up in here, Chief."

"I'm supposed to put you on hold, Glenn. I apologize in advance for hanging up on you."

Spike pointed to the phone, and I pushed where he pointed.

"Thanks, Chief," Paul said.

"Thanks, Spike; I couldn't have managed all that without you."

Spike gave a quick nod then bent down to rub Lucy's belly.

I covered my mouth to hide my smile. *I embarrassed him.*

Paul yelled from his office, "Chief, Glenn wants to talk to you. I put him on hold so you can pick up."

Spike pointed, and I picked up the handset then pressed where Spike had pointed.

"Maggie, I almost forgot: Jennifer wanted me to tell you that Ella and Moe took off Friday on short notice, and we suspect they eloped. They came into work this morning with big smiles and even more snuggly bubbly than before, and I'm not kidding. My stomach is still churning from the sight of our tough former police detective swaggering around here with a big grin on his face, and I don't think I'll ever recover from the sight of him and Ella while they nudged each other during our entire morning meeting. When Ella fluttered her eyelashes and Moe winked, I had to excuse myself for a breath of fresh air."

"I'm not sorry I missed it, but it's about time, don't you think? When do you think they're going to announce they're married?"

"It can't be too soon for me; they were annoying before, but this latest smiling, whispering, and swooning with kissy faces is worse."

When Julie returned, she dropped a quilt on her desk. "This is the softest one they had, and it doesn't have any holes. Is this what you had in mind, Chief?"

I felt the quilt. "This is wonderful; thank you. Let's go, Palace Guard; you lead."

"Wait a second, and I'll roll it like a sleeping bag, so it will be easier for you to carry," Julie said.

Julie gave me the quilt. "Put it under your arm while you run. Do you want me to run along with you? You might have to walk instead of run, though, so I can keep up."

"You can hold down the fort. I'll be fine."

Palace Guard ran at my pace. When we neared the man's spot, Palace Guard slowed then held up his hand for me to wait. He went around the corner of the building then motioned for me to join him.

The shivering blob was next to a grate that was blowing warm air. I frowned. *It doesn't seem that cold to me.*

"I brought you a blanket; are you sick?" I asked.

"It's nothing; I got a bad chill." The man broke into a wet cough that took away his breath. When he finally quit coughing, he wheezed. "I've had this cough for a couple of days." He wheezed again, and I heard bubbly gurgles from his chest. "I'm hoping it's not pneumonia."

I pulled out my phone. "Call the office."

When Julie answered, I said, "I have a sick man. Do you think Paul could take him to the hospital for me? We'll cover the bill; make sure the hospital knows that, and they'll need to clean him up."

"I'll be right there. I'll take him."

Before I could protest, she hung up. I waited on the curb until Julie pulled in and parked her car in the alley next to the man.

"Henry, we're going to take you to the hospital," I said.

"I don't have any money; they'll just evaluate me and give me some medicine then toss me out, and it's too far for me to walk back. I'd never make it."

"No, they won't," Julie said. "We found you a special grant. They'll do the right thing and won't ask you for any money."

"You're sick, Henry; I want you to go to the hospital," I said.

Henry coughed as he spoke and struggled to his feet. "You want me to go, Maggie, I'll go."

Julie and I walked him to her car and helped him into the front seat. Palace Guard and I jumped into the back, and Julie sped to the hospital. She parked at the emergency department entrance then ran inside and returned with a wheelchair.

After Henry told the registration desk his first name and said he had no address, Julie took over, and I pushed Henry's wheelchair close to the visitor's seats while we waited.

Henry whispered, "Hold this for me, Maggie. I don't want anybody to take it away from me."

I took the small paper sack he handed me. *This is pretty light; must be his smokes.* I dropped it into my backpack.

When Julie joined us, she whispered, "Henry, I'm your cousin's daughter, and your only living relative. I told them your last name is Perez, because that's my maiden name. Is that okay with you? It's the only way I can visit you because you're so sick."

"Call me Uncle Henry, Julie; that'll cinch it with the medical crowd."

"Got it, Uncle Henry."

A nurse came out of a set of double doors and called out, "Henry Perez."

"Right here." Julie pushed Henry's wheelchair toward the nurse who held one door open.

"This way, Mrs. Perez."

Julie and Henry disappeared behind the double doors.

"Henry said it was too far for him to walk; is it too far for us to run?"

Palace Guard nodded.

"I was afraid of that."

My phone rang. *Julie.*

"I called Paul; he'll pick you up in twenty minutes, so you don't have to run back to the office because I know that's what you are planning to do, but it's too far," she said.

"Thanks, Julie."

After we hung up, I crossed my arms. "I would have complained, but there are blobs headed this way, and I don't want to look angry."

Palace Guard raised his eyebrows then crossed his arms and scowled   at me.

I glared at him. "Is that what I looked like?"

When Palace Guard rolled his eyes, I uncrossed my arms then wiggled my nose to rearrange my face.

"The thing is, I found Henry and Julie took over. I should have been the cousin or niece."

A blob came out of the hospital. "Miss Perez?"

"Is something wrong with Uncle Henry?"

"No, he's settled in his room, and your sister is with him. These are his clothes and things that we removed in the emergency room before we gave him a quick shower. I was told to throw them out, but sometimes our homeless people get upset if they don't have their street clothes, so I put them in a hospital bag."

The blob put the handles of the bag into my outstretched hand. "Thank you; I know Uncle Henry will be looking for them when he's well."

The blob continued, "Your Uncle Henry reminded me of a prominent doctor I worked with for years. The doctor walked out of the hospital and never returned after his wife came into the emergency room after a terrible crash on the interstate. She didn't make it; I've often wondered if he left because he blamed himself for not being able to save her."

"My mom is a retired nurse; seems like she told me about a doctor who did that a while ago. What was his name?"

"It's been a while." The nurse shook his head. "I could have told you two minutes ago, but it's slipped my mind."

The nurse mumbled as he slowly walked back into the hospital, "This is going to bother me the rest of the day..."

Paul pulled in behind Julie's car then stepped out of his car.

"I'll be right back. I'll move Julie's car to a parking spot."

He hopped into the driver's seat and drove her car to the visitor's lot.

While I waited for Paul to return, the nurse was out of breath as he rushed out of the hospital. "Wallace. It was Doc Wallace." He took in a deep breath then exhaled. "It came to me just as I reached the elevators."

He shook his head as he went back inside. "How could I have forgotten old Doc Wallace?"

After Paul joined me and Palace Guard at his car, he said, "I didn't want to deal with a towing bill or a ticket. Julie must have been in a rush when she parked."

On our way back to the office, Paul asked, "Can you catch me up on why you and Julie were at the hospital, and who is Henry?"

I told him about finding Henry and calling Julie, and Julie's slick trick of making sure she could stay with him at the hospital.

"Sounds like there's more to Henry than just being what we'd think of as a typical old man living on the streets," Paul said.

"I think so too."

"He couldn't have a better advocate at his side, could he? Julie will make sure he receives proper medical care and is treated with respect."

Palace Guard poked my back, and I nodded. "Julie's definitely ferocious."

Paul snorted. "She likes to be in charge, but I'll bet the hospital staff knows how to manage that. Bob and I are meeting in the morning at a diner he enjoys, but Becky doesn't really like. I'm pretty sure Julie and Becky made plans too, but I don't know what they are."

"I'll check with Julie; maybe that's something I could do if she's tied up with Henry."

Paul sniffed. "What's in that bag? Henry's clothes? Pretty ripe, aren't they?"

When we went into the office, Heather said, "You have a new black sparkly patch, Chief; I love it."

I touched my eyepatch. "I didn't know I had a black one; Jennifer Coyle made me a batch of new sparkly eyepatches."

"We need to talk," Heather said.

"Let's go into the meeting room; I'll be there in a second." I took the bag into my office and stuck it under my desk.

"I'll lock the front door, so we won't be interrupted," Paul said.

After we were in the meeting room, Heather said, "Bob and Becky left out an important detail: Vanessa had Tourette syndrome. I talked to the senior investigator, and he said he'd heard that there were more related murders, but he knew of only two, and both of them had physical disabilities. He gave me their names, and we'll follow up on them."

"I was disappointed when Justin was transferred to the office in Columbus, but I'd be worried about Tonya if they were here," I said.

"Her hearing deficit would have definitely made her a target if our suspicions are right, but what about Chief?" Paul asked.

Am I suddenly invisible?

"I'm not sure; she and Palace Guard run together regularly. She can do anything anyone else can do and better, except drive," Heather said.

"We could get her a self-driving car," Paul said.

"I think you've forgotten that she's right here," I growled.

"Sorry, Chief," Heather said. "I don't like that you're a potential target, but then I remember how many criminals have made the fatal mistake of thinking they could take advantage of what they perceived as your vulnerability."

"That doesn't mean we're not worried, though," Paul added.

"I'm having lunch with the senior investigator; I plan to tell him I'm not still with the FBI, so he won't feel blindsided later. He's checking with other jurisdictions for young women with physical disabilities who have been murdered, and I'll call Moe to ask what he knows," Heather said.

After Heather left the meeting room for her office, Paul's cell phone rang, and he answered. "Hey, Julie, we're in a meeting; what's up?"

Paul listened for several minutes. "Love you, honey."

He smiled. "Julie's on her way back; while the nurse helped Henry with his shower, Julie ran to a nearby big box retail store and bought boxers, pajamas, a robe, and slippers for Henry. When she returned, he had an IV in place with antibiotics and was receiving oxygen. After the nurse helped Henry change from his hospital gown to the fresh clothes, he ate a warm meal, and now he's sleeping. The nurse encouraged Julie to leave."

"Good news."

I went to my office and closed the door. *I could have stayed with Henry and not been tossed out.*

I stared at Palace Guard who was standing in front of the window.

"We don't belong in an office, do we?"

Palace Guard turned and narrowed his eyes as he studied my face then shook his head.

"Do you suppose we could find the abandoned building with the apartment that Henry talked about?"

Palace Guard shook his head vigorously.

"Spoilsport. So, what do you want to do?"

Palace Guard turned back to the window.

"Vanessa was a teacher's aide, but we can't go hang around schools," I said.

Maybe I can do something better.

I picked up my phone. "Call Tonya."

"Hey, Maggie. Do I bring money, Kiki, or both?" Tonya asked when she answered the phone.

"I'm not in jail, but hold on to that bail money because you never know, and it would be weird if Kiki didn't come with you. I've got a case I need to talk over with you."

"Mom's at the store, and Kiki's excited; hurry up before she burns my neck. She might be a tiny imaginary dragon, but she sure can breathe out some flames."

"Move off Tonya's shoulder, Kiki, because this case will fire you up for sure; it makes me angry every time I think about it."

"Kiki moved to her fireproof mat that Mom got her, and I put my phone on speakerphone. We're ready."

"The parents of a young woman who was murdered several months ago came to the office. Their daughter had Tourette's, and it appears the investigators are stumped. They heard about two other young women with physical impairments that had been murdered too, but they didn't have any details."

"Tell me about their daughter."

"Her name was Vanessa Collins; she was a teacher's aide at school and was finishing up her coursework for her degree."

"I've known Vanessa since high school; she was a year behind me. I heard she was murdered, but the police have nothing? How can I help?"

"I'd like to know more about her friends and her boyfriend, and who are the other women who were murdered."

"Vanessa didn't have what people usually mean when they say boyfriend. Her close friend, Fred, was originally Frederica; Vanessa and Fred have been a couple for a long time. It's a little odd that Vanessa's parents didn't say anything."

"They said Vanessa and her friends went hiking and camping several times a year."

"That's true. The group goes camping regularly; usually about eight people can arrange their schedules to take one of their four-day hikes. I know several of them, and they talk about how energizing it is to be outside, but I'm not as outdoorsy as they are, so I don't appreciate how great it might be."

"I'm going crazy in this office because I'd rather be outside," I said.

"So, go. Aren't you the boss of you? Go."

"That was a simple fix; why didn't I think of that?" I asked.

"Oh, really? Are you feeling sorry for yourself or something?"

I snorted. "Who asked you?"

Tonya laughed. "Kiki's rolling on her mat because you asked me, Gray Lady."

I giggled. "You and Kiki sure make it hard for me to be irritated by everything."

"Any other character defects of yours that we need to discuss?" Tonya asked.

"Oh, hush. Back to the question of who were the other young women who had disabilities and were murdered?"

"How quickly do you want a list?"

"Truthfully? Before the end of the week, but the sooner, the better."

"Okee-dokee. I'll see you first." Tonya laughed as she hung up.

I grumbled, "She did it again, Palace Guard."

I spoke into my phone. "Send a text to Tonya: 'No you won't, because I'll hear you coming.'"

"Reply from Tonya: 'Ha. Too late. You lose.'"

Paul tapped on my door then walked in and closed it before he sat in my visitor's chair.

"What's going on with you, Maggie?"

This is not good; he didn't call me Chief.

"Nothing," I said. "I'm fine."

"No, you aren't. It's me, Maggie. You're a great liar, but I'm an old liar, and I know all the tricks."

"So, maybe I'm not fine, but I'm better. I called Tonya and asked her about Vanessa, her friends, and other young women with impairments who were murdered."

"Talking to a good friend about murder always cheers me up too. What did Tonya say?"

"She'll check on the murdered women, and Vanessa and Fred are gay."

CHAPTER TWO

"Really? I'm surprised Bob and Becky didn't say anything, but they're either still numb from grief or didn't think it was relevant. Of course, it's more than likely that it isn't, but we don't know. Maybe Bob and I will have a man-to-man discussion tomorrow; we'll see. You know, you're really brilliant, Chief; as obvious as it is, especially since Julie and I are renting her mother's house, I wouldn't have thought about Tonya as our best resource to help us find other young women with disabilities who were murdered. I'm supposed to be a hotshot detective; that's embarrassing."

Palace Guard poked me and grinned, and I rolled my eye. When Palace Guard golf-clapped, I smiled. *I'm getting better at the eye-roll thing.*

"Did you just roll your eye, Chief? What did Palace Guard say?" Paul asked.

I tried to side-glance Paul, but it must have been a backwards eye roll or something because he laughed.

I sighed. "What are you working on other than harassing me?"

"That good, huh? Way to go, Palace Guard." Paul held up his hand, and Palace Guard smacked it.

Paul grinned as he stared at his hand. "Felt it."

"I don't believe either of you. What are you working on?"

"Heather has all the good contacts, so I contacted some of my sketchier acquaintances from the old days. One of them heard of a crazed freelancer who was scaring the local community and cutting into the money of the successful, established, loosely organized kidnapping network. Ouch, terrible choice of words, wasn't it?" Paul-blob shook his head. "So, this freelancer is kidnapping young women and killing them. My friend isn't sure that the freelancer contacts the parents or appropriate purse strings, so we don't know if anyone is refusing to take the freelancer seriously or if the freelancer doesn't contact anyone, which, either way, puts the kidnappings for murder into a completely different class."

"Anything on the freelancer?"

"Not yet, but I'm digging just like you are, Chief. You're awfully young to be old school, but welcome to the old gumshoe society: the club of misfit detectives."

"I didn't know there was such a thing, but it makes sense to me, and thank you."

"You're welcome, and what's really bothering you?" Paul asked.

"I hate being in an office, sitting in meetings, and watching while everyone else works."

"I get it. Heather is a solo; she always has been. She's trying hard to be a part of the team, but we're slowing her down. We need to be a resource for her, and not a stumbling block, so she can be effective and do what she does best without supervision. I'll talk to her and let her know she can forge ahead in her own way," Paul said.

"Julie's jumping from one self-assigned task to another," I added.

"She always has; she's a hard worker, but she sometimes misses a thing or two when she loses focus."

"That reminds me, when Bob and Becky were here this morning, I asked if there was anything else, and they were quiet for a few seconds, then Becky claimed there wasn't. Becky's tone told me she was hiding something, but it's possible both of them were."

"It's not a surprise to me that Julie didn't mention that; it's the sort of detail she misses. You and I have worked together in the past. Let's get you out of the office. Go with me to meet Bob in the morning for breakfast; we can leave from the office."

"Wouldn't that put a damper on Bob?"

"It could, but it also could give us an edge. If he's being recalcitrant, you can go to the ladies' room, then he'll be under the pressure of a time constraint to tell me anything he doesn't want to say in front of you. You tag with me, and I'll tag with you. You need a driver; I need to hear your insightful, far-fetched theories, so I can consider possibilities that are outside my police detective experience. We have to stick together so we can remember that neither of us is the norm, which makes us great." Paul rose from his chair. "You have anything else for me, Chief, while I'm in a philosophical mood?"

"Other than I'd never accuse you of being philosophical? Nope."

"Seriously, thanks; I think I needed to be set straight as much as you did."

"You're good; you know that, right? What's our next move while we wait for more information that may or may not help us?"

"You rein in Julie, Chief. I'm going to take a nap." Paul went to his office and closed the door.

I stared at his door. *Did Paul just desert me?*

When Julie came into the office, she said, "What a morning; I haven't had a chance to call Becky yet."

"Do we need to hire someone to take care of the phone and office?" I asked.

"Chief, that's my job." Julie-blob sat at her desk. "Oh no; we have ten phone messages. I forgot I had turned off the ring volume on the phone when we went into our meeting."

"Before you return calls, give me Becky's number, and I'll call her; I want to talk to her myself. Then make a list of all your tasks that you can't accomplish, so I can contact an agency to hire someone to take over. We really shouldn't be locking the front door just because we're in a meeting or not answering the phone during the day."

"You are absolutely right, Chief; that is so unprofessional. We need to focus on what's important. If you need extra help with what you're doing, I say bring someone in, but I don't need any help. I can manage the office while everyone is in the field or in meetings."

"I really appreciate that, and I appreciate how much help you were with Henry this morning. It's nice to know that you'll back me up in emergencies."

"You're welcome, Chief; Henry was definitely an emergency, but I went a little overboard and lost a bit of my focus. Don't worry about the office; I've got it covered. I'll send you Becky's number."

I went into my office and closed the door as my phone buzzed with two texts: the first one was from Julie, and the message was a phone number; the second one was from Paul. I added Becky's number into my newly created phone group I named 'Clients' then listened to Paul's text.

"Knew you could do it with your usual sledgehammer diplomacy. Well done."

I giggled. "Send a text to Paul: 'I accept my prestigious award in the same spirit in which it was bestowed.'"

When Becky answered, I said, "Hi, Becky, it's Maggie."

"I'm so excited to hear from you personally. Thank you for calling me; did you know you're a celebrity for those of us who are library fans? My best friend is a retired librarian, and she and I have followed your cases since the library explosion in Harperville. She didn't really know Olivia that well, but did meet her at one of the state conventions years ago. We were horrified when we heard how badly injured you were in Columbus, but my best friend told me you would soldier on, and she was right."

I smiled. *Wait until I tell Paul I'm a celebrity; no, bad idea: he'd never let me live it down.*

"Thank you, Becky; that's so sweet of you. Is there a time you and I could get together? Maybe lunch today or tomorrow?"

"There is this cute little café that I love to go to, but Bob says it's too frilly for him. I could meet you there at noon. Wait, should I come get you?"

"No, Paul always drives me; is it okay if he eats with us? He'll be as awkward as all get-out, so he'll be very quiet and won't pay a bit of attention to our conversation, while he hopes no one notices him."

Becky laughed. "Taking one for the team, right? That's actually very kind of him to watch your back, but that's his real job, isn't it?"

"It is, but, you know, kind of keep it quiet."

"Oh, absolutely; after all the close calls you've had, I can understand how important Paul's job is. I'll text you the name of the café. Do you want the address too?"

"If you have it; otherwise, we can look it up."

I can't wait to tell Paul how important his job is.

After I received the text from Becky, I tapped on Paul's door.
"I'm busy, unless you're Chief."

I stared at the door. "If I open it, is that an admission?"

Palace Guard raised his eyebrows then nodded.

Paul chuckled as he opened the door. "I told you we weren't the norm; nobody else would have caught that. Come on in; what's up?"

"We're going to meet Becky for lunch at noon at a frilly café that she likes."

Paul groaned. "We did this in Tennessee. Can I be crass again?"

"I told Becky that you would be mortified and would hope no one would recognize you."

"That means I can wear sunglasses and a hat and pull down the brim to hide my face: works for me. I've got the perfect hat in my trunk. Can we stop on our way back to the office and pick up a burger and fries for me?"

"Only if I can order fries and a chocolate milkshake."

"Told you in Tennessee we both had a dark side."

"You were right; I'll forward Becky's text with the name of the café and the address. Come get me when you're ready to go."

"What have you got going on?"

"Something's been bothering me; we can talk on the way to lunch."

"Okay, let's go to lunch," Paul said.

"Isn't it too early?"

"We'll just ride around. Are you and Palace Guard interested in going to a gun range?"

"Always. Let's go."

"Give me a minute to make a phone call, and I'll be ready."

In my hurry to go into my office, I bumped into a tall, solid man-blob and felt a holster at his side.

"Excuse me; do I know you?" I asked.

I quickly regained my balance with the help of my jo and glanced at Palace Guard who grinned. *Good, not a bad guy.*

"My fault; you moved faster than I expected, and yes, ma'am, but you may not remember me. I'm Noah Baker; we met right before Kevin's graduation. I was with you when Della picked up the artwork from you."

"Lieutenant Baker?"

"Well, actually, it's Captain Baker now."

"Come into my office; I'm sure this isn't a social visit."

"No, ma'am, it isn't."

"Please don't call me ma'am again, Captain Baker. I've tossed FBI agents, police detectives, and dear friends to the ground for less than that." I held my breath. *Will he buy it if I pretend that was a test if he arrests me?*

Captain Baker laughed. "Got it, Gray Lady; call me Noah. Is it okay if I close the door?"

"Certainly; go ahead." I sat in my chair and raised my eyebrows as Lucy and Spike slipped into the room before Captain Baker could close the door.

"What a pretty girl." Noah reached down and scratched Lucy's ears.

Lucy dropped to her back for a belly rub, and he chuckled as he knelt next to her and obliged.

After he rose, I said, "Make yourself comfortable. How can I help you?"

As he sat in the visitor's chair, he said, "It's personal, not official. Is that okay?"

"You're stalling, Noah; there'd be no reason for you to drop in to see me for something official." I sighed. "Sorry, I think I have office fever, and I've become a little snappish."

"You were right; I lost my nerve for a second there because I was worried you weren't handling any cases yourself. I've been reluctant to share this with anyone, but when I heard you had opened an agency, I knew I could trust you."

Noah rose and began pacing in front of my desk. "I'm engaged to a wonderful, talented yoga instructor who specializes in yoga for seniors and people with disabilities; in fact, her studio isn't too far from here. I requested a transfer to the area last year so I could be closer to Sophie Rose. We have been engaged for a little over six months and have had trouble nailing down a date for the wedding because we've been trying to schedule around the families. We're seriously considering eloping, so our mothers can plan family get-togethers independently of each other after they forgive us for not having a big, costly wedding."

"I understand; we did almost the same thing. Short notice, simple wedding, and a small celebration, then we left town." I cocked my head and tried to focus to see Noah, but was unsuccessful. "Sophie Rose's clients are seniors and those with disabilities?"

"It's been a passion of hers to reach out to nontraditional yoga students. She was a backseat passenger in a crash on the highway. Her uncle was driving, her aunt was in the passenger's seat, and both of them were killed. Her leg was crushed; the surgeons couldn't save it, so she has a prothesis. She took ballet lessons for a while to strengthen her muscles then found someone willing to teach her yoga when she was fourteen."

"Not many people know what they want to do at such an early age," I said.

"She's definitely one of a kind, but I might be prejudiced."

I guessed Noah might have smiled, so I smiled.

"One of Sophie Rose's students showed her a slip of paper she found on her car a few weeks ago: all it had on it was the number thirteen. The young woman thought it was very curious, and so did Sophie Rose, who didn't tell me about it until the girl disappeared four days later."

Noah stopped pacing and sat. "I took a call late Friday afternoon about a reported body in a ditch on a little-traveled country road and found her. No one knows this, including the parents, because we're keeping details of her murder quiet, but the number thirteen was carved into her abdomen, and there were deep, repeated stab wounds in her chest."

"What was the young woman's disability?"

"Sophie told me she had a bad stutter," Noah said.

"There's more, isn't there?"

Noah exhaled and rose to pace again then stopped near the door. "Am I driving you crazy with the pacing?"

Is he going to bolt? I waited.

He returned to his seat. "Sophie Rose told me this morning at breakfast that she found a slip of paper under her car windshield wiper on Friday when she left work. The only thing on the paper was a number, fifteen. I'm thinking about taking an extended leave so I can protect her."

"Do you suppose we could tag team her protection? Does she live alone?"

"She has a two-bedroom apartment because it was cheaper than a one-bedroom, which I found strange when I first met her because she doesn't have a roommate. It came in handy because I could stay with her when I came to visit before I finally transferred here."

"Do you have your own place? I'm not being nosy; I'm trying to consider all our possibilities."

"When I moved here, I rented a house because Sophie Rose wants a dog."

"I have a couple of ideas; do you suppose we could get together this afternoon?"

"I can take some time off; Sophie's last class ends at three, so we could come by after that."

"That's great."

Noah rose. "I'd like to shake your hand, Gray Lady."

I held out my hand, and we shook.

After he left, Paul came into my office. "Your door was closed. What's up?"

I told him about Noah, Sophie Rose, and the murdered woman.

"Are you thinking we should talk to Heather?" Paul asked.

"Exactly. We're overloading our schedule today, aren't we?"

"I was complaining about not being busy, so I'm not about to say anything about our schedule. I'll contact Heather to see if she can meet us here about three. That should give us plenty of time with Becky at lunch." Paul snorted. "So much for letting Heather set her own schedule. Are you ready to go to our frilly café?"

"All I need to do is grab my coat and backpack."

"I'll let Julie know where we're going," Paul said.

When I joined him at the front door, Julie said, "Enjoy your lunch. You have a sandwich here if you need a snack later, Paul."

"Thank you; I might need it."

On our way to the café, Paul asked, "Is Palace Guard with us?"

"He's riding in the backseat."

"Thanks for going along, Palace Guard," Paul said. "I'm going to need moral support, so I don't die from cutesy overload."

"You didn't tell Julie about our planned fast food run, did you?" I asked.

"No way. She's on a healthy food kick; my idea of eating healthy is a double cheeseburger and large fries instead of a triple burger and jumbo fries."

I snickered. "Maybe the café will have potato chips."

"Don't get my hopes up," Paul grumbled as he pulled into a parking lot.

"I forgot to ask earlier. Do you have your earbud, so you can hear anything I record with my jo?"

"Sure do. We're five minutes early. Do you want to go in?" Paul asked.

"I think it's a good idea; if Becky's not here, you can pick out the best place for us to sit."

When we went into the café, Paul whispered, "I don't see her, but I see where I'd like to sit."

"Sit wherever you like," a woman called out in an almost musical voice.

I took Paul's elbow, and he led me to his selected table.

When the woman came to our table she asked, "Are you expecting more people?"

"Yes, ma'am," Paul said.

"What would you like to drink while you're waiting?"

"Hot tea for me," I said.

"Coffee; I don't need any cream or sweetener."

"I'll be right back with your fresh coffee, a pot of hot water, our tea box, and four menus."

"Thank you," I said.

"What kind of hot tea do you like?" Paul asked.

"I like peach tea, but if there isn't any, then regular tea is fine."

"Becky's here." Paul-blob waved.

"There you are; have you been waiting long? I was immersed in a page-turner of a book and lost track of time." Becky sat next to me.

"We just ordered our drinks," I said.

Our server returned with our drinks and a tea box on a tray. After she set our cups in front of us and the teas in front of me, she handed us menus. "What would you like to drink, ma'am?"

"Coffee with cream and sugar," Becky said.

While Paul looked at the menu, I asked, "What's good?"

"The lunch portions are on the skimpy side, but they are tasty. They have wraps and salads too, so it depends on what you like."

"I found a cheeseburger and fries," Paul said.

Becky tittered. "The owner told me she keeps the burger and fries on the menu because some of her ladies don't drive, and if there wasn't anything here for husbands to eat, the ladies wouldn't come here very often."

"That's smart," Paul said. "I like this place already."

"Maggie, I always have the chicken wrap; it's fantastic," Becky said.

"That sounds interesting," I said. *Interesting, but a huge potential for messy.*

"Chief, they have fried shrimp and sweet potato fries."

Paul's a genius; he found finger foods for me.

"My favorites."

Our server hurried to our table. "Have we decided?"

After we ordered, the server said, "Sir, we have a basket of magazines on the table near the back. You might find something you'd enjoy reading while you wait for your lunch."

Paul followed the server to the back table then returned to his seat. "Their selection of magazines is perfect. I found two fishing magazines I haven't read."

He opened the first one and read.

He's not reading; he's listening.

"The owner told my friends and me the last time we were here that she subscribed to some men's magazines; I'll have to tell Bob about them," Becky said. "I'm glad we're taking a little extra time to talk."

"Good; Julie's managing the office and will forward any important calls to Paul, so we won't have any interruptions."

The server brought our food. "Enjoy."

After we had eaten, and the server cleared the table and refilled the coffee cups, Becky said, "There are a few things I haven't told Bob because he obsesses over details sometimes, and I always hate to call his attention to Vanessa. I worry he resents her more than he should..."

Becky's voice drifted off, then she cleared her throat. "I'm trying to keep that under control; back to Vanessa: she was having some trouble at school. She never minded that the children sometimes mimicked her and laughed because the teacher that she worked with used those times as a teaching moment, but some parents were cruel and mocked or complained about her where she would hear them. She talked to the principal who emailed all the parents about respecting those who had disabilities, but it didn't slow down the worst of them. I heard Fred tell her she needed to toughen up, but Vanessa became furious and didn't speak to Fred for a week, and things remained strained between them in the weeks before she died. She was seeing a therapist to work on ways to minimize her uncontrollable outbursts, but their progress was slow, and the blowup with Fred really set her back. I've worried that I should have done more..."

"I'm really sorry, Becky. It must have been hard on you; I know my mother would have been worried sick."

Becky patted my hand. "I knew you'd understand."

Becky sipped her coffee. "I think Vanessa found someone who understood her because the week before she disappeared, she was staying out until three and four o'clock in the morning. She was an adult and had always made good choices, but I was still worried that someone may have taken advantage of her at a vulnerable time."

I furrowed my brow and nodded. *She still hasn't told me what she wanted to tell me.*

I kicked Paul's shin, and to his credit, he didn't flinch as he quietly rose and took his magazine to the men's room.

Now's your chance, Becky. I pushed the record button on my jo.

Becky whispered, "She and I installed tracker software on our phones long ago as a safety thing for both of us. The police gave her phone back to me. Would you like to check it? I can send you the login and pin number."

Would I ever.

"If you feel comfortable with me checking it, I'd love to," I said.

"It should go back about a month before her death," Becky put a phone on the table, and I slipped it into my backpack.

"It will be safe in my backpack," I said.

"There's one other thing that I wasn't supposed to know. She started seeing a new therapist, except she referred to him as her guide. I wonder if any of her friends would have more information about him, but I did write down his phone number when she repeated it back to him. I'll text you the number."

We sat in silence for a few moments before Becky said, "There's something that has been worrying me for a long time, but I'm probably just being silly..."

The server interrupted Becky. "More coffee?"

Becky cleared her throat. "May I have our check now, please?"

"No, ma'am. The gentleman already took care of that."

I pushed the button to stop the recording.

After the server left our table and hurried to the back, she whispered, "The older lady just asked for the check, sir."

"Thanks, here you go."

He tipped her for being his lookout.

Paul sauntered back to our table as Becky rose.

"Thank you so much for lunch, Paul. I enjoyed it very much."

After Becky left, Paul asked, "Did everything go well?"

"Very; I'm ready when you are."

Paul, Palace Guard, and I left the café.

As Paul pulled onto the road, he said, "The food was good, but I need a vanilla shake. Do you want a chocolate milkshake?"

"Absolutely. What do you think about what Becky told me?"

"Becky's been worried about Vanessa for a while, but she hasn't discussed any of it with Bob, which surprised me because of how Julie described them this morning; I'd like to know what she was going to say before she was interrupted," Paul said.

Palace Guard nodded.

"Palace Guard agrees. Do you think we'll hear the same thing when we meet with Bob in the morning?"

"I would have said no earlier, but now I have no clue. Unfortunately, I didn't have my earbud turned on this morning; I'm going to listen to the recording when we get back."

"We'll turn the phone over to Heather when we get back." I slurped the last bit of my milkshake.

"It's a little after one o'clock, so I have time to listen to Bob and Becky from this morning. What are you going to do?" Paul asked.

"I can research the phone number of Vanessa's new guide. I thought Becky was going to send me a list of Vanessa's friends;

maybe she sent them to Julie. I'll check with Julie. If she didn't, I'll call Becky for the names and numbers and ask her if she's talked to Fred since Vanessa's death."

CHAPTER THREE

After Paul parked at the office, the three of us went inside. Lucy raised her head, and I hurried to her and stroked her face.

"Missed you, sweet girl," I whispered.

"Thanks for lunch, Chief," Paul said.

"I'll take the receipt," Julie said. "I assume you included Becky's meal too."

"Sure did. Here's the receipt. I don't have a receipt for a tip though. It was twenty dollars cash," Paul said.

"I'll send you a statement to sign then reimburse you from our miscellaneous expenses," Julie said.

Paul hurried to his office.

I rose, and Lucy closed her eyes. *Julie is really in her element with this accounting stuff.*

"Julie, did Becky send you the list of Vanessa's friends?" I asked.

"Yes, I got it just a couple of minutes ago. Do you want me to follow up with them?"

"No, I'd like the list, so I can do it myself."

"I'll forward it to your email." Julie's voice had a tinge of disappointment.

"Julie, I can't tell you how much I appreciate you for taking care of the finance side of the house. You really do an outstanding job of staying on top of all the details," I said.

"What? This stuff is easy."

"For you, maybe, but I'd close the office tomorrow if I had to take care of it. You definitely fill a critical role for the agency."

"I do? Thank you." Julie-blob rose from her chair and hurried to the meeting room.

"Was it something I said?" I whispered.

Palace Guard rolled his eyes.

After we went into my office, my phone buzzed the text from Becky with the phone number of Vanessa's guide. I turned on my laptop and searched for the number.

"I keep coming to a dead end, Palace Guard; maybe this isn't a phone number at all, which makes it even worse."

I pulled out Vanessa's phone. *I wonder if there are any answers here.*

"What's your impression, Palace Guard? Did Becky hold anything back that we don't already know?"

Palace Guard shrugged.

"I don't know, either, but I don't believe we heard the full story of Vanessa and Fred."

Palace Guard nodded.

When Julie sent the list of Vanessa's friends to me, I forwarded the email to Paul. *I'm not sure I have the energy to research these. I'll talk to Paul.*

Paul stopped by my office door. "I got the email you forwarded to me. Did you want me to take these?"

"I think I do because I want to focus on that phone number for the guide. I'm not certain 258-9623 is a phone number, which sends off explosions in my mind."

"You're the right one to chase it down if it has gotten under your skin. Let's go into the meeting room; Heather's on her way."

Heather came into the office dressed in all black. "I felt like being goth this morning and have had a great day. What's going on?"

"You can listen to the recordings at your leisure or for bedtime listening pleasure, but here's a quick update of what I know." Paul gave her a quick summary of the meeting with Becky.

"There are a quite a few holes there, aren't there? What do you want me to take on?" Heather asked.

"I have a little something to add." I told her about Noah Baker, Sophie, and Sophie's yoga student.

"You win, Chief. I'm a total slacker. This simple investigation just exploded. What do you want me to do?" Heather asked.

"We need to toss around some ideas; it seems to me we have old cases we can use to profile the killer and the victims, but we also have the unique opportunity of knowing who the next victim, or the one after that, of the killer will be."

"You're the obvious one of the three of us to become one of Sophie Rose's students," Paul said. "We need to know her schedule. I'll start a list; I'm not the greatest list-maker, but I've learned from the best. After we decide what we want to do, I'll turn over my notes to Julie, so we'll all have a copy."

"Noah would make things simpler for us if he could convince Sophie Rose to move to his house," Heather added.

"Actually, you're right. If one of our goals is to provide twenty-four-hour protection for Sophie Rose, it would be helpful if we could count on Noah covering some of that time," Paul said.

"Add it to our notes because we don't want to lose that thought," I said.

"We absolutely need Sophie Rose's schedule," Heather said. "Chief, you were a volunteer at a Senior Center; maybe you could volunteer as a helper with Sophie Rose's classes for the seniors."

"Added," Paul said. "So far, it sounds like we're suggesting you attend all the classes, Chief. Are you okay with that?"

"I think so; I wonder if Sophie Rose runs in between classes? I wouldn't mind having a second running partner."

"I added her daily routine to our list then drew an arrow to her schedule," Paul said.

"I wonder how reliable Noah's schedule is. We assumed he would be home at night, but how often do his hours fluctuate from his schedule?" Heather asked.

"I would think fairly frequently, but we do need to have an idea of how much at least, so we can plan." Paul wrote on his notepad.

"Let's shift," I said. "Noah and Sophie Rose will be here sometime after three. How do we want them to help?"

"I'd like for Sophie Rose to become a harder target to track," Heather said.

"It would be easier on my nerves if Noah can stabilize his schedule, at least for a while," Paul said.

"I'd like to know who is investigating the yoga student's murder because Noah or I may have the contacts to help us," Heather said.

"This is a little different because Captain Baker will be a great asset to our team; we'll have to protect him from looking like he's involved, though," I said.

"Absolutely; my undercover methods aren't necessarily standard procedure," Heather said.

"We've got a little time before Noah and Sophie Rose are here. I'm going to follow up with Vanessa's friends," Paul said. "Heather, could you listen to the recordings from Chief's meeting with Bob and Becky this morning then the lunch meeting? You might catch something we missed in our summaries."

"After Noah and Sophie Rose leave, if we don't come up with any tasks that require immediate action, I'd like to visit Uncle Henry in the hospital. Paul, I'd like Heather to take me because Uncle Henry seems to be partial to girls," I said.

"That's a good idea because I won't have to explain to Julie where we're going then tell her to ask you why she can't go," Paul said.

Palace Guard grinned, and I smiled. "I knew I could count on you to understand."

"You'll explain to me later. I have recordings to listen to before our meeting." Heather left for her office.

"Anything else, Chief?" Paul asked.

"Uncle Henry gave me a sack to hold for him; I'd forgotten about it until now."

I reached into my backpack for the sack then opened it and pulled out a card. Palace Guard leaned over my shoulder and raised his eyebrows when he saw what I had in my hand.

I gave the card to Paul. "Is it an ID? Does it say Henry Wallace?"

"How did you know?"

I told him about the nurse at the hospital and what Henry said about a man dragging three women up a fire escape.

"We are getting a tangle of loose ends that may or may not be related to anything," Paul said.

I nodded. "Welcome to my world. I didn't have any luck with the guide's phone number, so I'll hand it off to Heather; it's more of Heather's specialty anyway, and I'll give her Vanessa's cell phone too. I called Tonya, and she's going to pull together a list of the young women with disabilities who were murdered."

"Tonya's a great resource for us, particularly since she isn't anywhere close, so we don't have to worry about her."

When we went into the meeting room to wait for Noah and Sophie Rose, Julie asked, "Are you two having a meeting? I think we need to set up the meetings on the calendar, so we don't have any conflicts."

I shook my head. "That wouldn't work for us, but maybe we do need a conference-style phone on the table. What do you think?"

"I'll research the price range and features we might use; we don't need anything complex." Julie turned to her computer.

"Well done, Chief," Paul said after we were in the meeting room.

Heather joined us as Noah and Sophie Rose came into the office.

"I remember Noah Baker: very talented," Heather said. "Sophie Rose moves like a trained ballerina."

After Julie escorted Noah and Sophie Rose into the meeting room, and all the introductions were over, I said, "We've been investigating another case similar to the murder of your young yoga client, Sophie Rose. The common threads are the physical disabilities and the slips of paper with the numbers on them. We think it's important for you to have someone with you at all times. We have several ideas, but we work better as a team, so we'd like to hear your ideas too."

"For example, it would help if we had a fairly detailed idea of both of your schedules," Heather said.

"I'll start," Noah said. "I work the day shift: on at eight and off at five thirty, except I usually go in around seven, and it's frequently closer to seven by the time I get home."

"Even though my first class is at ten, I go the studio around eight thirty to do my administrative tasks and to prepare myself for the day. My last class of the day ends at three, then I return phone calls and run to the bank before I go home."

"What about weekends?" Paul asked.

"Neither of us work weekends," Noah said. "We go to the range, work at my house on the yardwork and garden; the weekend goes by too fast."

"That's the truth," Sophie Rose said. "I've been spending most of the week and the weekends at Noah's because he has a nicer kitchen than I do, and with three bedrooms and two baths, I have had my own bedroom and a private bath."

"How far is it from Noah's house to your studio in comparison to your apartment?" Heather asked.

"His house is actually two minutes closer," Sophie Rose said.

"Is that right?" Heather asked.

Palace Guard rolled his eyes; Spike wiggled his eyebrows at Heather, and I glared at Spike.

"Am I missing something?" Noah asked.

"Probably," Paul said, "but so am I. It's nice to have company for a change."

"We've been talking about combining resources for a while, haven't we, honey?" Sophie Rose said. "Maybe it's time."

"It would be easier for your new team, Captain," Heather said.

Noah laughed. "Are y'all asking me for my hand in marriage?"

"Yes, we are," Sophie Rose said. "So?"

"Let's move you in as soon as we leave here and get married this weekend," Noah said.

"It's a date. Does having someone with me at all times include the time while I'm working?" Sophie Rose asked.

"I'll spend the day with you at the studio, but I don't think I'm interested in yoga," I said.

"We'll talk, Gray Lady; I need to know what you want to work on," Sophie Rose said.

"I want to run every day, and my attitude needs a little adjustment," I said.

"My job," Sophie Rose said.

"We'll see what works as far as the end of your day, Sophie Rose, but we don't want you driving home alone," I said.

"What do you need from me?" Noah asked.

"I need for your schedule to be more solid," Paul said. "We can't operate effectively if we can't count on you to be home at a certain time and to leave no earlier than your normal schedule either."

Noah nodded. "I've been volunteering for extra duty for so long it's almost expected of me; I'll stop."

"Do I owe you extra for that, Paul, or wasn't I supposed to mention it in front of you-know-who?" Sophie Rose asked.

Noah chuckled. "Point taken."

Heather elbowed me; I elbowed her back.

"We like that Sophie Rose person, Captain," Heather said, and I nodded.

"You have good taste, so do I. Anything else for us?"

"Noah, if you can wait until seven thirty before you leave for your office in the mornings, Larry can drop me off at your house."

Heather added, "Larry is Gray Lady's code word for Kevin; we've all picked it up from her."

"Good to know; I was confused for a second there," Noah said.

Paul rose and opened the meeting room door. "Julie can give you all of our phone numbers."

"Save our numbers and call or text any of us anytime if you have a question or a problem comes up," Heather added.

After they left, Heather said, "I don't like that gap of number fourteen. Are you ready to leave, Gray Lady?"

I grabbed my backpack and computer as I headed to the door. "Let's go, Lucy."

After we were in Heather's car, she asked, "Are we dropping off Lucy and Spike at your house?"

I nodded. "They've been pretty cooped up all day; Lucy needs some outside time, so she can clear away all the squirrels from our property."

When we went inside through the side door, I refreshed Lucy's water while Lucy and Spike went out back.

Heather said, "I'm in awe of this kitchen. It must be a dream to cook in."

"I don't have stove privileges yet. Larry thinks I'll set myself on fire."

"I can understand that," Heather chuckled. "Show me around your house."

"The house is old, but you'd never know it because it's been well cared for. We have the large kitchen, a large dining room that we use as a computer room, the great room with a fireplace, a half bath close to the dining room and the great room, three bedrooms, a guest bathroom, and the master bedroom and bath."

"Is it okay if I peek around?"

When Heather returned, she asked, "Was the house furnished when you bought it?"

"The previous owners moved into a condo on the beach and offered us all the furniture as part of the deal. Our real estate agent told us to jump on it because most of the furnishings were high-quality furniture that we could never even find these days."

"She's right; the front porch is very inviting. Is there a back porch?" Heather asked.

"There's a back porch and a large gazebo with a bar for evening cocktails. This house is ready to party." I snickered. "Which is more than I can say for the owners."

Heather snorted. "You and Larry are such party animals."

"Where are you staying?"

"I found a clean, moderately priced hotel near the office that serves breakfast."

"Why don't you stay here? You'd have plenty of privacy."

"I'd love to, but don't you think you should check with Larry?"

I pulled out my phone. "Send a text to Larry: Is it okay with you if Heather stays at our house?"

Larry replied immediately, "Absolutely."

"Okay, will I be allowed to cook? I never have a chance to cook for anyone besides myself."

"Anytime you want. Bring your things here tonight."

"I'll check out of the hotel in the morning, so I'll have time to pack tonight."

"Perfect."

On the way to the hospital, I asked, "Will you stop by the studio and visit me?"

Heather snorted. "You're not going to jail, Chief."

"It feels like it; I can push a button on jo to catch you up on what's going on, but I won't hear from you or Paul unless you call or text me."

"That's a good idea. Paul and I need a way that we can communicate with each other and you too. I'm going to make a quick call after we're at the hospital."

Palace Guard and I climbed out of the car, then we eavesdropped while Heather remained in the car. "Hey, it's me; remember the jo? I need two more audio transmitters that work with the same earbuds, and I'll need a third earbud."

When I didn't hear anything else, I whispered, "Is she listening to someone on her phone?"

Palace Guard nodded.

Heather continued, "That's perfect. I'll buy lunch."

As we walked to the hospital, Heather said, "I have a lunch date at a gas station tomorrow; Paul told me I have an expense account. I'm being a big shot and buying lunch. I'll have something for you and Paul tomorrow afternoon."

I giggled when Palace Guard rolled his eyes.

"What did Palace Guard do?" Heather asked.

"He rolled his eyes when you said you'd be a big shot and buy lunch at a gas station."

"I'm the only one in my crowd with an expense account," Heather said. "I might even give my techie friend a bonus of his choice from the ice cream case."

Palace Guard scanned the waiting area when we entered the hospital.

He's on high alert.

"Uncle Henry's in room 312; I don't want to startle people by looking like I can see." I took Heather's elbow, so she could lead me to the elevator, and Palace Guard could concentrate on our surroundings.

When we walked into his room, Henry said in a much stronger voice, "You're a sight for sore eyes, Maggie. Today's black patch day?"

I smiled. "Sure is, but I didn't know it until after Julie told me what color my patch was this morning. Uncle Henry, this is my best friend, Heather. We work together."

"Nice to meet you, Heather, and thanks for bringing my niece to visit me. Come sit by me, Maggie, and we can talk."

While I sat in the visitor's chair, Heather quietly closed the door. "So, what do you two want to know?" he asked.

"How are you doing? And where was that apartment with the fire escape that you were telling me about?" I asked.

"I'm doing a lot better; they're pumping antibiotics through this IV and serving me regular meals. You still have that sack I gave you?"

"Sure do," I said. "Do you want it back?"

"Oh, no; that would mean a death sentence for me here if someone found it. Henry Perez is perfectly safe. I didn't let them shave my beard, and that helped too."

"When do you expect to be released?" Heather asked.

"It depends; it could be as soon as tomorrow afternoon, but I might decide to have a relapse to draw it out to the end of the week. I'll have to take you on a tour of my favorite haunts after I'm better. You don't see many fire escapes these days, do you? Kind of picturesque in a macabre sort of way."

"Where do you plan to go when you're released?" Heather asked.

"Ahh, that's to be determined. Shelters aren't safe for an old man, which is why I was on the street. I was pretty good at staying out of sight."

"Send Larry a text, Heather," I said.

"Done."

"How do you do that, Uncle Henry?" I asked.

"Old people are naturally invisible. You have other skills that go far beyond sight, though, Gray Lady. You notice what people are saying, and not just the words, but the tone too."

"You're right; in fact, my sense of hearing seems to have heightened," I said.

"I heard back from Larry," Heather said. "Larry said of course."

I smiled. "Heather's staying with us at our old house. It's not quite a bed-and-breakfast, but dinner's included, so I guess it's better than a B&B."

"What's the catch?"

Heather snickered. "You'd be spending your days in the office with Julie, and she'll talk your ear off."

"I'll have to tell you about the time I lost my hearing aids, Heather. I think I'll be fine, but are you two sure about this?"

I glanced at Palace Guard, and he nodded.

"We certainly are," I said.

"Julie's on my contact list. As soon as the medical team tells me I'm ready to be released, I'll tell the hospital to call Julie."

"If it's tomorrow afternoon, I'll pick you up, and depending on how late in the afternoon, Maggie will be with me," Heather said.

"Will there be any people around that I don't know?"

"Not at all. Maggie's kind of a loner, but you probably already guessed that, and her husband, Larry, is what my grandma called nice people; there will be only the four of us and Lucy, who is a sweet, old short-haired German pointer. I'm volunteering to cook dinner tomorrow. Any requests?"

"Warm food and good company."

"We can guarantee that's what you'll have. We'll let you get some rest and see you tomorrow," Heather said.

As we were on our way to the car, Heather asked, "What was in his sack?"

"His driver's license. He's Doctor Henry Wallace. When I asked him what his name was, he told me they called him Doc, but his name was Henry."

I told her what the nurse told me about Doc Wallace then continued, "He was lying on the sidewalk when I first saw him, and he called out for Gray Lady. Before I ran back to the office to grab something for him to wrap up in, he told me he saw a man drag a woman up the fire escape to an apartment, and I should stay away from that street."

Heather-blob shook her head. "He was that ill, but he was concerned about your safety. What an amazing person."

"I think so too."

"Does Palace Guard agree?" Heather asked.

As Palace Guard nodded, I said, "Yes."

"That cinches it for me; I don't have to sit in the hallway all night with a shotgun across my lap after all."

"Let's check in at the office before you drop me off at home," I said.

"Is something going on?"

"I have a feeling."

"Oh man; that's the second thing I hate to hear you say," Heather said.

I held onto the dash as Heather swerved and sped through traffic. *Good thing I can't see because I'd probably be screaming.*

I glanced back at Palace Guard, and his knuckles were white from his tight grip on the back of the front seat.

After Heather screeched into a parking spot, I said, "Don't run in. Let Palace Guard check first."

Palace Guard raced inside then motioned for us to continue. When we reached the door, he motioned for me to stay outside and for Heather to continue.

"Palace Guard wants you to go inside, but with caution. I'll be behind you when he releases me."

Heather went inside. "Oh, no!"

Palace Guard moved out of my way, and I stepped in and smelled the distinctive iron odor of blood as Heather tapped on her phone.

"I'm calling from the Gray Flanagan Agency. We found a woman on the office floor; an attacker cut deeply into her abdomen, and she is bleeding profusely," Heather said.

Palace Guard motioned to me to open my backpack then pointed at my spare change of clothes. I knelt next to the woman and stuffed my clean clothes into the wound like a trauma dressing.

Too heavy-weight to be Julie.

"Julie?" Heather called out. "Chief, the meeting room is locked." I heard light scratching, then Heather said, "Not anymore."

"Julie? Are you okay? Chief, Julie's unconscious, and her hands are bound."

I pulled out my phone from my back pocket and dropped it next to my knees. "Call nine-one-one."

When the dispatcher answered, I said, "We have a second unconscious woman at the Gray Flanagan Agency who is bound and gagged."

Palace Guard pointed to Paul's office then made an angry face.

"Bad guy?" I whispered.

Palace Guard nodded.

I slowly rose then Palace Guard guided me around the woman on the floor. When I was behind Julie's heavy desk, I crouched down in a position where I could see Heather.

I put my index finger over my lips and motioned for her to stay down before I called out, "Heather, stay with Julie. I'm going out to my car that's around the corner and get more bandages."

I motioned again for Heather to stay low then turned my attention to Paul's office.

I heard the office door handle turn, then Palace Guard showed me the small rock in his hand, and I nodded. He held up one finger then two fingers; when he got to three, I rose and fired a few feet above where I heard the rock hit the floor.

CHAPTER FOUR

After the sound of a thud as a body dropped onto the floor, Heather joined me and whispered, "Good shot, Chief. You and Palace Guard stopped him. Can I go into Paul's office now?"

Palace Guard nodded, and I copied him then listened to the comforting wail of approaching sirens.

"Is there any blood on his hands or clothes? Any signs that he was the killer?"

Palace Guard shook his head.

"Hello? Hello?" a voice called out from my phone.

I forgot I still had the dispatcher on my phone.

"I'm here; we're okay. The intruder is dead," I said.

"Is that you, Gray Lady?" the dispatcher asked.

Why do I feel like I'm in trouble?

My phone was still on the floor, but I didn't want to pick it up because my hands were sticky with blood. "Yes."

"Thank you, hon. We had a frantic GBI agent on the phone."

"Oh boy, I am in trouble."

"Sorry, hon, but you sure are." The dispatcher snickered.

Heather raced past me to Paul's office. "Paul's not here, but I think our bad guy was rifling through his files."

She looked into her office then went into mine. "He was still working on Paul's office and hadn't made it to mine yet; your office is a wreck. I don't think he found what he was supposed to find in your office, so he went to Paul's."

I shuddered, and Heather put her arm around me. "I don't recognize the young woman in front of Julie's desk. The sight of the number fourteen that was cut into her stomach caught me off guard. She's still breathing, Chief. You stopped the bleeding, so she might have a chance. I'm going to cut the straps around Julie's wrists. Why don't you sit down?"

After Heather led me to the waiting area seats, she hurried to the meeting room then returned to my side when three blobs burst into the office.

"Heather? Where's Maggie?"

Larry.

I sighed as Larry rushed in.

"It's not my blood, honey." I shuddered. "I need to clean my gun before the blood dries."

Larry put his arm around me. "Shhh. It's okay, sweetie. They'll take your gun as evidence. We'll get you another one."

More blobs with stretchers rushed into the office; I flinched at the swell of increasingly loud noise and the smells of the growing number of people in the office that had suddenly seemed to shrink and close me in.

"Heather and I were on our way to our house, so she could drop me off, but I had a feeling." I put my hands in my armpits to stop them from shaking. "When I told Heather I had a feeling, she drove like a maniac to get us here."

Larry rose but kept his hand on my shoulder. "Captain, can I take my wife home? She's in shock."

"Certainly, Kevin. We'll talk later."

"I can give you a full statement of what we saw when we arrived," Heather said.

"Thank you; your shot?" the in-charge man asked.

"No, the shot was my wife's," Larry said.

"He's right," Heather said.

"Your wife is Gray Lady? I'll come to your house later for her statement."

"That's a good idea; she'll be fine at home."

"Agent Ewing?" another man asked. "Did you see that?"

Larry exhaled. "No, I didn't; thanks."

Larry knelt next to me and hugged me as he buried his face in my hair.

"Larry, we don't know where Paul is," I said.

"Give me a second, sweetie. I'll check on Julie."

Larry followed a stretcher out of the building then returned to my side and called Paul.

"Paul, there was an incident at the office. Julie was ambushed and knocked unconscious; she s coming around, but the ambulance is taking her to the hospital for evaluation. You're welcome to come to our house later for supper."

Larry smiled as he looked at me. "Yes, Maggie and Heather are okay, and Maggie stopped Julie's attacker."

I tugged at Larry's arm. "Just a second; Maggie wants to talk to you."

"Paul, someone with the man brought number fourteen here and dumped her in front of Julie's desk then rifled both our offices. My attacker wasn't our murderer, though, because he didn't have any blood on his clothes or hands."

"Thanks, Chief; I can't imagine what he could have been looking for. What about Julie's files?"

"Larry, are the file cabinets behind the desk still closed?"

Larry strode to the cabinets. "Sure are." He tugged on each drawer. "And still locked."

"I don't know if you heard him, but Larry said all of Julie's file cabinets are locked."

"The keys are in the bottom left drawer of Julie's desk; if they're still there, take them with you, Chief."

"Will do."

"I heard him." Larry strode to the desk. "Got 'em, honey."

"Larry found them," I said.

"Good; talk to you later." Paul disconnected.

Before we left, Larry said, "Heather, gather up your things then come to our house. You can pack up the rest of your clothes tomorrow. I planned to heat up one of my three casseroles that I cooked this weekend, so don't stop to eat."

On the way home, I leaned back in my seat and sighed. "What was it that the man asked if you saw?"

"Julie's desk had a bullet hole. The man shot at you, but your shot threw off his aim; you still might have been hit, except Julie bought the furniture, didn't she? It was an old, solid, wood desk."

"I guess I owe her an apology, but I can't because I'd have to tell her I thought she was being cheap when she insisted on old furniture."

"What do you think the man was looking for?" Larry asked.

"I don't know, but maybe what he was looking for wasn't in our offices because almost all our files are on our laptops and our cloud that we all share. I have my laptop in my backpack, and I'm sure Paul keeps his with him too."

"Are you okay now?"

"The smell of the blood was overwhelming; I wanted to run outside. When all the people and the stretchers came into the office, it felt like the walls were closing in on me; I couldn't breathe. Did you hear the call on the radio? The dispatcher told me a GBI agent wanted to know if the Gray Lady was okay."

"When the call came in, I didn't even need to hear the address; I knew it was you. I jumped into my truck and yelled family emergency as I left the office. I called nine-one-one on my way. Sweetie, now I'm thinking you need to go to GBI training, so we can work together. We've already said Paul and Heather can take care of the cases at the Agency."

"I'd get kicked out for cheating." I snickered.

"You would." Larry chuckled. "If they didn't kick you out first for correcting the instructors when they were wrong, although I don't see the bad side of that. I'd love for you to take a couple of them down a peg or two before you were invited to leave. Maybe I can get an assignment from GBI to keep an eye on you like the old days, except I didn't do that great a job."

"We had fun working together," I said. "I think that's what we miss the most."

Palace Guard nodded.

"We really were a team, including you, Palace Guard," Larry said.

When we reached the house, Larry said, "Take a warm shower, and I'll wash your clothes in cold water. I told the paramedic to toss the clothes you used to stop the bleeding. That was really genius."

"It was Palace Guard's idea. Are you going to have a beer with me, so both of us are off duty when the boss guy shows up to take my statement?"

After I climbed out of the shower, Larry opened the bathroom door. "Feel better?"

"Much, thank you," I said.

"You look better." He leered then dodged the towel when I tried to snap him.

"I hate saying this, Naked Maggie, but I suppose you have to get dressed; I've put the casserole in the oven, started a fire in the fireplace, and opened our bottles."

While we relaxed on the sofa, I stroked his cheek then kissed him. "You're getting a little scruffy. Is your beard still red? Thanks for telling Heather to come here."

"It was self-preservation; you would have worried about her, and Spike would have pestered me to go check on her. At least this way, Heather can enjoy her evening chastising Spike instead of being tense while she waited for an attack."

I snuggled against Larry while we sipped our beer and shared beer kisses until Lucy howled on the front porch.

"What on earth? Lucy never howls." Larry hurried to the front door, and I followed him.

When he opened the door, Larry smiled. "I should have known."

I nodded as Heather parked in front of the house while Lucy howled, and Spike danced his wacky dance.

Heather climbed out of her car then lifted out a duffel bag from the backseat. "What a reception! I don't think I've ever heard Lucy sing like that before; nice dance, Spike."

Spike froze and gaped at Heather as she walked past him and into the house.

"Did you see Spike's wacky dance?" Larry asked.

"Didn't have to; I knew that's what he was doing," Heather said. "Do I get to pick my room?"

"Sure do; there aren't any sheets on the beds, but each bedroom has a set of sheets in the closet, courtesy of Jennifer and Ella," I said.

"Naturally. Did they volunteer Glenn and Moe to help you move in?"

"We didn't have much to move, but Glenn's truck was loaded down," Larry said. "When my mother shows up, we'll have so much stuff, we'll never be able to move out unless it's to a bigger house."

"I need to be off duty too; does a beer before supper come with my vacation package?" Heather asked.

"Your travel agent snagged you the bonus special with the open fridge included," Larry said.

Heather chuckled as she dropped her duffel bag in the hallway; she sighed, and her tone became serious. "We need to talk."

"I'll grab you a beer," Larry said.

When he returned and gave Heather her beer, she saluted him with her bottle then took a long drink before she spoke.

"We need a big change in our plans. We can't have Henry here because you're a target, Chief. It was actually genius that Julie used her maiden name because that removes Henry from any association with the Gray Flanagan Agency, but I can't think of where Henry could go where he'd be safe. We could talk to Jennifer or one of my old friends in Harperville, but that wouldn't be ideal for Henry to be so far away because he trusts the Gray Lady. I'm not sure he has trusted anyone in a long time."

I exhaled. "I agree that being here would be a tremendous risk for Henry, but I don't have any other options either."

"I got this." Larry swaggered to the back door and went outside with Palace Guard behind him.

"Well then, Mrs. Ewing, I think the mister has taken charge of our problem."

"Looks that way, doesn't it?"

Heather finished her beer. "I'm going to pick out my room and unpack a few things. Holler when Larry comes back in, and I'll slide down the hall in my socks because I've never had the chance to do that before; I don't want to miss anything."

Spike followed Heather to the hall then waited.

"Are you planning to stop her if she slides too fast?" I asked; Spike's face reddened, then he shrugged.

When Heather joined me in the great room, she said, "I picked the bedroom that is next to the bathroom. It's the biggest one, and did you know Jennifer and Ella set up the small bedroom next to it as a comfortable work area with a desk and a TV? I have my own private suite, so I can work and don't have to hang out with you boring married people all the time unless I'm feeling social."

"I didn't know that. What if we have more than three guests at a time?"

Heather snorted. "If Jennifer and Glenn, Ella and Moe, and Larry's folks show up, then you, Larry, and I would go to the beach."

Larry and Palace Guard came inside. "Did you say we're going to the beach? When?"

I rolled my eye. "After the weather warms up."

Spike nodded.

"I talked to my supervisor, and he called someone else; the bottom line is we've arranged for Henry to stay at a safe house. After GBI catches the killer, he's welcome to come here, if he likes, but he'll be safe wherever he goes."

Heather elbowed me. "After GBI catches the killer: got that, Chief?"

Larry continued, "Sweetie, we'll need you and Heather to pick up Henry from the hospital tomorrow, so you can explain the situation to him."

"We can do that, but what about Sophie Rose?"

"My supervisor liked your idea of someone at the studio with Sophie Rose, so the yoga studio will have a new office manager tomorrow morning. My supervisor asked me if you wanted to work for the GBI, by the way, and I politely said you didn't."

Heather chuckled. "Politely?"

"More or less; anybody else ready for my special chicken casserole?"

While we ate, I said, "Heather, we found a personal chef that was really great, but after Paul and I decided to start the Gray Flanagan Agency, I realized I didn't want to hang out at home while she prepped and cooked meals three days a week."

"I've been making casseroles, and Maggie eats them, so we're fine; you'd never guess it by how slight she is, but she is not a picky eater: she'll eat anything," Larry said.

"I really miss cooking; can I take over a few days a week, so I can cook in that amazing kitchen?" Heather asked.

"Be my guest," Larry said. "I have no imagination at all in the cooking arena, but I can keep us from starving."

"What about rent? I don't want to be a freeloader here," Heather said.

Before I replied, I glanced at Palace Guard, and he narrowed his eyes then side-glanced Heather.

I have to respect Heather's need to contribute.

"I'll call my lawyer's administrative assistant, Shantelle, and ask her for a rental agreement. Would that work?"

"Yes, I know Shantelle; she'll be fair to both of us," Heather said.

After Heather and I cleared the dishes, and Larry loaded the dishwasher, Heather said, "I'm going to set up my laptop and turn on the TV in my living room for a little relaxation before I collapse."

"We have ice cream for dessert," Larry said.

"Right after dessert," Heather added.

We finished our ice cream; when Heather was halfway down the hall, Lucy woofed, and headlights lit up the driveway.

Heather rushed back. "Are we expecting anyone?" she growled.

"It's probably the captain from the police department; he wants to interview Maggie," Larry said.

"He was a sharp guy; can I sit in or at least eavesdrop?"

"I don't think he'd allow it, but the sound from the kitchen is as good as having a front-row seat at a theatre," Larry said.

Heather raced to the kitchen and then called out, "Say something."

"She certainly was in a hurry, wasn't she?" I whispered.

"Dang, this is a wonderful house," Heather said.

"Since when did you develop a sneaky side, Wicked Cowboy?"

"I've had years of training by the best." Larry patted my bottom then kissed me while he opened the door.

"Eww," Heather said.

"Maybe you shouldn't be spying around corners too, Heather." Larry chuckled.

"Good to see you, Agent Ewing. Is now a better time for me to talk to Mrs. Ewing?"

"Come in, Captain. She was overwhelmed by all the people in her office, but she's fine now."

After we were seated, the captain said, "Tell me what you saw when you went into your office, Mrs. Ewing."

I furrowed my brow and cocked my head. *Is he making a joke to start off on a light note?*

Palace Guard rolled his eyes.

Larry cleared his throat. "Captain, my wife tends to be very literal, so you might want to rephrase your question."

"To answer your question, Captain, after I smelled blood, I saw a blob on the floor."

"A blob?" Captain asked.

He sounds as confused as I was. I think I got even.

Spike threw his arms into the air in triumph and danced his victory dance, and I coughed into my elbow to keep from laughing.

Palace Guard shook his head as he stared at the captain then Larry, who frowned while he bit his lip.

"Help me out, Agent Ewing; I'm lost," the captain said.

"I can help you," I said. "My left eye has been removed, and I have only a little sight in my right eye; basically, I can tell the difference between night and day. I call people blobs because I see vague figures, which is why I told you I saw a blob, but the first sensation I had when I walked into the office was the overwhelming odor of blood."

"So you didn't know if the person was a man or woman?" Captain asked.

"Right, or even if they were a close friend or a stranger," I said.

"Okay, I think I'm starting to understand why you reacted to the entire scene so intensely. So, did..."

"Captain, why don't I tell you what I did, then you can ask me questions? We'll save a lot of time," I said.

"Thank you, Mrs. Ewing, for the reminder that I need to adjust my questions for the person I am interviewing. I used to be good at that. Unfortunately, I've obviously been behind my desk too long." He exhaled. "I need to get out more."

I nodded then told him about Heather picking the lock to the meeting room while I stuffed the woman's wound with my clothes to slow the bleeding then called for an ambulance.

The captain interrupted me. "How did you call the emergency number?"

"I told my phone to call nine-one-one."

"I should have realized...I'm sorry for interrupting."

"I heard someone moving quietly in Paul's office, so I moved behind Julie's desk for cover. I knew it wasn't Paul because he would have called out, or if he was gagged and alone, kicked something to get my attention. When I heard the knob turn, I was in position to shoot. I heard a click, then I fired at the same time the attacker did. Not long after that, more and more people swarmed into the room, and I became completely disoriented by the sound of growing hysteria, the smell of fear from all those people, the feel of the sticky, coagulated blood on my hands, and the sickening, distinctive odor of iron on my clothes. I felt trapped until I heard my husband's voice."

"Wow, I didn't understand earlier, but I do now; thank you, Mrs. Ewing. Is there anything else you'd like to add?"

"You'll think of more questions later, I'm sure, but thank you for listening to me."

The captain rose, then Larry shook his hand at the door.

After Larry closed the door, he said, "You are remarkable, gunslinger. Hey, Heather, want to join the big kids in another beer?"

"You betcha." Heather carried three bottles of beer when she came into the great room.

CHAPTER FIVE

I woke the next morning to the alluring aroma of coffee and hurried to the shower. After I dressed and selected an eyepatch, I grabbed my jo and headed to the kitchen.

"No running naked through the boarding house in the mornings, Gray Lady," Heather called out; Larry chuckled.

"No fair making up rules before breakfast; where's my coffee?" I grumbled as I stomped into the kitchen.

"At your place at the table," Larry said.

"I found tortillas in the refrigerator and made breakfast burritos; they're in the oven and almost ready to serve," Heather said.

"How are my colors?" I asked.

"Eclectic," Heather said.

"You're wearing a red shirt and an orange sparkly eyepatch," Larry said. "You're radiating a sunny attitude."

"Good; I can be in disguise today as the cheerful Gray Lady. What's the schedule?"

"I called Paul last night, so he's caught up on the shift in plans. Julie regained consciousness completely before the ambulance reached the hospital, but they still put her through a battery of tests. They may keep her for several days for observation, but Paul hopes not because she's unhappy enough about not going to work today. I'm dropping you off at the office, then I'll go to my hotel and finish packing and check out," Heather said.

Heather pulled out the burritos from the oven. "Paul will be at the office when we get there and will take you with him to the diner to meet with Bob. I have an out-of-town lunch date, but I'll be back in plenty of time for us to pick up Henry then take him to his handler."

I inhaled the aroma of the hot burritos and forgot I wanted to be crabby. "That's good news about Julie; Paul must be relieved."

"I'll send you a text, Heather, as soon as I know where you'll meet up with Henry's handler, which I think is a far more superior word than escort, which is what I've always heard," Larry said.

Heather nodded. "I think it makes Henry sound like the rock star he is, as far as I'm concerned."

"I'm worried the killer is escalating because the amount of time between murders is rapidly compressing. He left the slip of paper with fifteen on it for Sophie Rose before he cut number fourteen," I said.

"I'll call Noah immediately; he can assign state troopers to assist GBI." Larry rose from the table. "Don't wait for me to eat breakfast; I might be a while."

Heather and I had finished eating and were ready to leave when Larry returned to the kitchen. "Noah assigned two additional troopers to assist GBI, so two agents can guard Sophie Rose: one will be undercover, and the second one will pose as her visiting sister and go with Sophie Rose to the studio and will stay at their house, so there are no gaps."

"Enjoy your burrito, honey. Are you and Lucy going out back, Spike?"

Lucy trotted to the back door, and Spike waved as they went outside.

I kissed Larry, then Heather and I left with Palace Guard staying closer to me than usual; I didn't mind.

When we reached the office, Paul was waiting for us in front of the building. "I talked to the lead investigator. After they have finished collecting all the evidence, he'll call me. We'll want to have the office cleaned thoroughly, but I'd like to go through Julie's files before we hire professional cleaners."

"I wonder if we can tell what the attacker was looking for in my office. Does the investigator know if there was a second attacker?"

"I don't know; that might be something Larry learns later," Paul said.

"I think there had to be," Heather said. "The attacker didn't look like he would have had the strength to move the number fourteen woman without assistance."

"While Julie was undergoing all the tests last night, I made a friend who told me the woman who was cut survived her first round of surgery. I owe her donuts."

"I'll be back in town before two." Heather hurried to her car and left.

On the way to the diner, I told Paul about the change in plans for Sophie Rose.

"That means you aren't going to be hanging out all day at the studio. What do you have in mind?"

"Tonya may have at least a partial list of victims after we've met with Bob. I don't think it's likely, but I'll ask Tonya if the murdered women could have known each other. There has to be a common thread of how the killer met all of them."

Paul nodded. "I'd like to start with Vanessa's guide. When you go to the women's restroom, I'll ask Bob if I can check her computer."

"I'll call Becky and ask her if Vanessa had a password book or a journal she wrote in. After breakfast, drop me off at the yoga studio. I'll ask Sophie Rose if she heard any of her clients mention a guide."

"I'll be interested in hearing what her reaction was. I'm glad Palace Guard will be with you. He'll see anything you won't, and your Gray Lady sensors will pick up any tension."

After Paul parked his car, I climbed out and inhaled the familiar smell of old grease and bacon. "Ahh. Reminds me of Reggie's Diner."

As we walked into the diner, I told him about how Kate taught me to cook breakfast for a table of four and have everyone's food ready to serve at the same time.

"Do you miss your diner days?"

"I really do. I understood exactly what you meant when you said you missed the hectic pace of working on more than one case at a time because the pace in a diner is nonstop, and there's no slack. If anyone gets behind in even one small thing, it throws everyone else off too, and no one will ever catch up."

I furrowed my brow and paused in the middle of the aisle. *Did the killer get behind, and now he's scrambling to catch up?*

Paul whispered, "Is everything okay?"

"An idea just popped into my head; I'll tell you after we leave."

Paul nodded. "Bob's waving at us."

I held onto his elbow as he led the way through a large group to Bob's table.

"I see you brought reinforcements, Paul." Bob chuckled.

I smiled. "My husband had to go into work earlier than usual, so Paul's my chauffeur today. I hope you don't mind that I'm crashing your meeting."

"Not at all, Gray Lady. I understand you have like a sixth sense or something, so you may notice something that's right in front of me, but I can't see."

After both Paul and Bob ordered the farmhand breakfast, and I ordered a cinnamon roll, Bob asked Paul if he'd watched the game last week. I had no clue what game he was talking about, but Paul answered him like he did. I listened to Bob's tone as he talked.

He's not avoiding any discussion about Vanessa because he's grieving or stressed; he's hiding something, and he's afraid I'll see what it is. I put on my best bored face and turned my head toward the window like I was listening to something outside.

When our food was served, Bob and Paul dug in, and all conversation ceased.

While they ate, I nibbled on my cinnamon roll, then asked, "Bob, was Vanessa an aspiring author? Did she write a lot?"

Bob dropped his fork on the floor, and Palace Guard held up two thumbs.

That's an affirmative. He dropped his fork to buy some time, so he could decide how to answer.

"Not all that much," Bob said as the server set a fresh fork next to his plate, "but she occasionally wrote a short story or worked on what she called her novel when she was in junior high school. Why?"

"No special reason; it just seemed like she had a really creative talent for teaching and cooking. I'm sorry I didn't know her; she reminds me of my best friend who is a very talented teacher, but she also paints remarkable watercolors of wildlife."

"Ask Becky about all the journals we have with Vanessa's stories from elementary school. Becky was convinced she definitely had talent."

Thought so.

After Bob turned back to his breakfast, I rose and mumbled, "Excuse me."

"Ladies' room is straight ahead of you: first door on your right after you pass the counter," the server whispered.

I smiled. "Thank you. I was afraid I had gotten turned around."

"You are doing great, honey."

I walked slowly and tapped my jo to make sure the aisle was clear in front of me. When I went into the women's restroom, I exhaled. *That was exhausting.*

I pulled out my phone then turned down the volume. "Send a text to Sophie Rose: 'I have questions but only for your ears.'"

Sophie Rose replied, "I'll go to the restroom at nine thirty and call you. My sister is a snitch."

I giggled. *I knew I like Sophie Rose for a reason.*

I waited a few more minutes, then washed my hands. When I stepped out of the restroom, Palace Guard was waiting, and he followed me as I slowly tapped back to the table.

As I neared the table, Paul said, "And that was why I never went fishing with Julie's dad again."

When I reached my chair, Paul rose and helped me sit.

"Y'all care for anything else?" the server asked.

"Just the check," Bob said.

"I'll get the check, Bob; I appreciate your help," Paul said.

"Are you sure? I'm afraid I wasn't much help, but let me know anytime you have any questions, and I'll do my best to answer them."

After Bob left, Paul paid the check. On our way out to his car, Paul asked, "Did you notice how Bob stared at you? I wonder if he has some eye problems himself because it didn't seem like he blinked at all. He reminded me of a cheetah staring at a small antelope, but don't tell Julie I said that; she'd accuse me of reading some of her books. What are we doing the rest of the day?"

"I'd like to pick up a fruit and cheese tray from a deli and take it to Sophie Rose's studio, then we could go to the hospital and visit Julie."

Paul started the car then backed out of the parking spot. "Why a fruit tray? It would be easier to find donuts or cookies."

"I think donuts or cookies would be welcomed by the students, but Sophie Rose might disapprove."

"I'm not asking the right question." Paul exhaled. "Why do we have to go to the yoga studio?"

"You and Palace Guard saw Sophie Rose; could you tell by the way she walked or by the clothing she wore she had a prothesis?"

Palace Guard raised his eyebrows then shook his head.

"Not at all; what did Palace Guard say?" Paul asked.

"Same as you."

"At least I'm in good company, but what does that have to do with taking a fruit tray to her studio?"

"Because we can't just walk in and gawk; I want to know if you and Palace Guard can tell whether she has a prothesis when she's in her yoga outfit."

"I didn't give it a thought, so I must have assumed we could, but that's not necessarily true, is it?"

"It's been bothering me," I said.

"Julie and I found a great bagel and deli shop; we'll see what they have this morning."

When Paul opened the deli door, the tantalizing aroma of fresh cinnamon bagels greeted us.

"Come on in," a woman's voice called out. "Browse a while and give a shout when you've decided what you want. I'll bring out blueberry bagels in a few minutes."

"We were thinking about a fruit and cheese tray for a yoga studio," Paul said.

"What's the occasion?" A woman-blob asked as she carried out a bin.

The distinctive aroma of everything bagels surrounded the woman like a cloud of onion and garlic. "The owner is a college friend of mine; she doesn't know I'm in town, so we thought we'd surprise her and her students with a treat," I said.

"I have mini-bagels; they're a hit with the young yoga crowd. Why don't I fix you up with a nice tray of strawberries, chunks of cantaloupe, grapes, whipped cream cheese, and blueberry mini-bagels?"

Palace Guard nodded.

"That's perfect, thank you," I said.

"Help yourself to the coffee; I'll have that tray ready for you shortly."

When the woman brought out a tray, she asked, "What do you think?"

"It's a work of art," Paul said. "They'll love it."

After we were in the car, Paul said, "You were fast with your credit card. Julie would have approved the expense on the business card."

"We need to get you a card you can use for expenses with your name on it; I realized I claimed the gift was personal, and it would have raised questions in the woman's mind if you paid for it with a business account."

"You're right, Chief. It wouldn't have worked if I had casually pointed to you and told the woman you were the boss, so it was okay for me to use the company credit card because I wasn't cheating on my expense account."

I giggled. "Like that wouldn't have raised even more questions in the bagel lady's mind."

Paul laughed. "Couldn't you just hear me trying to explain why an old, grizzled guy like me had a young, blind woman, who was obviously very kindhearted, as a boss?"

I giggled. "Fishiest story I've heard except for the last bit of the fish story you told Bob at the diner."

"That was a classic," Paul said. "It always goes over well with the sports minded crowd, and it's easy to substitute fish with turkeys or wild boar to suit the audience."

"Wild boar?" I asked.

"It's a thing; we're at the yoga studio. Guess I'll have to save my wild boar story for another time."

"What time is it?" I asked.

"Eight thirty. Why?"

"I've got a date at nine thirty." I opened the car door and climbed out.

While Paul followed Palace Guard and me to the front door, he mumbled, "Something else for me to remember to ask about."

"Door's locked."

I tapped on the door, and a blob I didn't know opened the door.

"We're not open," she growled. "Who are you?"

"Gray Lady! This is a surprise," Sophie Rose pushed past the woman at the door. "Please forgive my sister; she takes after our mother, who had, you know, troubles. Come on in."

"I thought you might enjoy surprising your students with a National Yoga Day treat."

"How on earth did you know that? This is absolutely wonderful. Can you stay?"

"I wish I could, but we have errands to run."

"My students will be very impressed; thank you."

"Where do I put the tray?" Paul asked.

"Right here on my desk."

After Sophie Rose and I hugged, Paul, Palace Guard, and I left.

As we headed toward the hospital, Paul said, "You and Sophie Rose were amazing. Even though I know better, I would have thought you've known each other for years."

"She's fun," I said. "Was she wearing yoga pants?"

"If that's what you call the skinny leggings, then she was wearing yoga pants, and her legs looked the same to me. What about you, Palace Guard?"

Palace Guard nodded.

"He agrees with you."

"It was a treat watching the two of you in action. I almost felt sorry for that poor officer who had to play the part of Sophie Rose's sister. What was it you said you'd tell me after we talked to Bob?"

"Remember when we were talking about scrambling to catch up? Don't you think that's what's going on with the killer?"

"Help me; I don't get it," Paul said.

"He went from thirteen to fifteen then tried to murder fourteen but was unsuccessful."

"His scrambling is making him sloppy," Paul said. "How can we take advantage of that?"

"I don't know, but I'll think about it. How many cars were in the yoga studio parking lot?" I asked.

"Two. Why?"

"One must be Sophie Rose's car and the other one, her sister's. Were they the same color?"

"No, do I need to care about that?" Paul asked.

"Not yet."

When we arrived at the hospital, Paul waited for another car to back out of a prime spot that was close to the hospital in the visitors' lot then parked. "Are you going to visit Henry?"

I shook my head. "Unfortunately, I need to stay away from him until Heather and I pick him up this afternoon. I don't want to lead anyone to him."

Paul paused as he reached to open his door. "Does that mean you think someone is following you?"

"Not necessarily, but if they are, I'm not leading them to Henry."

"What's our plan?"

"You visit Julie; Sophie Rose will call me at nine thirty; I have some questions for her. When Heather and I pick up Henry this afternoon, I have more questions for him; I'm hoping for some answers."

As we walked toward the visitors' entrance, Paul said, "I'm obsessing over the question of how we take advantage of the killer being stressed to the point of becoming sloppy. How do we put more stress on him?"

I stopped in the middle of the road to think, and Paul pulled me back onto the curb as a car sped toward the emergency entrance.

"We need to force his hand. If we assume I'm number sixteen, which is a possibility, how do we preempt him?" I asked as the hospital doors whooshed open.

"I wish I didn't understand what you're saying, but I do, and I'll worry about it. Where are you going to be while I visit Julie? Shouldn't you go with me?" Paul asked as I turned toward the chairs for visitors.

"I'll sit in the waiting room; it's the most private for a conversation and the most public for security."

"If you get yourself kidnapped or killed, I'm the one that will have to answer to Larry, Julie, and Heather, and I can't take the pressure. You have to come with me."

Paul gets so dramatic sometimes.

I crossed my arms. "I'm staying here. I don't want to step into a hallway to have a so-called private conversation with Sophie Rose; it would be too easy for someone around the corner or in a nearby room to listen."

"Julie has a private bath; no one would be able to hear you unless they were in Julie's room with their ear pressed against the door. I wouldn't let that happen, and neither would Palace Guard."

I glowered at Paul while we waited for the elevator. *Paul is an annoying man; he has an answer for everything.*

When we went into Julie's room, she said, "I knew you'd come to sneak me out of here, Chief. The doctor told me I had a mild concussion, but she wouldn't let me go home last night, even after I reminded her several times that she's the one who said mild, and Paul ignores me when I ask him nicely to tell me where he hid my clothes."

Paul snorted.

"Don't give me that attitude, mister; maybe I forgot to say please, but I didn't yell as loudly as I did last night," Julie said.

"The doctor will be here at ten; we'll see what she has to say," Paul said.

"I should be dressed when she gets here, so she'll know I'm okay to leave."

"I'm going to grab some coffee. Would you like a cup too, Chief?"

"I'm fine."

After Paul left, Julie said, "Good, he'll be gone for at least a couple of minutes. Right before you got here, I overheard two nurses chatting in the hall as they passed my room; it sounded like the experienced nurse was filling in a recently hired one on the hospital inside gossip. She told the newbie to be careful about ever being in the elevator alone with any of the male hospital staff, doctors, or volunteers, especially one certain person, then I missed his name because they walked too fast, and I was too slow getting to my door before they were out of my hearing range. I wanted to run down the hall after them, but I don't have any slippers. My socks would slip on the floor if I ran, and my hospital gown would have flapped open in the breeze; while I'm not overly modest, I would have been far too conspicuous. I couldn't say anything in front of Paul because he hates it when I share what I hear even if I'm merely reporting the facts."

"That was really interesting."

"I thought so too, but then I wondered if there's always that one person in every large establishment that everyone knows to avoid."

I shrugged. "Or a perfectly innocent person who wonders why everyone at work shuns him."

"Exactly."

Palace Guard squinted at Julie then raised his eyebrows as he glanced at me.

I nodded. *Julie confuses me sometimes too.*

"Before Paul gets back, see if my clothes are in that cabinet next to my bed," Julie said.

When I tapped my jo in an exaggerated search for her bed, Palace Guard stood back; after I bumped into her bed, I asked, "Am I close?"

"Oh for goodness sake, where's Palace Guard?" she asked.

"He must have gone with Paul to check something."

"Typical man," Julie muttered, and Palace Guard grinned.

"Your doctor is down the hall, and your nurse told me you're next; that's thirty minutes earlier than we expected." Paul strolled into Julie's room.

Paul's actually not all bad; he just told me it's close to nine-thirty.

"Do you suppose it would be okay if I use your restroom, Julie?"

"Certainly, Chief; go right ahead."

Palace Guard guided me to Julie's restroom. "Thank you, Palace Guard; it's much easier to get around with your help."

"No kidding," Julie muttered.

I found the shower then a bench seat inside the shower and sat while I waited. When my phone rang, I answered.

"Hi Gray Lady, ready for some potty talk?" Sophie Rose asked.

"I'm sitting in a shower on a shower stool, so keep it clean, missy."

Sophie Rose and I giggled.

"We're so funny. Whatcha got?" she asked.

"Have you heard any of your students talk about a new therapist or guide?"

"Vanessa was going on about a new guide, and one of the girls told her she had a guide too, and her guide was amazing. They argued briefly about who had the best guide, and one of the others told them to shut up because they weren't supposed to talk about their guide where other people could hear them."

I gaped at the phone. "I didn't expect two others; did you get any indication of what the guide did?"

"The young women talked like having a guide is a status symbol or being selected to join a secret club; is it possible they are being groomed?"

"I don't know, but it sounds plausible to me. Do you know who the other two were?"

"Sure do; would it help if I text you their names?"

"Very much so."

"I'll see what else I can find out."

I shuddered. "It might be better if you didn't."

"If you're worried about me, you met my sister, and she's not nearly as bad as my cousin that you didn't meet. I'll be safe."

"Send me the names of those you know have a guide. I don't know exactly how it will help, but I feel like I'm getting closer."

"I'll send you a text after my ten o'clock class."

"What do you call your guide?" I asked.

"Maggie, I don't have a guide, but if I did, I'd call him a dead man because you are on his trail."

"I've been a little out of sorts; thank you for reminding me I needed to adjust my attitude."

"Your husband and my fiancé are in law enforcement, and we live with the fear that this might be the day they don't come home; we have to stick together."

Like Parker. A tear slipped down my cheek.

I don't want Larry to die. I brushed away the tear. *Tears dry; the fear never goes away.*

"You tell me what you want me to do, and I'll do it; besides the fact that I want to help, you love stirring up trouble as much as I do, and that's half the fun," Sophie Rose said.

I told Sophie Rose about my theory that the killer got behind or off schedule and got out of order. "Any killer that kills so methodically must be in complete turmoil right about now, and I think in his rush to get back on track or catch up, he's making mistakes; for example, is it possible he made a mistake by putting the number fifteen under your windshield? Do any of your students have a car like yours?"

"I don't know because I've never paid any attention. I wonder if my sister will get suspicious if I go out to the parking lot twenty times today to see if there is another car like mine there?"

I smiled. "Whatever it takes."

"That's my philosophy too. Maybe I'll just ask my sister to check for me."

"Even better." I giggled, and so did Sophie Rose.

"I don't see things all that clearly, but I can't tell at all that you have a prothesis," I said.

"Of course you can't. As much money as the insurance company spent for it, I can't tell either, and that's almost not a joke," Sophie Rose said. "What's your point?"

CHAPTER SIX

"I know I'm bouncing from one thing to another, but that's how I think, so if the number on your car was not a mistake, how would the killer know you have a physical infirmity?" I asked.

"That is an excellent point, and I have no answer; I never consider talking about it because my artificial leg is just another part of me, even if it isn't the original one I had when I was born. I don't talk about my right thumb, even though it is a little larger than my left, because it's just a part of my body, and that's exactly what my leg is," Sophie Rose said.

"That's interesting because that's how I feel about my sight: it's just who I am."

"Noah's family knew about the crash and my injuries not long after we first started seeing each other, but I'll bet most of them have forgotten because they have no filters and would bring it up at every family get together if they remembered. Anyone in my doctor's office would know if they checked my file; same with my physical therapist and my prothesis team. You're being quiet, Maggie; what are you thinking?"

"Every time I ask a great question, four more even more complex questions pop up. How do I push the killer into making one last mistake, so we can be ready for him?"

"I don't know the answer, but you tell me what you want me to do, and if you want to join one of the classes today, you might hear something."

"That's a great idea; for some reason, when people realize I can't see, they often assume I can't hear either."

After we hung up, I washed my hands in case Julie was listening then opened the door.

"Julie's gone for one more test; the doctor signed her release papers, and I've set out her clean clothes on her bed. How was your call?"

"Still no answers other than the ones that lead to more questions; do you suppose you could drop off Julie at home then take me shopping for yoga clothes? I feel a need for lessons at Sophie Rose's studio."

"Julie would enjoy going shopping and could help you find what you want in half the time it would take me, and that might wear her out enough to take a nap this afternoon. She didn't sleep at all last night, so I didn't either."

A blob pushed Julie's wheelchair into the room. "I'll give you a few minutes to dress unless you want me to help you, Miz Vargas. I'll bring you your discharge papers that the nurse went over with you and take you to the discharge exit where Mr. Vargas will meet us with his car."

"I'll be fine; if I need any help, my husband will help me."

"You got yourself a good man, Miz Vargas." The woman locked the wheelchair into place then closed the door as she left.

"These are clean clothes; that was really thoughtful." Julie rose from the wheelchair and quickly dressed. "Did you take home my clothes from yesterday, and that's why I couldn't find them? Why didn't you just tell me?"

Julie continued before Paul could answer her, "Did she say I was supposed to find her when I was ready to leave?"

"I don't think so, and you wouldn't want to miss her," I said.

"Just sitting here and waiting is going to drive me crazy; maybe I'll just lurk in the doorway, so she can see me if she's nearby. I hope she didn't go on a break. I think I know where the breakroom is, but you're right, Chief, I might miss her."

"We're not parked very close, so we'll leave now to get the car, then we'll be waiting for you at the exit," Paul said. "Your phone is on your bedside table; it's fully charged. Text me if the plans change. Ready, Chief?"

After we reached the exit, Paul hurried to his car then pulled up near the door where I waited. When he joined me, I told Paul about the two other girls and their guides. "As soon as I get the text from Sophie Rose, I'll forward it to you, but I don't have any suggestions on what you could do with them."

"Have I told you how much I appreciate you give me a problem to solve without telling me how to solve it?"

I furrowed my brow. "If I already knew the answer, why would I waste your time?"

Paul chuckled. "You wouldn't, but you've described the basis of my frustration with working in an environment with a rigid structure."

I nodded. "I couldn't work like that either."

"Most people thrive with a clearly defined structure, but you, Heather, and I would wither if we couldn't color outside the lines."

After Paul helped Julie into the car, I said, "Julie, I have to have yoga clothes, I'm going to hang out at the yoga studio. Where's the best place for me to shop?"

"I know the perfect place, and I'll help you find exactly what you need to blend in, so you can be the Gray Lady of yoga."

While Julie gave directions to Paul, Palace Guard elbowed me then smirked.

"That's exactly what I need to be, and the best part is that I won't see myself in the get-up."

"Oh, you'll be really cute, Chief," Julie said.

I stuck out my tongue at Palace Guard, and he grinned.

When Paul parked, he said, "I'll wait in the car. I have a few texts and phone calls to make."

Julie picked out four outfits then hung them on a clothes rack while she inspected them. "What do you think? Shall we take them all?"

"I'd like to try them on to see how comfortable they are first."

Palace Guard pointed to two of them, and I copied him.

"I'll try on these two."

I tried on the first one; when I came out of the dressing room, Palace Guard shook his head.

"Thanks," I whispered. "I don't like this one either. How do I carry my pistol without being glaringly obvious?"

Palace Guard pointed to a small backpack that must have been for yoga gear; I gave him a thumbs up.

"That one's cute; what do you think, Chief?" Julie asked.

"It's not all that comfortable."

"Try on the other one, then I'll find more for you to try on for comparison."

After I put on the second one and didn't hate it, I came out of the dressing room.

Palace Guard smiled and nodded.

"This one's comfortable. I only need one, but I do like that yoga backpack."

"Sounds like you're getting the yoga bug. I picked out a yoga mat for you. Shall we find a couple more outfits for you?"

"I think one will be great for now," I said.

"There's plenty of room in this little backpack for your clothes, water bottle, and towel," the clerk said when Julie put our selections on the counter.

"I forgot about a water bottle and a cute yoga towel, Chief. I'll grab them for you."

After I paid, Julie instructed the clerk to cut off the tags and place my outfit, water bottle, and a small towel inside the bag.

While Julie chattered about her plans for the day, I slipped my waist band holster with its pistol into my new backpack.

When Paul parked at the yoga studio, Julie asked, "Do you want me to go in with you, Chief? I can tell you what Sophie Rose is doing with each move, so you don't get lost or confused."

"No, Sophie Rose told me I'd be fine." I grabbed my backpack and my yoga backpack and hurried to the door with Palace Guard's guidance.

I reached for the door handle, then Palace Guard corrected me a few inches, and as we went in, I pushed the video button on my jo.

The blob at the door sniffed, and I blinked at the intensity of disapproval in that simple sound while I turned in her direction then pushed the button on my jo to turn off the video.

Gotcha, crabby girl.

"We're so glad to see you, Gray Lady, aren't we, Sissy?"

The newly named Sissy grunted.

Palace Guard pointed to Sissy then narrowed his eyes and grimaced; I nodded then smiled at Sissy.

She knows something's up.

"I'll show you where the dressing rooms are; I've admired how quickly you have learned to orient yourself to your surroundings. How did you do that?"

"Self-preservation," I said.

"Of course, but more than that, you have developed such a flowing style in the way you get around," Sophie Rose said.

When we were in the dressing room, Sophie Rose gave me a quick tour. "We have a little time before the class starts. If you'd like to change clothes, then come with me to the office, I have some paperwork to take care of and would love the company."

After I changed and put my street clothes and boots into my backpack, I tapped my ear and raised my eyebrows at Sophie Rose; she nodded.

"Don't you look just the cutest in your new clothes; don't be surprised at how many compliments you'll overhear," Sophie Rose said.

I nodded. *The entire studio is bugged except for the bathroom.*

"You make me blush, Sophie Rose."

Sophie Rose twittered. "It's the truth; you might as well hear it from me."

Palace Guard mimicked a fake gag, and I giggled.

I took Sophie Rose's elbow, and she guided me to her office.

"The two large classrooms, the two dressing rooms, and the nice-sized foyer take up most of the building. My office is small, but it's perfect for me. The owner of the building put in a new security system last week that included an update to our fire alarm system. He replaced the back door with a security door that can't be opened from the outside. He told me he was worried about my clients, but I happen to know the fire marshal was planning to slap a hefty fine on him."

After we were in her office, she pointed to the wall behind her desk. "That poor fire alarm is supposed to be for my office and the two dressing rooms. The fire marshal will be here next week for a final inspection, but I don't think this will pass."

While I sat in the visitor's chair, she said, "Paperwork wears me out, and yoga energizes me. I could never be a fulltime office worker," she said as we sat.

Sophie Rose pulled out a file drawer and removed a folder then tapped on her computer while she hummed.

Sophie Rose sighed. "Time almost got away from me. Ready for your first class, Gray Lady? There will be three other new people in the class, so do what you can; no one is there to judge you."

After we went into the class room, I set my backpacks against the wall and was happy that the room was large enough for the eight blobs and me to have plenty of space.

When I glanced to my right, my eyes widened at Palace Guard who stood next to me; he was barefooted and wore yoga pants and his favorite soccer team T-shirt. *I'll bet he knows yoga. This might not be so bad, after all.*

While Sophie Rose explained what she was doing step-by-step, I copied Palace Guard.

At the end of the class, I whispered, "That was fun."

Palace Guard held out his hand, palm up at his waist, and I smacked it.

I picked up my backpacks I had left against the wall then filed out with the rest of the class and followed them into the changing room.

As I listened to the surrounding conversations, I rolled my eye at some of the catty remarks.

A woman a few feet from me whispered, "My guide told me not to mention this, but he told me my lucky number was seventeen, and I should watch for a sign."

"Really? My guide told me that I would hear about my lucky number soon. I'm excited for you; doesn't it seem like we have been waiting since forever for ours? What do you suppose the number means?"

When the first woman mentioned "guide," I pushed the video button on my jo to capture their conversation and to have photos of them. After they left, I dressed and joined Sophie Rose in her office.

"It sounds like the studio clears out quickly after a class. I think everyone changed then left."

Sophie Rose chuckled. "It's almost a stampede; I should have warned you not to get caught between them and the door. Two of them have baby sitters, and the rest of them go to a coffee shop for humble bragging, from what I understand. You were superb, Gray Lady; are you sure you've never had a yoga lesson before?"

"I haven't, but I did take a gymnastics class one time; now I'm wondering how many of our warmup and cooldown routines were actually yoga."

"They must have been."

I blinked when I heard Paul's voice in my ear because I'd forgotten about my ear bud. "If you can hear me, Chief, take a quick photo of where you are."

I pushed the video button then turned it off.

Paul continued, "In five minutes, I want you to cause a disturbance of some kind then grab Sophie Rose and run out the back door. I'll be waiting in my car."

"Sophie, I'm supposed to rest my eye for five minutes every hour. It's very annoying, but would you time me, so I don't fall asleep?"

"Sure; I'll set my alarm, so I won't forget."

When a cheerful tune played on Sophie Rose's phone, I grabbed my backpacks. "Sophie Rose, we're in danger; pull the fire alarm, then we have to get out of here as fast as we can. Paul is waiting for us in the back."

Sophie Rose pulled the fire alarm and grabbed her backpack. We raced to the back door while the loud clamor of the alarm filled the building.

When Sophie Rose pushed open the heavy door, I heard the pling of a rock behind me; I whirled and shot then raced out behind Sophie Rose.

Sophie Rose slowed when we were outside, and I bumped into her as Paul shouted, "Here! Hurry!"

After we jumped into the open back door of his car, Palace Guard sat in the passenger's seat before Paul sped away.

When we were several blocks away from the yoga studio, Paul veered into an alley then unexpectedly slammed on the brakes; Sophie Rose and I lurched against our seatbelts and instinctively reached for each other to stop the forward motion. We scrambled to unfasten the belts when Paul said, "Move! Get out and run to the street at the end of the alley; Heather will pick you up."

Paul roared away as the three of us raced to the end of the alley. Heather was waiting for us in the shadow of an abandoned building.

"I'm parked on the street. Take a breath, and we'll take a little stroll to my car. I'll tell you what's going on after we're on the road."

The three of us casually sauntered to Heather's car while Palace Guard scanned the alley then the street.

"Front seat, Sophie Rose," Heather said.

Palace Guard and I climbed into the back.

"Take off your eyepatch, Chief; it makes you too easy to recognize. There is a pair of sunglasses and a ball cap on the seat next to the door. Put them on."

I removed my eyepatch and put on the sunglasses and ball cap.

"Where are we going?" I asked.

"You and Sophie Rose are going to be split up at my insistence, and Larry and Noah agreed."

"I don't understand at all what's going on, but I'm not some wimpy civilian," Sophie Rose growled. "As long as I'm with Maggie, no one will know she's Gray Lady because everyone knows the Gray Lady is a loner."

"No," Heather said. "Chief would protect you, even if it meant sacrificing herself."

"You hit below the belt; you know that, right?" Sophie Rose said.

Heather nodded. "I learned from the best."

"I'm sorry, Gray Lady, but I refuse to be a liability. Call me if you need me," Sophie Rose said.

"I can do that," I said.

Heather exhaled. "I'm going to get into line at a popular drive-through about two blocks from here. Chief, slouch down, so you can't be seen from the outside. Sophie Rose, when my car reaches the entrance door, get out of the car and go inside the restaurant then head toward the restrooms. Noah will be waiting for you at a table. Your job is to forget anything you've heard."

After Sophie Rose was in the restaurant, Heather said, "When we round the corner, Chief, slide over the seat to the front and don't kick me in the head because I'll know it wasn't an accident."

While I slid into the passenger's seat, I asked, "What's going on, Heather?"

"A neighbor of the GBI agent who was assigned to be Sophie Rose's sister called the police when the agent didn't answer her door even though her car was parked in the driveway. The police contacted GBI who broke into the house because she was supposed to be on surveillance. There was blood all over her kitchen, but no sign of the agent."

Heather cleared her throat then continued, "Before the search for the agent began, the local sheriff received a call about a deer near the shoulder of a county road. A deputy checked and found the agent's body. The killer had slashed her throat and carved the number sixteen in her abdomen. Julie called the hospital, and she and Paul are going to pick up Henry right away. Paul identified number seventeen from the photo you sent, so the sheriff is talking to her parents to come up with a way to remove her from harm."

"What did you leave out?"

"That's it," Heather said.

I'll have to tell Paul that Heather's not in our league.

"So who was Sophie Rose's sister?" I asked.

"She was a paid killer and has been on everyone's top ten most wanted list. I recognized her from your photo and called Larry. He sent the police to the yoga studio. Tell me about your diversion."

"I told Sophie Rose I needed to close my eye for five minutes and asked her to time me. When the five minutes were up, I told Sophie Rose to pull the fire alarm, then we grabbed our things and ran to the back door. When Sophie Rose opened the door, I heard a rock hit the floor behind me, which is how Palace Guard trained me to shoot, so I turned, shot, and ran."

"Palace Guard, you are an amazing instructor. The police found the imposter in the hallway; her gun had two rounds missing from its chamber and was still in her hand. The police recovered one bullet from the wall next to the back door but haven't found the second one yet; she was dead from a shot in the middle of her forehead."

"I didn't even see her; I just shot and ran."

"Remember the girl with no number? The police are on their way to talk to her parents. Paul discovered the girl drives a car that is the same model, year, and color as Sophie Rose's car, so Sophie Rose was never the target. Chief, you're a wild card because you're getting one step ahead of the killer."

"I feel naked." I put on my eyepatch. "That's better. So where are we going?"

"I'll hand you off to a contact who will take you to a safe house."

"That's interesting; whose orders are those?"

When Heather didn't answer me, I said, "Larry."

"He wants you out of the picture as far as the killer is concerned."

"Ah, so you're working for Larry now."

"Don't be like that, Chief," Heather growled.

"I'm not a wimpy civilian, either, Heather; I promise I won't shoot anybody at the safe house, but you know I won't stay, don't you?"

Heather stopped for a light and turned toward me. "You have to, Chief."

"Why? What did you leave out?"

"Not a big deal."

"I suppose I have no choice then."

Palace Guard poked my shoulder, and when I glanced at him, he glared.

Heather exhaled. "I told Larry you'd take off the first chance you got. So, what are we going to do?"

"What's the no big deal? Whatever it is, it pushed you and Larry over the edge."

Heather shook her head. "The killer butchered the agent's right eye."

I shuddered. "I'm sorry to hear that. He's truly brutal, isn't he?"

"Brutal is definitely the right word," Heather said.

"Do you know where the safe house is?"

"No, but I can find out. What does Palace Guard think?"

"No big deal."

Heather chuckled. "Your fabrications are so transparent when you want them to be. If it's any consolation, Palace Guard, I understand."

"We know something else about the killer: he doesn't have a subtle bone in his body, does he?" I asked.

"No, he doesn't, and you're the only one in the world that would think of that."

"We don't know what he looks like. I need to talk to Henry because I think he does."

"Finally. You've come up with something I can work with. I have a safe house in downtown Savannah that I can use. We'll need to grab some groceries, and you'll have to tell Larry we're going underground."

"Me? Why me? It's your safe house, and you're driving."

"Yep, I'm driving. Call him, or I'll take you to the hand-off point, and you'll never know I abandoned you until I drive off."

Heather held up her hand, and Palace Guard smacked it.

"Palace Guard smacked my hand, didn't he?"

"Don't bother me; I have a phone call to make, even though I believe blackmail is morally and ethically reprehensible," I growled.

"Call Larry." My phone rang. "He's too busy to answer; I'll just hang up and text him."

Larry picked up before the second ring. "What's wrong, Maggie?"

"I have to tell you that Heather is going underground with me, so we'll be together."

"Thanks for letting me know, sweetie, but that was our plan; I'm really busy, so get straight to the punchline: why did Heather make you call me?"

"Because Miss Smarty Pants Chief decided she didn't want to cooperate and was planning her escape from the safe house, so we're going to Savannah; I have a safe house there," Heather said.

I hate my phone; there's no such thing as a private conversation if I forget to use my earbud.

Larry roared, "Maggie, this is one of your schemes, isn't it? Heather, drive her to our house; I'll quit my job and meet you there, then we'll move to Alaska."

I shook my head. *Alaska's too cold.*

"You have to find the killer, Larry; I'll take care of Chief," Heather said.

"I don't like this one bit, Maggie; why can't you cooperate for once?"

"I am; I didn't sneak off without Heather."

Larry hung up.

"That went well, don't you think?" I asked.

Palace Guard glared, and Heather laughed.

After she pulled into a parking lot, Heather parked near a store. "We need groceries; I won't be long."

I watched blobs go into the grocery store and other blobs that hurried out with their full shopping carts. I cringed when one of them rushed toward Heather's car, and Palace Guard patted my shoulder.

"I'm glad you're with me, Palace Guard."

I squinted as a familiar blob rolled a shopping cart toward the car. "Is that Heather?"

Palace Guard raised his eyebrows and nodded then tilted his head as he stared at me.

"I can't see her, but I recognize her walk, don't you?"

Palace Guard narrowed his eyes as he watched her then shook his head.

As she neared the car, I said, "I wonder if I'll recognize Paul too, now that I know what to look for."

Heather put four sacks of groceries into the back seat then ran the cart to the nearest cart corral before she hopped into the driver's seat. "We'll have plenty of food for four days, but I suspect Larry will either come up with something or catch the killer before then."

The closer we got to Heather's safe house, the slower and noisier the traffic became. The stench of old garbage filled the air; sirens, howling dogs, the occasional distant sounds of gunshots, and the cacophony of honking horns accompanied the constant rattle of trucks that seemed as though they had lost their will to live as they doggedly lumbered from one pothole to another.

"This is not what I expected," I said as Heather pulled into an alley then stopped in front of a one-car dilapidated garage.

"Jump out with your stuff and grab at least one sack if you can manage it; your door won't open after I pull into the garage."

While I climbed out, Heather set the other three sacks and her backpack outside the garage then parked her car in the tight space. After she pulled down the rolling door, we headed to the steps of the old house that didn't look much larger than the garage.

"Hey there, Pearl, who you got there? Is you royalty because that sister of yours looks like a pirate princess," an old woman said from a second-story balcony of the house across the alley. "You ever heard 'bout that famous pirate, Bonnie Calico Anne? She was as beautiful as she was fierce and brave. Welcome to the neighborhood, Calico. I'm Grandma Zee, the last of the great-grandmas."

Palace Guard poked me.

"Appreciate it, Grandma Zee," I said.

"Polite too, just like you, Pearl. Your mama woulda been proud of her girls. You movin' back for good, Pearl?"

I copied Heather as she bowed her head when Grandma Zee mention her mom.

"I'm in between jobs right now, so I'm not sure. I have some prospects, though, and expect to have something before the end of the week."

"You'll get exactly what you want, Pearl."

I raised my eyebrows. *I wonder if Grandma Zee is what some call a seer?*

CHAPTER SEVEN

"Thanks, Grandma Zee; I wonder sometimes." Heather led me into her safe house.

I inhaled the surprisingly soft aroma of old wood and magnolias as the house in the seedy neighborhood suddenly transformed into a welcoming home when we stepped inside.

"Getting a name from Grandma Zee was huge," Heather said. "Nobody in the neighborhood will mess with us, and nobody from outside the neighborhood will be allowed near our house. If anyone asks your name or who your people are, tell them you are Calico, and you're Pearl's sister. The rule is our Grandma Zee names are never spoken outside of the neighborhood."

"Why does Grandma Zee call you Pearl?"

"This house belonged to my mom's aunt; Mom and I spent our summers here as long as I could remember until we moved to Harperville when I was eight; after that, Mom put me on a bus and sent me here for the summers until she died my sophomore year of high school. Mom said Grandma Zee called me Pearl because I was the precious stone of this gritty neighborhood. My great-aunt and I stayed in touch until she died not long after I finished the academy and started working; I was surprised that she left the house to me, but I was grateful because I had wonderful memories of my mom being happy here. The rest of the relatives didn't think much of the house and were relieved to be shed of any responsibility for the rickety old shack, as they called it. After the lawyer sent me the keys, I packed a small bag and drove straight here after work in my short black leather skirt, a red crop top, and high-heeled boots. Even though I hadn't been here since I was fifteen, Grandma Zee recognized me right away and told me she was happy to see that I was working, supporting myself, and didn't have no babies. 'Can you imagine this beautiful home in the hands of one of those ignorant ruffians?' That's a direct quote of what she said. Have you ever heard of the pirate Bonnie Calico Anne?"

"In a way, I have. Grandma Zee took a little literary license with her historical information. One of the most famous women pirates was Anne Bonny, and she joined forces with Calico Jack, a flamboyant pirate of the Caribbean. The fact that Grandma Zee knew about them tells me she is probably better educated and more well-read than the community realizes."

"You pirate librarians come in right handy, Calico."

"I have some questions for Paul. Is it safe to text him?" I asked as I handed items from the grocery sacks to Heather.

"Why would you want to text him when you could talk directly to him?"

When I furrowed my brow, Palace Guard pointed to my jo.

Of course.

I pushed the audio button. "Paul, let me know when you can talk."

"Yep," Paul said.

It's still startling hearing Paul talk through the earbud.

"While we wait, I'm going to make cookies," Heather said. "Want to help?"

"I sure do; I miss cooking."

"Good, then you can help me cook our supper too. I'll put the flour, white sugar, brown sugar, and measuring cups and spoons in front of you. Tell me what you need as you go along."

"I think I can handle it without help."

"You heard her, Palace Guard," Heather said.

While I guesstimated, mis-measured, and mixed the butter and flour instead of the butter and sugar, Palace Guard smiled, and Heather and I laughed as she corrected my worst errors and suggested adjustments I could make next time.

After I put the cookies into the oven, Heather said, "If you tell me when you're ready for them to come out of the oven, I'll pull them out."

"Why don't you give me a house tour while we wait?" I asked.

"Let's start at the front door, so you'll have an idea of where the rooms are because we came in the kitchen door."

She led me to the front door. "This is the living room; most of the furniture is my mom's that I had in storage, but a few of the pieces are the ones my great-aunt wanted me to have. Her grandchildren sold or gave away the rest."

"Does the fireplace work?" I lightly rubbed my fingers across the hand-hewn wooden mantle.

"Sure does. It used to be the only source of heat until my grandmother put in an oil stove for her sister, but it's hard to get heating oil these days, so we'll have a fire in the fireplace after supper. If I wanted to live here fulltime, it wouldn't take much to put in a gas heater because the stove and hot water heater are gas. Before we go upstairs, let's go into the kitchen."

"The cookies smell ready," I said.

"What's up, Chief?" Paul asked as Heather opened the oven door and then pulled out the cookie sheet.

"Perfect," Heather said. "Go ahead and talk to Paul."

"Becky said she would give me Vanessa's journals," I said.

"Julie can call her, and we'll pick them up. They may give me some answers for all the gaps we have. What else?"

"Would you ask Julie if she saw more than one man?"

"I can answer that; she told me she didn't even see the man who attacked her. He grabbed her from behind, bound her hands behind her back, then pushed her into the break room. She stumbled and hit her head against the file cabinet. He must have locked her in so he could rifle through our offices."

"What are in those files?" Heather asked.

"Julie said most of the drawers are empty because the only paper documents we have are contracts signed by our clients; Julie scans them then sends the originals to the accountant, who sets up the accounts for billing and payment."

"How's Henry doing?" I asked.

"When Julie called earlier to let the hospital know she would be right there to pick him up, the nurse said his doctor was concerned about his heart and ordered another test; the nurse said someone would call Julie as soon as Henry was ready for release. We're still waiting for the test results," Paul said.

"Julie can't pick him up," I said. "Julie Vargas was just released from the hospital; she can't go back a few hours later as Julie Perez."

"She's right, Paul. Chief and I need to pick up Henry. We'll meet you at our back up drop off point that you and I designated earlier."

"We'll let you know when Henry is released. I'll be in touch," Paul said.

After we turned off our transmitters, I said, "This is perfect. I wanted to talk to Henry, but it had to be privately. I have some questions that I thought Julie could ask him, but I'm not sure Henry will talk to anyone except me."

Heather said, "I'll show you the bedrooms, then we'll grab a couple of cookies for the road and head to the hospital."

When we reached the stairs, Heather said, "There's a small bathroom tucked in the corner of the hall behind the stairs."

As we climbed the steep stairs, I asked, "Aren't we going to wait for Paul to tell us that Henry can be released?"

"Nope; you'll play your blind niece card, so we can take Henry away from the hospital before anyone knows he's gone."

I glanced at Palace Guard, and he nodded.

"I think Henry knows the killer; if you're thinking the killer could be connected to the hospital, Palace Guard agrees with you."

When we went into a small bedroom, Heather said, "This bedroom was my aunt's room. After she died, one of my cousins and I replaced the old bed with a new queen-sized one; he had planned to spend a weekend getaway here with his wife, but they never did because she didn't like the neighborhood. I always wondered what Grandma Zee called her, but I was afraid to ask."

Heather stopped at the next door. "The bathroom has a beautiful clawfoot tub, but my mom told my grandma there had to be a shower in the house before I could stay here without her because she was positive I wouldn't rinse my hair adequately after I shampooed unless I took a shower. I hate to admit it, but she was probably right because I was too impatient for all that careful rinsing nonsense. My grandma had a plumber friend of hers put in the small bathroom with a shower downstairs and told her sister that she was getting too old to climb the stairs to use the restroom."

When we went into the second small bedroom that overlooked the street, Heather said, "Mom and I always stayed in this room together. There were two old-fashioned wrought iron bedframes with coiled steel springs and cotton mattresses and were just as uncomfortable as they sound, but Mom and I never cared because we were here. I updated the old springs and mattresses but kept the bedframes because they reminded of the stories Mom told me after we went to bed."

"I love your memories here; no wonder you kept the house."

"Ready to break Henry out of the hospital?"

"Sure am."

"Are you girls leaving without eating first?" Grandma Zee asked as Heather hurried to her garage.

"Just a quick excursion into town. We'll cook after we get back."

"That's good. It's asking for trouble to go clubbing without eating first."

As Heather weaved through traffic at a break-neck pace, she said, "The only time I've ever been clubbing was when I was working; you'd never be able to take the noise."

I held onto my armrest and the console next to me to keep from being slammed against the door. "Guess we'll have to skip."

"That won't be hard; they don't usually open until after we're asleep, anyway. We're almost at the hospital. I'll park, then we can go in together. You know Henry's room number, right?"

"Yes," I said.

After Heather swerved around a garbage truck then floored the accelerator to pass it before she hit the oncoming furniture truck, I glanced back at Palace Guard. His face was pale, and he clutched his armrest with one hand and had the palm of his other hand firmly planted on the roof.

We would never be on a daredevil driving team.

When Heather parked at the hospital parking lot, Palace Guard jumped out and stood by my door as he put his hand on his heart and gasped for air.

"No need for the drama," Heather muttered.

Palace Guard raised his eyebrows as he stared at her.

After we were in the elevator, it crept to the third floor, then the door slid open.

"We should have taken the stairs; we'd have been on our way out by now," Heather said.

As we passed the nurse's station, a woman said, "I'm glad you're here, Miss Perez. Your uncle has been released, but someone must have decided on one more test because he's not in his room. You can wait for him there, if you like. I'm sure he won't be very long. The doctor didn't like his heart rate on his new medicine earlier, but that's been adjusted, and he's fine now."

As we hurried to Henry's room, Heather whispered, "Has Julie heard anything from the hospital?"

"No, do you want her to call them and ask if he can be released?" Paul asked.

"No, that's okay; just asking."

"I don't like this at all," Heather said.

When we went into the room, Heather said, "What do we do?"

Palace Guard pointed to the bathroom door that was in the room. I raised my eyebrows, and he nodded.

Heather and I hurried to the door, and Heather tried to open the door.

"Locked," she said.

"Henry, are you in there?" I whispered. "It's me, Maggie."

Heather picked the lock and opened the door, and I exhaled with relief when I saw Henry-blob.

"You're been released; do you have anything to take with you?" Heather asked.

"Just this worthless goodie bag." Henry handed it to Heather.

Heather peered into the plastic sack. "You're right about that. We'll just leave it. Henry, your collar is askew. I'll fix it for you."

"Thank you."

Heather removed a small object from his collar then bent down and removed another small object from the cuff of his pants.

"Do you have a jacket, Uncle Henry?" I asked.

"No, this is all they gave me."

"Are those new glasses?" I asked as we headed to out of the room.

"Yes, but I never wore glasses before; I don't see what difference they make."

No one was at the nurse's station when we left. Heather hurried ahead to the elevators while Henry, Palace Guard, and I followed her at a slower pace.

I heard her on my earbud. "Paul, we're at the hospital. I removed two bugs from Henry's clothing. I suggest a change of clothes and shoes for him. You have fifteen minutes before the handoff."

"We'll be there."

By the time we reached Heather, she was in the elevator with her finger on the open button. After we joined her, Heather said, "Your glasses are dirty; I'll clean them for you."

Henry gave his glasses to Heather, and she held onto them.

When we were on the main floor, Heather said, "I'll go to the car then pick you up under the canopy. There was a light mist earlier."

After she disappeared, Henry said, "She's quite the go-getter, isn't she?"

I nodded. "She doesn't do anything slowly."

While we waited for Heather, Palace Guard tapped on his ear then pointed to Henry.

"Do you have new hearing aids, Uncle Henry?"

"They gave me a pair to try out, but they itch my ears."

I held out my hand, and he removed them then gave them to me. I pushed the audio button on my jo. "Your hearing aids probably itch because they're new."

"Give them to me when I pick you up," Heather said. The sound of the interstate was loud in the background when Heather spoke.

She must have put the bugs inside her car then walked close to the road.

"Did you hear, Paul?" Heather asked. "Can you meet us at the gas station two blocks from the hospital with the clothes? I can fill up, and you can go inside then to the restroom. Chief and Henry can go inside, and he can get the clothes from you then change and leave with you. I'll join Chief inside for a few minutes and ditch the bugs before we leave. I'll write Henry a quick note, so he knows what's going on."

After Heather parked under the canopy, she opened the back door for Henry then handed him a note while I climbed into the car.

"I have to stop and get gas. Anyone need to use the restroom?"

"I do," I said.

"So do I," Henry said.

Heather drove slowly to the gas station and caught every light on red along the way. I glanced at Palace Guard, and he rolled his eyes.

"Traffic was terrible," Heather said as she pulled up to a pump.

"We won't be long," I said.

"I'll park after I fill up and come find you," Heather said.

After we climbed out of the car, Henry offered me his elbow, and we strolled inside together.

I pushed the audio button. "Lots of people in here."

"I'm waiting," Paul said.

Henry led me toward the restrooms, then we separated as he went into the men's room, and I went into the women's.

"I gave him the bag, and he's in a stall changing." The sound of an extra-loud, high-speed hand dryer in the background almost drowned out Paul's voice.

"There's Julie. We didn't see anything we needed in the store after all," Paul said.

"We need more ice cream and beer," Heather joined me as I stood in front of the large ice cream case. "I'll grab some cold beer; you pick out the ice cream."

I pointed to a gallon of ice cream and glanced at Palace Guard, and he shrugged; when I pointed to a different gallon carton, he nodded, and I picked it up.

"Vanilla caramel?" Heather asked. "Interesting; let's check out and head to our castle."

After we were in the car, Heather started the engine and pulled away from the gas station. "Who picked out the ice cream? It's my favorite."

"Palace Guard."

Heather sped north on the interstate and veered across three lanes of traffic to exit at the last minute before she headed back then drove her usual break-neck speed to her house. I glanced at Palace Guard, and his eyes were closed while he held onto the back of the seat and his arm rest.

That might be the smartest thing to do, but I'd rather know when I can scream.

She stopped outside her garage to drop me off, then after she rolled down the garage door and locked it, we headed toward the house.

"Hey there, girls. I never knew your daddy was related to Grandma D. I hate that Grandma D is gone, but she went just like she told me she wanted: with her guns blazing," Grandma Zee said.

Heather and I automatically bowed our heads at the mention of Grandma D.

"How did you hear about Grandma D and Daddy?" I asked.

"I'm not supposed to tell you, but Honey Boy told me he was your cousin on your daddy's side. I sure was surprised to see him. Grandma D thought the world of him and his wife. Do you know his wife? I heard they call her the Gray Ghost, but nobody ever told me why."

"Not very well, but everybody gets busy, and we don't visit as much as we used to when we were kids," Heather said.

"Well, Honey Boy has a surprise for you two, and I won't spoil it, but you'll be happy to know you won't be cooking tonight after all. Don't let on that I told you."

I smiled and waved.

"Thanks, Grandma Zee; he does love to pull surprises on us, so we'll let him have his fun," Heather said.

As we headed to the house, Heather asked, "I remember when Larry was your cousin. Is Honey Boy Larry?"

"That's his Grandma D name. You can't say nothin', Pearl. You made the rules."

"You're right, Calico. Names stay here."

When she unlocked the door to the house, she asked, "So what do you think of that wife of his?"

"I heard she was really smart and terribly modest, but kind of elusive, which is why they call her Gray Ghost," I said.

We giggled as we went inside, then Heather said, "Whoa, I smell fried chicken."

Larry hurried out of the kitchen, and I raced to him; he caught me up and hugged me.

"I've been undercover for a few weeks," he said. "Imagine my surprise when my guys told me Grandma Zee was tickled that Pearl and her sister Calico were back home. When do I get to hear the story?"

"After we eat or while we eat, just not now." Heather put the ice cream into the refrigerator. "I'm famished for good fried chicken; what else do you have? I'll set the table."

"Fried chicken, chicken livers, fries, hush puppies, coleslaw and rolls. I lost all my self-control when I got to the front of the line at the chicken takeout. Are we off duty tonight? I brought beer."

"We were planning on it; we picked up beer and ice cream," I said.

While we ate and sipped our beer, Larry said, "Tell me about Pearl and Calico."

Heather told him about being named Pearl when she was a toddler then told him about Bonnie Calico Anne, the Pirate Princess.

"Was there really a Pirate Princess?" Larry popped another hush puppy into his mouth.

"We have a Pirate Librarian; give ole cuz the story, Calico," Heather said.

I told Larry about Anne Bonny and Calico Jack.

"I see where Calico came from." Larry nodded. "Honey Boy isn't a pirate, but I treasure the name because it came from Della."

When we all pushed back from the table, Heather said, "There's plenty here for tomorrow. I'll wrap it up then tackle the dishes."

"I'm the dishwasher expert here," Larry said.

"I'll help clear the table," I said.

After Larry and Heather washed, dried, and put away the dishes, Larry started a fire in the fireplace.

While I sipped my hot tea, and Larry and Heather drank their second beer, Larry said, "Tell me what you did today, and then it's my turn."

"This won't be in chronological order, so you'll have to keep up." Heather told him about the earbuds.

"I need an earbud," Larry said.

"Yes, you do." Heather picked up her phone and sent a text. "We'll pick it up tomorrow. You'll be on the same frequency as Paul because he's my boss, and he's doing all the ground work for us. Are you okay with that?"

"Paul? Of course, but shouldn't you check with him before you spring me on him?"

"Good idea. Tell Paul, Chief," Heather said.

I pushed the button on my jo. "Paul, Heather has something to tell you."

Larry chuckled. "I only laugh because she does that to me all the time, Heather, and it always catches me off guard."

Heather grumbled, "Grandma Zee told us they call your wife Gray Ghost; I sure am glad I didn't correct her because she got that right; she comes out of nowhere, doesn't she?"

"Are you there, Heather?" Paul asked.

"Your boss is impossible," Heather said. "Larry jumped the fence and is joining us. If you say no, we'll feed him ice cream, then send him on his way."

"In the morning," I added.

"Right, in the morning, because he brought us fried chicken and hush puppies."

"He stays," Paul said. "If he'll keep an eye on the two of you, maybe I can get some work done."

"Paul's going to think about it, honey," I said.

Larry nodded. "He said I'm in, didn't he?"

I wrinkled my nose then told him about Sophie Rose and what Paul discovered.

"Tell him about Henry, Chief," Heather said.

"I'm certain Henry saw the killer and recognized him. I need to talk to Henry and thought I'd have a chance tonight, but Heather found bugs on him."

Heather explained the handoff of Henry to Paul.

"What's your plan, sweetie?" Larry asked.

"I don't know; maybe I will in the morning."

"Your turn, Honey Boy," Heather said.

"You know about the agent who was supposed to be Sophie Rose's sister, right?"

"Yes, and we heard about the special message for Chief," Heather said. "We intend to stop him before he gets close to her."

"I was pulled from my undercover assignment; my supervisor told me I could lead the investigation to solve the murders, and he would give me a team. When I told him I couldn't work this with a team unless the team was undercover and willing to do whatever it took to stop the killer, he told me I couldn't work for him. I was ready to be fired because I decided my next step was to find you two. I called Paul, and he picked up Lucy and Spike."

"Are you fired? If you are, I'll take that second beer after all, so we can celebrate," I said.

Larry snorted. "He told me someone else has been asking for me to take over the case, so guess who I'm working for."

"Really?" I asked. "You agreed to work for Kate?"

"I'm on loan," Larry said.

"How did you make that leap?" Heather asked. "I was sitting right here and heard exactly what you heard, Pirate Princess, and I definitely did not hear anything about Kate Coyle or the FBI."

"Who else could it have been? Who else would want a team that gets results and fast?" I asked.

"Larry, Paul and I don't work for Kate; we work for Chief," Heather said.

"Technically, you work for Gray Flanagan Agency, and I am one of the two owners."

Heather growled, "Fine, the stuffy part of me half-works for you, but the action part of me works all-in for Chief."

Palace Guard peered at her and scratched his head.

"I have no idea of what I said, either, Palace Guard," Heather snickered.

"How long have you been seeing Palace Guard and Spike?" Larry asked.

Heather shrugged. "Who says I have?"

Palace Guard raised his hand, and Heather automatically jumped up and smacked it.

Larry rolled his eyes, and I covered my mouth to keep from laughing while I pushed the audio record button on my jo. "I've added Paul to the conversation, Larry."

Larry nodded. "Back to Kate: Heather, you and Paul will remain employed by the Gray Flanagan Agency; Kate contacted Shantelle, and Shantelle and I signed a contract for the Gray Flanagan Agency to perform services for the FBI through Kate. All of this is just administrative trivia; you still work for Paul, Heather."

"The bottom line is we're working together, right?" I asked.

Larry smiled and nodded.

"We aren't focused on solving any murders. We are driven to stop the murders. Is that okay with Kate?" I asked.

"She's counting on it," Larry said.

"How involved will she get?" I asked.

"I told her you'd walk away if she tried, and she said she knew that and would stay out of our way," Larry said.

"What do you think, Heather?" I asked.

CHAPTER EIGHT

"I don't trust Kate, but we definitely need Larry. I'd feel better if you reviewed the contract, though, Chief," Heather said.

Larry nodded. "I sent it to Paul; I thought he was the most impartial."

"After he's reviewed it and asked Shantelle any questions he might have, he'll hand it off to Julie, and she'll tear it to shreds for any loopholes. If Julie says it's okay, it's a solid contract, and I'm okay," Heather said.

"You'll hear back from us first thing in the morning," Paul said.

I nodded. "You know what we need?"

"More ice cream?" Larry asked.

"Always, but we need someone working at the hospital."

"Kate could swing that," Heather said.

"On it." Larry picked up his phone and put it on speakerphone.

When Kate answered, Larry said, "You're on speakerphone. Heather needs a job at the hospital."

"Environmental aide okay?" Kate asked. "Heather, show up at the hospital employee entrance at seven thirty and tell them you lost your ID. Your name is Annie Smith, and they'll have your driver's license and employee badge. If they ask you to verify your birthdate, it's Maggie's. Anything else?"

Palace Guard, Heather, and I shook our heads, and Larry said, "That's it."

Kate hung up.

"She'll find a way to find out what we're up to," I said.

"It won't be through us," Paul said. "Check your things for a tracker."

"Will do," Heather said, and I turned off the audio.

I rose, and Heather checked my clothes and my shoes. I handed her my jo, and she and Palace Guard examined it closely.

When Palace Guard held up his thumb, Larry and I nodded.

Heather picked up my backpack then held it up. "Look what I found."

Larry put his arm around me. "There's a bullet hole in your backpack, sweetie."

Heather checked the other side. "There's no exit hole."

"Where was your backpack?" Larry asked.

"It was next to Julie's desk."

Heather dumped out my backpack onto the table.

"What's that?" Larry pointed to the pile.

"Chief, it's a small, mangled circle of metal with wires and a bullet embedded in it." Heather handed it to Larry.

After he and Palace Guard examined it, I held out my hand with my palm up, and Larry gave it to me.

I felt the mass with my fingertips then found the bullet. "I don't know what it is, but it's definitely broken."

"That guy was a better shot than we thought." Heather finished rummaging through my things, then I repacked my backpack.

Heather checked her backpack. "So far, so good. Where's yours, Larry?"

"In the kitchen."

Heather hurried to the kitchen; she dashed to the stairs a few minutes later. "All clear down here."

Palace Guard followed her.

When they returned to the living room, Heather tapped her transmitter. "All clear."

"Thanks," Paul said. "Did you find anything?"

"We found a bullet hole in Chief's backpack and the second bullet from the office stuck in a mangled piece of metal inside her backpack. I couldn't tell if it was an audio transmitter or a GPS locator, but it's trashed."

"That's good news; that means whoever put it there hasn't been able to track Chief since the shooting," Paul said.

"I'll send it to my techies to analyze." Heather tapped her transmitter again, and it was off.

"Where's your truck, Larry?"

"I have an old car in a self-service storage unit a couple of blocks away."

"Good, I'll be leaving early for work; I'll pick up your earbud on the way; if you'll meet me at the hospital employee parking lot, I'll give it to you. What do you have in mind for tomorrow, Chief?"

"I want to visit Henry, Lucy, and Spike," I said.

"I'm your chauffeur," Larry said. "We can go there after we meet Heather at the hospital if it's not too early. What else?"

"Is Sophie Rose still under guard?"

"Technically, no; GBI reassigned her undercover guard to the murder of the agent, and the two troopers were released from their temporary assignments to GBI," Larry said.

"Noah has probably assigned one of the troopers to guard Sophie Rose," I said. "That's tricky; we can't ask Noah how reliable the trooper is, but I need to talk to Sophie Rose."

"I understand and don't have any solutions right off, but let me take that one," Larry said.

"On to more important things. If you two get up early enough, I'll have breakfast ready," Heather said. "Any requests?"

"Bacon," Larry said.

Heather sniffed the air then crossed her arms. "Larry, you smell good; ditch the deodorant, and you can't shower tonight or tomorrow, so you'll have a chance to ripen. Chief, you're allowed to smell nice and flowery."

"Thank you; that's exactly the kind of thing I didn't learn in the classroom," Larry said.

"That's awful," Heather said. "You can't just dress like you belong where you are; you have to smell, walk, and talk like you belong. Grunts and partial sentences will get you by, and you can't walk with your shoulders back; drop that self-assured attitude in the way you hold your head while you scan everyone around you. Slump a little, narrow your eyes, and be suspicious of your surroundings like everyone is out to get you because they are."

"That's a tall order." Larry narrowed his eyes.

"Too bad; do it." Heather headed up the stairs. "Goodnight."

Palace Guard and Larry practiced slumping while they narrowed their eyes and glanced surreptitiously around the room until my head jerked, and I opened my eye.

"Okay, sweetie, let's go to bed."

"I can shower tomorrow morning," I mumbled as we went upstairs.

"Don't rub it in, Calico," Heather called out from her room.

Larry grunted, and I rolled my eye.

We have to catch that killer, so I can have back my literate, talkative, cop husband.

• • • ● • ● ● • • •

I rolled over to snuggle against Larry, but he wasn't there. I opened my eye, and it was dark. After I sat up in the unfamiliar bed, I remembered we were at Heather's house; I inhaled as I stretched. *Bacon?*

I quickly dressed then made the bed while Larry and Heather whispered downstairs; I sneaked down to join them, but one of the steps creaked.

"Coffee's ready; better get down here quick if you want breakfast, Calico," Heather said.

When I joined them in the kitchen, I grumbled, "Why didn't you wake me when you got up?"

Larry grunted; Palace Guard slouched in a corner; he narrowed his eyes then gave me a quick upward nod.

Heather pointed to a chair. "Sit down; breakfast is ready, and you needed your beauty sleep more than a shower."

I leaned over my plate and breathed in the aroma of bacon, a fried egg, and pan-fried potatoes.

Heather stood at the refrigerator. "Do you want ketchup for your potatoes, Chief?"

"Yes, please."

"So, now we're all smiles and polite with the pleases when there are fried potatoes involved." Heather refilled our cups before she sat to eat her breakfast.

"I'm going to get my car." Larry was the first to finish eating.

"Walk fast, like you have somewhere important to go; don't run, though, because you don't want to look like somebody is chasing you. Pull into my driveway then head out the way you came in. I'll be right behind you, but I'll take a different route to the hospital than you do; you'll get there a few minutes ahead of me, so wait near the employee entrance like you're waiting for somebody to get off work."

After Larry left to get his car, Heather and I finished eating then washed and dried the dishes.

"Grab your things, Calico. You have to be ready to leave as soon as he gets here, so I can get to work on time."

I put on my sweatshirt and picked up my backpack. "What color is my eyepatch?" I asked while I listened for an old car.

"Calico," Heather said.

"Why did I ask, Palace Guard? I should have known she'd say Calico."

Palace Guard nodded.

"Where's your scowl, Soldier Boy?" Heather narrowed her eyes. "Are you taking your coat, Calico? The weather's a little chilly, but it might turn cold sometime today or tonight."

I grabbed my coat before we went outside, and Heather locked the door to the house then opened the garage door. When Larry pulled in the driveway, I jumped into his old car, but Palace Guard waited for Heather to back out and waved goodbye.

"Isn't Palace Guard going with us?" Larry asked.

"No, he's decided to stay with Heather today. He must expect trouble at the hospital."

Larry frowned as he backed out of the driveway. "How can he keep her safe?"

"The weekend before she started her new job, Palace Guard trained Heather to throw a knife with deadly accuracy, and he and Spike taught her how to fight dirty; that was before she could see them. Heather will pay attention to whatever Palace Guard tells her to do, and he won't let her walk into any dangerous situations unprepared."

"Spike's going to have a fit." Larry chuckled.

"I know."

Larry's phone buzzed a text. "I need a phone like yours that will read me my texts."

"Yours probably does; I think it's a setting; I'll ask Heather."

"No, I'm sure you're right; I'll figure it out."

I bit my lip, so I wouldn't snicker. *He's too proud to let Heather help him.*

After Larry stopped his car near the employee entrance at the hospital, he pulled out his phone and read the text.

"You're not going to like this. Noah wants me to meet him at the diner where we had coffee last week: a private conversation, just him and me."

"What are you going to do? Leave me at Paul's with grumpy Spike?"

"That's a pretty good plan; I don't have anything else."

"Here's a better plan. I go with you, except I lay flat on the backseat, so I can't be seen."

"I have Honey Boy's earbud. See you in two," Heather said.

Larry stepped out of the car, then after Heather parked, he strolled to the employee entrance; with perfect timing, he reached the door and read one of the notices. After he shook his head and abruptly turned, he bumped into her.

Smooth; it was almost a ballet.

He scowled, and if I hadn't been watching as closely as I could, I would have missed her blob-hand near the pocket of his jacket as she lost then regained her balance.

"Watch whatchyerdoin'," she growled.

He grunt-snorted then returned to the car and pulled out the earbud from his pocket and inserted it into his ear.

"That was slick," I said as he drove away from the hospital.

"She's good, isn't she?" Larry said. "Text Paul to see if now is too early for you to talk to Henry."

"I'll just ask him. You'll hear all of us through your earbud. The first time I heard Paul's and Heather's voices through my earbud, I thought they were talking in my head."

I pushed the audio record button on my jo. "Paul, I'd like to talk to Henry. Is it too early for Larry and me to drop by your house?"

"Not at all," Paul said. "We just finished eating."

Larry shook his head. "Dang, you're right, sweetie. That was startling; thanks for the heads-up."

Heather said, "I've been warned about the elevators, but no one has mentioned a specific person yet. Word got around that I had been working at another hospital in Atlanta but had boyfriend problems and asked to be transferred here to be close to my sister, so everyone is being sympathetic to my situation and not asking any questions. Pretty slick of Kate. Gotta go."

"Can the transmitters work from an elevator?" Larry asked.

"We need to know," I said. "Heather, let us know the next time you take an elevator; we need to be sure you can transmit from one."

"Going in," Heather said.

"I don't hear Heather; do you, sweetie?" Larry asked.

I shook my head.

"Third floor," Heather said.

"We didn't hear anything while you were in the elevator," I said.

"Not good, but at least we know," Heather said.

I pushed the off button on my jo.

"I just realized I could tap my earbud to turn on and off the audio, but I've gotten used to my jo that records audio and video," I said.

After he parked, Larry opened my door.

"I'll need your elbow, honey; I don't have Palace Guard to guide me."

"If you'll be okay here with Paul, Spike, Lucy, and Julie, I have a couple of things I'd like to do before I meet with Noah."

"I'll be fine; what are you going to do?"

Paul answered the door, and I side-glanced at Larry as he sighed with relief.

"I'll see you later, sweetie." Larry gave me a quick kiss then hurried to his old car.

After I went inside, Lucy rushed to me with her entire back end wiggling. I sat on the floor with her and hugged her while she covered me with kisses, and Spike beamed.

Paul closed the front door. "Larry's done a good job of going undercover."

"He's working on it; he got a lecture from Heather last night, so he made a few corrections."

Paul nodded. "Heather's definitely the expert. Is Palace Guard with you?"

I shook my head.

"Makes sense for him to go with Larry since you're here with us," Paul said.

I nodded my head. *Maybe we can leave it at that.*

"We're in the kitchen, Chief," Julie said.

After I rose from the floor, Lucy and Spike led me to the kitchen.

"Lucy does a pretty good job as a seeing-eye dog, doesn't she?" Paul asked. "Maybe it would be useful if I find a harness with a handle for you and comfortable for Lucy, then she can go anywhere with you, and you'll have Spike along for protection."

"That would release Palace Guard and open up possibilities, wouldn't it?"

When I went into the kitchen, Henry was sitting at the kitchen table with a bowl in front of him. "Are you here to rescue me, Maggie? Julie put me to work: I'm almost finished peeling a ton of potatoes."

"You old faker," Julie said. "You volunteered, and you know it."

"Sure, volunteer or get tossed out into the snow."

Paul chuckled. "Chief, they've been going on like this nonstop, and I'm not sure which one of them enjoys it more."

Henry rose and washed his hands. "All done, Julie."

"About time; I can't believe how you managed to make peeling a couple of potatoes such a grand production."

"Let's go out back and relax on the porch, Maggie. My ears could use a rest," Henry said.

Lucy and Spike went outside with us; after we were settled on porch chairs, Henry said, "I'm really enjoying the banter with Julie, and Lucy is a sweetheart. Paul said he needs me to stick around because I keep Julie entertained; that must be a polite way to say aggravated." Henry chuckled. "So, tell me why you're here, other than you're one of my favorite people."

I pushed record on my jo. "I have some questions."

Henry nodded. "Go ahead."

"Remember before you went to the hospital, and you told me you saw the man dragging women up a fire escape?"

"No," Henry said.

I giggled. "Of course, you don't; what a bonehead, rookie question, right?"

Spike nodded his head.

Henry laughed. "I certainly didn't expect you to make me laugh; you are definitely not a rookie of any kind, Maggie. So, what was your question again?"

"You know who he is; tell me about him."

"That wasn't much of a question." Henry rose and walked across the yard to the fence; Lucy followed him, and Spike followed Lucy.

When Henry returned to the porch, he sat in his chair. "He was a doctor at the hospital where I worked: not the best, but not the worst, either. My wife called him a predator, though, and I always thought she was being a little tough on him. In the old days, we would have called him a skirt-chaser."

I furrowed my brow and peered at him. "I don't know what that means."

"He had almost an obsession when it came to the younger women; the nurses and other women in the hospital said he was too friendly, especially in the elevator when no one else was around, and there was no way to escape."

"Whatever happened to him?"

"It's kind of a long story," Henry said.

"I'm not going anywhere."

"He became fixated on two young nurses; both of them told their supervisors but quit when their supervisors didn't take them seriously. One of the older nurses who was a close friend of mine told me he joked in the operating room about being so irresistible, he had to fight off those two nurses; after that, he became bolder. When the Director of Nurses reported him to the Medical Board, he disappeared. I heard he became the administrator of a long-term care facility, but I don't know if that's true."

"This weather is nice, isn't it?" Henry sighed before he continued, "Not long after that, my wife...was gone. I worked for a month or so then left everything behind: my job, my house, my adult children, and everyone I knew. I lived on the street and assumed I'd be dead in a year, but I wasn't, and my grief and survivor's guilt deepened and pushed me farther into the black hole of depression. I felt like a total failure: I didn't want to live, but I wouldn't die. When I saw him on the fire escape, I recognized him right away, but I was a coward. He was bigger and much younger than I was, and I knew he'd hurt me if he noticed me, but Maggie, when I saw you, something clicked, and I had to warn you."

Henry shook his head, and the tone of his voice became stronger. "It was like my wife reached down and backhanded my chest like she used to when she was irritated with me and told me to straighten up so I could save the Gray Lady."

"So, what's next for you?" I asked.

"Julie and Paul want me to stay with them, and I might. I'm willing to give it a little time to see if I wear out my welcome."

"I think that's wonderful. Will you go to work with Julie?"

"Julie said there's a not-for-profit medical clinic down the street from her office that needs help. I could volunteer with them once or twice a week. I used to love to draw, and I did a couple of sketches for Julie. When I did a sketch of Paul, she made me sign it. I'd say she was just being nice, but we're talking about Julie here. I wouldn't mind getting back into my art." He shrugged. "We'll see what works, but I'm willing to tackle this thing called living again."

"What was the doctor's name?"

"I like how you work, Gray Lady: just as sweet as you can be, then you go straight for the throat." He chuckled. "Willard Barnes; they call him Willy."

"Does he live in that apartment?"

"Not on a regular basis; he just shows up from time to time."

"You told me to stay away from the street, but I'm not clear on exactly which street or where the apartment is."

"I'll draw you a map so you can send Paul to check it out."

"Can you sketch Willy for me too?"

"A week ago I had forgotten I knew how to draw at all, but according to Julie, I'm pretty darn good at it, so I'll do that for you this morning."

As we went into the house, Lucy and Spike dashed past us; I pushed the off button.

"Julie gave me a box of pencils for sketching and an art pad. She said I had to have a hat to protect my head from the sun when I went outside to draw, so she was going to get me a beret. Paul told me I better tell her what kind of hat I wanted, or he'd start calling me Henri. I asked for a cowboy hat, and she got me a nice one."

I giggled. "Aren't you surprised she didn't run out back and hand you your hat?"

Henry chuckled. "Don't say that too loud; she'll put it on her list."

"Is it getting warm out there?" Julie asked. "How about some sweet tea?"

"Sounds good to me," Henry said, and I nodded.

After the three of us sat at the kitchen table, I drank down half of my glass of tea, then asked, "Where's Paul?"

"He's in his office working on something or other. I'll show you," Julie said.

Henry slid his sketch pad from the middle of the table to his seat then picked up a pencil and began drawing a few lines.

Julie led me past the living room. "His door is closed. He says I get too rowdy in the kitchen when I toss pots around when I'm trying to decide which one I want to use. I think it's just an excuse."

Before we reached the closed door, Paul opened it. "Come on in, Chief. I need your perspective on my latest theory."

"I'll leave you two to work; I love to watch Henry when he sketches. It looks like a bunch of lines to me, then like magic, he's drawn a landscape or a person. He made a sketch of Lucy dozing in a sunbeam on the kitchen floor; you'll have to show it to Larry, Chief. It's really good." Julie closed the door as she left.

"I have dozens of loose ends to follow, but I dropped everything to listen to you and Henry. It was really enjoyable, and I'm on the trail of Doctor Willard Barnes. I did find entries in one of Vanessa's journals that were interesting in a macabre sort of way. It was a collection of poems titled 'The Guide to Happiness by the Numbers.' I'm sure she wrote the poems because the style is so similar to the rest of her journal. Her number from her guide was twelve; most of the poem revolved around the kindness of the guide to give her such a special number. The poems were terrifying in light of what happened to Vanessa."

Paul picked up one of the journals from his desk. "I won't read all of them, but here's one of her shorter poems: 'My twelve will make me complete; Guide will set me free; I live only for my guide; Count the days to twelve."

I shuddered. "I'm glad you have the journals; Becky would be devastated to read them because she'd be certain she could have done something to save Vanessa if she had read them earlier."

"I have to return them, you know," Paul said.

"Pick one that we can give to Larry; maybe the GBI team should see at least a sampling before we return them," I said.

"I'll give you two. Larry and Heather are more qualified than I am to decide whether we send all, none, or a sampling of the journals to GBI. I want to carry them to the backyard and burn them."

"I didn't think of burning them; that's my favorite solution, by far."

"Remember when I said I was glad we don't take divorce cases? Let's pick up a few so we can get back to the normal world of people hating each other and taking revenge by emptying a joint bank account."

I snorted. "You wouldn't last one day on a divorce case."

"True, but it doesn't hurt to daydream about the days that dragged down my spirit with boring, angry people who are not accomplished serial killers."

"You don't have anything else, do you? Please say you don't."

"I don't; what else do we have that could be a priority for me without completely wounding my soul?"

"When Henry finishes our map and the sketch of Willard Barnes, I'd like to go with Larry to look for Barnes."

"Why couldn't I go?"

"Do you look as seedy as Larry?"

"Worse. I have dark circles under my eyes because it's allergy season. I haven't shaved in two days, and I have clothes that are forty years old and stained."

I frowned. "I don't know…"

"We'll let Henry decide. I'll go change."

"I'll meet you in the kitchen."

"You're okay from here?" Paul asked.

"All I can do is run into a wall or furniture; as long as I can't fall down any stairs, I'll be fine."

When I went into the kitchen, I stumbled over a chair and caught myself with my jo before I went facedown across the floor.

"Good save, Maggie. You're on a mission: what is it?" Henry asked.

"Paul and I need to know if he will blend in at the neighborhood where the apartment is."

"I worked on the sketch of Barnes, but I realized I never got a good enough look at the full face of the man while he went up the fire escape to actually sketch a portrait, and that's all I've ever sketched of people. I decided to draw Barnes as he looked the last time I saw him years ago, but my memory was hazier than I expected."

"I appreciate whatever you can do."

Henry gave me a folded piece of paper. "I'm not very happy with this; I'll see if I can sketch the man climbing the fire escape."

"Thank you." I stuck it into my backpack.

When Paul came into the kitchen, Henry said, "You've got the right clothes and the stubble on your face is perfect, but Paul, you look like an old undercover cop. How long were you a detective with a police force?"

Paul exhaled. "Long enough, I guess. What can I change?"

"Now that I look at you again, do you have any idea how many old, undercover cops there are in that neighborhood? You'd actually fit right in."

Paul chuckled. "Maybe I need a different niche."

CHAPTER NINE

"You could go for tourist. All you'd need to do is change your clothes. Some of those tourists look like they're trying too hard to blend into a neighborhood and end up looking like an old, undercover cop in tourist's clothes."

Paul laughed. "Are you serious?"

"I don't joke about tourists because they give me, actually make that gave me, money, burgers, and fries, and I don't joke about old cops because their sense of humor dried up years ago."

"Don't listen to him, Paul. He gets addled when he drinks too much sweet tea," Julie said.

"Sweet tea gives me clarity of thought," Henry said. "You should have more respect for your elders."

"So, when did your sense of humor dry up, old man?" Julie asked.

"Let's go to my office," Paul said. "They drive me crazy."

Spike nodded as he and Lucy followed us.

After Paul closed his door, I said, "I sure don't understand it, but it seems like to me they're having a great time."

"My mom's family was like those two," Paul said. "Dad told me it was because they were superstitious. If a demon heard them say nice things to each other, the demon would become jealous and cause a terrible tragedy to strike them; usually a death. They also never used a baby or a child's name but called them by something generic like the boy or the girl because the demons could only take the life of a child if the demon knew the baby's name."

"So are you ready to go in your disguise as a tourist in disguise as an old undercover cop in disguise as a long-time resident of a specific section of sidewalk?"

"I'm not sure exactly what you said, but I don't think so. One thing I learned from Henry's lesson is that I've never been undercover, and neither have you. We're stepping into the big league where Larry and Heather shine, not us. We'll have to come up with something else for us to do."

"Let's go to a park; I need to run," I said.

"I hope that was a joke, but it wasn't funny."

"I'm serious. I think the apartment is where Barnes takes the young women when they're drugged or unconscious, but I don't think that's where he cuts them. It would be too conspicuous to haul them upstairs just to slash them with their numbers then drag their exsanguinating bodies down the fire escape or even down the interior stairs. I need to run, so I can think."

"If I put it up for a vote, what do you think Larry and Heather would say?" Paul asked.

"Ouch; that was a low blow."

"I hate to admit it, but you might be onto something: we need to do something completely different. I hate this part even more: the answer might be in the journals."

"How can we read them without getting pulled down by what we know?" I asked.

"I don't know; let's ask the experts."

"Heather and Larry?" I asked.

"Nope; Julie and Henry."

"Okay, but you'll have to take the lead on this because I can't figure out what to ask them," I said. "Let's go."

After we walked into the kitchen, Paul and I sat at the table.

"We need help with a problem, and we decided it doesn't make sense to go to the apartment because neither one of us can pull off undercover. We need to find the killer in our own way. We have some journals we could read that might point us directly to the killer, but most of the content is very depressing. How do we read the journals without being drowned in sadness?" Paul asked.

Julie joined us at the table.

"I don't know if this will work, but do you suppose if you read them aloud, the words won't stay inside of you?" Henry asked.

"Paul, I have a portable text to speech reader in my computer bag," I said.

"That's a possibility; where's your computer bag?" Paul asked.

"At home," I said.

"We don't know if your house is being watched. If I go there, I could be followed back home."

"No, you couldn't," Julie said. "You're a fantastic driver; you'd lose them, and you could drive my car. We haven't used my car in a while."

"It seems a little risky for something when we don't even know whether it will work," Paul said.

"Give me what you want read, and I'll read it to you," Henry said. "I've already been to the bottomless pit of depression; I'm immune; or another option is Julie: she's immune because she would be too busy reading to pay attention to what she's saying."

"That was very insulting, old man, but I'm not denying the accuracy," Julie said.

"Let's give it a try," I said. "Julie, do you want to read to me?"

"I'd love it," Julie said.

"Henry, you and I could go into my office. I have a comfortable chair next to the window. I'll bring you two journals, Julie."

While Julie and I moved to the living room, Paul brought us two hard-back journals and a spiral notebook.

"This is only a test, Chief; don't take this as an endurance race. You two can call a halt at any time," Paul said.

After Paul left, I told Julie, "You can't read ahead because you'll lose me and your place, and I'll get confused."

"I agree; are you ready?" Julie picked up a journal and opened to the first page and read with her fingers marking where she was reading and her hand covering the remaining page.

After she turned the page, she said, "This is total drivel, and I feel like I'm intruding on Vanessa's privacy. I'm going to read faster until you tell me to slow down because I came to something that interests you."

When Julie resumed reading, I had to concentrate to catch all the words.

After she had read the first half of the journal, Julie said, "We need a break. How about some fresh air?"

"Should we suggest a break for Paul and Henry too?"

Julie called out, "We're taking a break."

Paul and Henry came out of the office. "Good idea," Paul said. "What do you think so far?"

"It's brutal to read because it's so repetitive, and I feel like I'm going agonizingly slow." Julie poured four glasses of sweet tea.

"It would go much faster if you'd turn us loose to read; if we come across anything that's different from what we've read so far, we can let you know," Henry said.

"The two of us could read in the kitchen," Julie said. "If either of us finds something, we could show the other then alert you."

"And if either of us becomes too involved in what we're reading, we'll stop," Henry added.

"What do you think, Paul?" I asked.

"I think they could handle it, and that frees us to do some research and leg work."

Paul carried the journals and notebooks into the kitchen and dropped them onto the table. "They're not organized into any logical order."

"The two I had are dated on the back page; did you notice that, Julie?" Henry said.

"It will take me two minutes to get them into chronological order, so we can follow the flow of Vanessa's thoughts."

"Do you have any of those paper sticky memo pads or tabs that we can use to mark spots we want to come back to or which journals we've read?" Henry asked.

"I run a full service operation here; of course, I do, and I was planning to do that right after I finish organizing these, so quit trying to get ahead of me," Julie said.

While Julie and Henry bantered about the best way to organize and mark the journals and argued about their comparative reading skills, Paul and I went into his office.

"I'd still like to have my computer," I said. "What do you think about taking Julie's car?"

"Not much; I don't see why you'd need your computer so much that it would be worth the risk," Paul said.

"I think it would be fine, but I can wait until after we hear from Larry; he's meeting with Noah to see what they can work out, so I can talk to Sophie Rose, then we could get my computer."

"What do you want to talk to her about?"

"I'm not really sure, but it seems like we've overlooked a few possibilities that would help us find the killer; maybe Sophie Rose will have some ideas."

Paul's phone buzzed a text. "This is from Larry. He asked if I heard him. I don't think so. Did you?"

"No; that's not right."

Paul answered Larry's text then his phone rang.

Larry spoke quietly, and quickly, but I heard him. "I only have a second. I tried to get in touch with Heather and didn't hear anything. I think we have a system failure. Noah and I will be leaving the diner soon; I'm going to the hospital."

Larry hung up, and Paul asked, "Did you hear that?"

"Yes, let's go to the hospital."

"Larry's going; we don't need to."

"You can get there faster than he can. One more experiment. Go outside."

Paul closed the door as he left.

When I was certain he wasn't close enough to hear me, I pressed record. "Does my jo work?"

Paul returned. "I heard you. Did you hear my reply?"

"No; one more experiment."

Paul left again.

I tapped my earbud. "Does my earbud work?"

Paul waited longer the second time before he returned. "Did I come back too quick? I was waiting for you to say something."

"I used my earbud. Take my jo outside; this is the record button."

Paul grumbled, "This is a conspiracy to get me to walk more."

When Paul returned, he asked, "How did that work?"

"I didn't hear you. I think the failure is in the newer earbuds. You have the original that Heather gave you for my jo, don't you?"

"Yes, that means I can hear you, but no one else can; and none of us can hear the others. I'm convinced; let's go."

As Paul drove as fast as he dared to the hospital, it seemed like we were crawling after riding with Heather.

"What's our plan, Chief?"

"I'm trying to figure out how we could go in without looking like we're together."

"If I walk a foot or so ahead of you and whistle or hum you could follow me. I could say oops, or something like that when I stop," Paul said.

"Let's try it out."

"Okay; I'm not going to tell you where we're going because you're too familiar with the house. Before we start, a front from the north is blowing through, and it's turned cold; put on your jacket and bring along your backpack because you should always have it with you."

Paul whistled softly through his teeth, and I followed him but used my jo as a cane to make sure I hadn't inadvertently veered toward a piece of furniture or a wall.

"Oops," he said, and I stopped.

"That was good, Chief." He began whistling again, and I stayed close to him.

"Back off a little bit, Chief. You wouldn't be walking that close to someone you didn't know."

I nodded, and he continued whistling.

I think we're walking around the sofa.

"Oops," Paul said, and I stopped then heard the door open.

Yay, we're going outside!

"Three steps, no railing," he mumbled.

I stopped to zip up my jacket, then while I used my jo to find the edge of the steps, he quietly whistled and walked away from me; after I cleared the last step, I quickened my pace.

No complaints from Paul; I must not look like I'm trying to catch up with him.

The cold air took away my breath, and it seemed like we'd trudged for miles against the bitter wind.

"We walked around the block and are in front of our house," Paul said.

After we were inside, he said, "You did a good job with your jo. How did it feel?"

"It was wretchedly cold out there. I felt a little awkward at first going at such a fast pace with my jo and without Palace Guard to guide me, but after I became a little more confident, it was great."

"Good, I'll tell Julie we're leaving."

Before he pulled out of the driveway, Paul's phone buzzed a text. "It's from Larry. He said he'd pick you up at our house a little before noon for a picnic in a park. Does that make any sense to you?"

"No, because it's a terrible day for a picnic, but maybe we're meeting with Noah and Sophie Rose for lunch."

"That makes sense."

On our way to the hospital, Paul said, "When we get there, I want to find Heather, so I can ask her if there's anything I can do to get the earbuds back in service. Maybe there's somewhere here in town that I can take them, so an electronics technician can troubleshoot and fix them. What are you going to do?"

"I'm going to sit in the visitors' waiting room near the elevators; I want to hear what people are saying."

"What are you listening for?"

"A needle in a haystack, which is extremely difficult because they are incredibly quiet."

Paul snorted.

After he backed into a parking spot, Paul said, "We're in the middle of the visitors' lot. After you get out of the car, stand in front of the car next to us. I'll walk past you, then you can follow me."

I zipped up my jacket against the chilling wind before I stepped out of the car; after I slipped my arms through the backpack straps, I tapped my jo on the pavement in a semicircle search pattern while I listened to Paul's off-key whistling and followed him across the parking lot and into the hospital.

After we were inside and away from the doors, Paul said, "Oops, chairs."

I heard the ding of the elevator.

"Will you be okay?" Paul whispered, and I nodded.

After he left, I sorted through different voices as those around me spoke quietly about the condition of a patient or in frustration about waiting for someone who wasn't there, so they could visit a patient in the hospital together.

I saw blobs run into and out of the nearby elevators, and other blobs trudge to and from the elevators. *I never realized how easy it would be to tell the difference between staff and visitors.*

While I watched the elevators, I was startled when Palace Guard blocked my view.

"I am really glad to see you," I whispered.

He smiled and nodded vigorously then motioned toward the elevator.

"This is great to have you back to guide me," I said quietly.

He patted my back as we stood in front of the elevators as they emptied then filled. After several people came out of an elevator,

Palace Guard guided me to it as a man rushed into it, and I put my jo in the way before the door could close. Two young women raced into the elevator as the door closed then began its slow ascent.

The man left when the door opened on the second floor.

One of the young women said, "We saw you go into the elevator right after that man did. Our supervisor told us to never get into an elevator when only one man is there."

"She said it happened ages ago," the other woman said, "but it must have been horrible because everybody knows that the only way to be safe is to always have a friend with you."

"Some people say the elevators are haunted, and other people say there is a stalker in the hospital. We don't want to be the ones to find out which group is right."

The second young woman continued, "The stalker even has a name." Her voice dropped to a whisper. "I have nightmares about Willie."

"That sounds terrible. Is he really still around?" I asked.

"It depends who you ask. I heard one of the older nurses say that she was certain that one of the volunteers is Willie," the first woman said. "Oh, here's our floor. Are you getting out here?"

"Yes."

"Visiting hours aren't for another half hour here, but the visitors' waiting room is very nice, and your patient's nurse will come get you."

"Thank you," I said.

"We'll show you where it is. Do you hold onto my arm or something?"

"That's exactly right. You wouldn't believe how many people try to grab my arm and pull me."

"You need to learn karate, so you can throw them to the ground."

"You're absolutely right; wouldn't a nice crunch when their nose slams onto the hard floor be glorious?"

The two young women giggled, and I smiled. Palace Guard rolled his eyes.

After they left, I asked, "Am I stuck here?"

Palace Guard glanced at the ceiling in feigned serious thought.

"Come on," I growled. "Don't tease me."

Palace Guard shrugged, then we left. We waited at the elevator until two blobs headed toward us.

"Honey, did you want to take the elevator to the lobby? Have you been standing here very long by yourself? Are you waiting for someone? You have to...oh...sorry, I didn't notice your cane. It's wonderful that you are getting around so well," a woman said.

The four of us went into the elevator, and the woman continued chattering about celebrities who were blind and the one girl in her neighborhood when she was a child who had very bad eyesight and wore thick glasses, but the woman never teased her like everyone else did.

"It's so impressive how well you people do," she said before she and the other blob hurried away when the elevator door opened.

"She was embarrassed that she didn't notice my cane right off."

Palace Guard raised his eyebrows.

"I was trying to give her the benefit of the doubt."

Palace Guard furrowed his brow and held his nose.

I snickered. "I don't believe me either."

Palace Guard led me to the same visitor's chair that I had occupied earlier, and I sat.

I asked, "How is Paul going to find me?"

Palace Guard pointed to the elevators, and Paul-blob hurried to join me, then Palace Guard disappeared.

"Heather gave me her earbud and a name and address. Larry will meet us at the house, and I'll take his earbud, Heather's, and yours to see if they can be fixed. Heather told me to drop off mine, so it could be checked too, but I need to know what you want me to hear."

"Sit next to me a second."

Paul sat and stretched out his legs. "Whatcha got, Chief?"

"Can you take this to Heather?" I handed him the folded paper from Henry, and Paul unfolded it.

Palace Guard peered over Paul's shoulder. "Sure, who is it?"

"It's Willy when he was quite a bit younger; Henry sketched him for me."

Paul refolded the paper. "I'll be right back. Do not move, Chief." Palace Chief followed him.

I frowned. *I'm pretty sure the chief gives the orders, not the bossy operations guy. I'll have to check on that.*

When Paul returned without Palace Guard, he said, "Heather will be at our house a little after four."

On our way back to his house, I asked, "Has Heather seen anyone that might be Willy?"

"No, but at least now she has a better idea of who she's looking for."

"I'd really like to have my computer," I said. "What time is it?"

"It's almost eleven thirty. We need to head back to my house so Larry can pick you up for your lunch date."

"I hope Sophie Rose can understand me when my teeth chatter while I'm trying to talk."

"Tell Julie you need a blanket; she'll give you one, or you could ask her for a cup of hot tea while you wait for Larry."

"Hot tea sounds good." *I'd rather the weather just warmed up.*

After we went inside, Julie said, "It must be miserable out there. Would you like some hot tea, Chief?"

"You're a mind reader, Julie; thank you."

While Julie heated the water, she said, "Becky called me earlier; she told me she's been talking to some of the other mothers and may have found something. When I told her how busy you are, she said that you probably already talked to the teacher or librarian anyway."

Paul slipped into his office while I sat at the table with Henry who was heads-down while he worked. "Heather appreciated the sketch you did, Henry."

"I'm glad I can help."

"What are you doing now?"

"I'm rough-sketching Paul and Julie on a sailboat at her suggestion; I'm putting in some shading to make the waves really rough. We decided I should practice sketching people I had around me, so I would have them available as a reference."

"You can do that? You don't have to have the person pose the way you want them to, so you can sketch them? That's amazing; I'm really sorry I can't see it."

"After I got started, it wasn't as hard as I thought. Think of the two of them on a sailboat on a large lake. Both of them are wearing life jackets. The wind has suddenly come up, and Julie's hair is whipping around her face while she hangs onto the tiller with both hands. Paul is fighting to bring down the mainsail, and both of them are laughing over their adventure on the lake. Behind them, the sky is dark as a curtain of heavy rain moves across the lake toward them. They are racing the storm to the shore."

"Wow, thank you, I can see it."

"You're making that up." Julie stood behind Henry and leaned over his shoulder to peer at the paper. "I don't see any of that; all I see are lines and shading."

"Give it time, girl; you'll see it when you want to," Henry muttered.

I furrowed my brow. *See it when I want to; that's interesting. Is that why I can see Larry, Lucy, Spike, Palace Guard, and Kiki?*

I snorted. *Doesn't explain why I see Gary Sloan, though.*

Lucy yipped and rushed to the front door. I tried to follow her, but I fell over a footstool and instinctively threw out my right arm to catch myself. My arm hurt, and I groaned as I got up. *Toughen up, buttercup, or you'll get hauled off to the hospital.*

I exhaled and rubbed my arm to will it to stop hurting then pressed it against my abdomen while I picked up my jo. Larry burst into the house and grabbed me into a big hug. I winced but held my breath, so I wouldn't cry out in pain.

"Ready to go, sweetie?"

"I sure am."

"You'll want your coat. I'll grab it for you."

"Just throw it over my shoulders; I'm sure your truck is warm by now."

"It's plenty warm, that's for sure; I've had the heater running full blast for you. I'll grab your backpack."

"We're on our way," Larry called out. Lucy raced to the door and Spike followed her. "Lucy decided she's going with us."

"Enjoy your lunch," Julie said. "When do you expect to be back?"

"We might have a long lunch; don't look for us to rush back," Larry said as he escorted me out the door and then to his car.

After he helped me into the passenger's seat and backed out of the driveway, Larry asked, "What happened to your arm?"

"I took a dive; I think I fell over a footstool, but it's fine."

"We'll see."

It's never a good thing when he says that. Maybe he'll forget.

"Which park are we going to? Does it have like a pavilion or something, so we can be out of the wind?" I asked.

Larry chuckled. "Believe it or not, I'm ahead of you: change in plans. We're going to Noah's house. Noah is picking up some gumbo, etouffee, and whatever else he can order from a Cajun food truck."

"That sounds great."

"Do we need to splint your arm?"

"No, it'll be fine," I said.

After Larry drove through the noisy city traffic, we were on a smooth road, and I heard only an occasional vehicle going the opposite direction.

"Do they live out in the country?" I asked.

"More like on the outskirts of town; they live in a neighborhood, but the houses aren't very close to each other."

After Larry parked, he opened the back door for Lucy, and I took his arm while Lucy sniffed the yard, and Spike stayed with her.

When Larry and I walked together to the door, I inhaled and sighed. "Smell that wood smoke; isn't it wonderful?"

He said, "There's smoke coming out of their chimney. They may have to throw us out."

Spike nodded then motioned for us to go inside without them.

"I am so glad to see you," Sophie Rose said.

"You're a sound for sore ears." I giggled, and so did Sophie Rose.

"Come on in," she said. "Is that Lucy in the yard? She's beautiful. Shouldn't she come inside?"

"She'll let us know when she's ready," Larry said.

"We'll eat as soon as Noah gets here because when he called me and told me what our choices were, I told him to get all of them, so we're having a Cajun buffet for lunch. Come into the great room; Noah started a fire in the fireplace for me this morning, and I've been feeding it logs."

When I sat down, Sophie Rose asked, "Do you need a splint or an antacid?"

"I'm fine."

"Heart attack? I know the number to call for nine-one-one."

I giggled. "You're being a little nosy."

"Yes, I am. What of it? Which one? Ambulance or a home treatment?"

CHAPTER TEN

I sighed. "I tripped and tried to catch myself."

"It's a natural reaction; let me see." Sophie Rose joined me on the sofa.

"I don't think I could outrun you without falling over another footstool, so go ahead," I grumbled.

Sophie Rose gingerly felt my arm. "I don't see or feel any deformity. I'll splint it unless you're more comfortable with a professional splinting it."

"I was an undercover paramedic," Larry said.

"Well, there you go; your choice, Gray Lady."

"Whatever," I grumbled.

"Nice attitude," Sophie Rose mumbled. "I'll be right back, then Larry and I will toss over who gets the honors."

Larry sat next to me on the sofa and kissed me. "Sorry."

"No, you're not; Lucy's ready to come in."

"I was being polite." Larry rose and opened the door, and Lucy and Spike came inside.

"I'm being crabby," I said.

"So far, so good, sweetie, but I'm still sorry about your arm."

Lucy trotted to the rug in front of the fireplace and flopped down.

When Sophie Rose returned, she said, "Larry, why don't you put the splint on Gray Lady's arm, and I'll get an ice pack. I didn't feel any swelling, but it will help with the pain."

Sophie Rose slipped the ice pack on my arm and under the splint, then sat across from us. "The splint will hold your ice pack in place. Gray Lady, you have one eye and the use of one arm; I have one leg. Just to let you know, I'm not taking this as a personal challenge."

I snickered. "So, I win?"

Sophie sighed dramatically as she placed the back of one hand on her forehead. "I suppose."

"You two are a mess." Larry chuckled.

Noah came into the house with two large sacks. "We've got a week's worth of food here. Anybody hungry?"

Lucy stayed close to Noah as she followed him into the kitchen. After all of us were seated at the kitchen table, Larry served my plate for me while Lucy wiggled under the table to lie across my feet.

"You have a small bowl of gumbo with a spoon in the bowl close to your left hand, and the rest of your food is on the plate in front of you. It's all finger food; your napkin is on the right side of your plate. I didn't put anything on your plate that I haven't seen Chef Daryl cook, so I'll let you tell me what everything is," Larry said.

I giggled. "If I mess up, you have to promise me you won't tell Chef Daryl."

"That would be embarrassing, wouldn't it? It depends on how crabby you are after we eat."

"I believe that's called husband subtlety," Sophie Rose said. "Speaking of which, is it okay, honey?"

"Go ahead," Noah said. "I can't take the stress of watching you trying not to say anything."

"Noah and I decided we'd better get married before we had to explain to Heather once again why we weren't married yet, or one of us tried to back out."

"That's not exactly what I had in mind, but this is your story, as long as you agree you were the one who was about to back out."

"No way. So, this morning we visited a nice judge and were married."

I giggled. "That's wonderful; when are you going to tell your parents?"

Sophie Rose popped another bite into her mouth.

"Yum, good," she said. "We thought we'd send them postcards while we're on our honeymoon and sign them Captain and Mrs. Noah Baker."

Larry chuckled. "I sure am glad I wasn't sipping my tea. I can just imagine my folks' reaction if we'd done that."

"Well, my partner in crime had the same reaction as you, except my timing was better, and he was drinking his coffee; we're going to visit them separately and swear them to secrecy," Sophie Rose said.

"Which means they will swear all the rest of the families and friends to secrecy, but we'll start getting requests for a list of what we'd like for wedding gifts before we get home," Noah added.

"How's the food?" Sophie Rose said. "Is it as good as your chef friend's?"

"It's fantastic," I said. "I have missed good Cajun food."

I took a bite of something. *Shrimp*.

"I removed the shrimp tails, sweetie. How are they?"

"They're cooked perfectly. Do we have any sauce?"

"I'll put some sauce on your plate at six o'clock," Larry said.

After I ate another shrimp, I asked, "Do I have a crab cake?"

"We have mini-crab cakes," Noah said.

"Larry put three at three o'clock on your plate," Sophie Rose said.

I bit into one. "Yum."

After everyone finished eating, Larry cleared the table while Sophie Rose loaded the dishwasher, and Noah put the leftovers into the refrigerator.

"We're having a feast for the next two nights at least," Sophie said.

"Larry, I've got a few things to go over with you in my office," Noah said after he'd put away all the food.

After Larry and Noah left, Sophie Rose said, "Let's go into the great room; I'll bring a fresh icepack, and we can enjoy the fire."

When we walked into the room, I moaned at the warmth. "This is wonderful. That fireplace is really great, isn't it?"

"I love it; I can't remember why I didn't have sense enough to move here earlier. Make yourself comfortable on the sofa."

Sophie Rose carefully placed the icepack on my arm then sat in the chair next to the sofa. "That Noah guy has superb taste in houses. So, what did you want to talk to me about?"

I pushed the audio button on my jo. "I need to know everything you know about your criminal sister."

"That's interesting; you're the only one who has asked me that, and I've been through the wringer, in a polite way."

Sophie Rose thought a minute then said, "She had that cop-look when she came into the salon. In retrospect, I don't know if it was so much a cop-look, or the look of someone who has been in women's prison and was able to assume the persona."

"That's interesting because I had the same sense when I met her: that she was a hardened cop."

"That's it. She asked me about my routine; again I thought it was because she was a cop and being thorough. Now, I think she was just being thorough. One thing about her: she didn't like surprises. It really threw her when you showed up at the door; I think she recognized you."

"I don't really know how," I said.

"Oh, I do; think about it, Gray Lady: how many other one-eyed young women have you met lately? She told me her boss was very particular and wouldn't have assigned just anyone to the job: that's what she called it. She said she'd never had a job outside of Atlanta until she got the call about this one. She wanted to know if I'd ever seen any snakes in the studio because she was deathly afraid of snakes."

"Snakes? That's odd that she thought you'd have snakes in the studio."

"Not really; a lot of people from Atlanta think we're part of a swamp."

"Did she say anything more about her boss?"

"She told me he thought he was a ladies' man, and he had a brother; she didn't trust the brother because there was something off about him, like he had no soul, then surprisingly, she crossed herself."

"Really?"

"I was certain she was superstitious when she told me the brother was obsessed with numbers, but I was completely lost when she told me the boss goes up, the brother comes down, and it's all about the numbers."

"Sounds like she talked about the boss and his brother a lot."

"I didn't really notice at the time, but you're right, she did. When you came to the studio, I was on my way to welcome you, but she beat me to the door and was red-faced with anger. I was startled by her abrupt change of mood when she asked, 'What's she doing here? Not a good sign.'"

"I don't understand that at all. Why was I not a good sign?"

"I have no idea; while you were changing, she crossed herself again and said, 'It's going to be bad; she's messed with the numbers.'"

"What else?" I asked.

"She told me she was assigned to the job for one day unless the plan changed, and she hoped it wouldn't because she wanted to go back to Atlanta where there weren't any snakes or numbers. When I asked her what the plan was, she became defensive and claimed she never mentioned a plan."

"No snakes or numbers? I definitely don't get the correlation."

"She sounded like she was equally afraid of both."

"How could she be afraid of numbers?"

"I have no clue; her radical change in behavior and tone puzzled me, and I still don't understand."

Sophie Rose paced to the fireplace then to the window and paused as she gazed outside. "It's even more baffling because she was speaking from her heart and was completely sincere before you came to the studio." Sophie Rose paced to the doorway then back to the fireplace before she circled the sofa. "I keep feeling that I somehow missed a key point because she talked super-fast about so many topics."

"If you're going to pace, let's put on our coats and go outside; you're making me nervous."

"I think that would help," she said. "There's a beautiful trail that weaves through the neighborhood, but it seems like it would be as smart as going into a basement in a horror movie."

I smiled. "My best friend from high school and I were in the same apartment building after college. We'd argue every weekend about which movie we'd see, and Taylor always wanted to go to a horror flick, but I hated them because I couldn't understand why they never had sense enough to stay out of the basement where the monster was."

"Noah doesn't allow monsters in his backyard, so we can pace there. Would Lucy like to go out too?"

"She'd love it."

After I put on my coat, I remembered to turn off my audio.

While we walked across the yard, I kicked the leaves to hear them rustle and inhaled the wood smoke from Noah's chimney that reminded me of a campfire.

"We'll enjoy being outside when it's spring and the azalea and gardenia blossoms are out. I enjoy the brilliant colors of the flowers, and you'll love the soft fragrance of the gardenias," Sophie Rose said.

"Does Noah have a garden?"

"Of sorts," Sophie Rose said. "He plants pumpkin seeds every year, and they take over his yard, then when they are ready for picking, the deer jump the fence and chow down at the pumpkin buffet."

Larry opened the back door. "Are you doing cold therapy now? I'm not pushing, but I was wondering if you were ready to leave."

"I'm ready; call me if you think of anything else, Sophie Rose."

"Will do; I might even call if I don't think of anything else," she said.

"Works for me."

On the way back to Paul and Julie's house, Larry's car sputtered then stalled when he stopped at a traffic light.

After he coaxed it forward when the light changed, he said, "This old car is the best ever; I've already gotten two tickets today: one for the loud muffler, and a second one for a tail light being out. The tickets are on Kate's dime."

"Aren't you worried about two tickets on your driving record, though?"

"I would be, but my undercover work for Kate includes a driver's license."

"You are fantastic at undercover, honey; you never have any slipups because you go all in."

Larry smiled and squeezed my hand. "Thank you, sweetie."

When I glanced behind me, Spike fake-gagged.

"I saw that, Spike," Larry said.

Spike silently snapped his fingers.

"Yes, you were definitely busted," I said.

Spike held his wrists together and held them over the seat, and Larry laughed. "Cut it out, Spike. I have to drive; besides, I can't arrest you because I'm undercover."

When Larry parked in the driveway, Julie came out of the house. "I've been watching for you; Heather texted Paul. He's gone to the hospital. He thought you'd be fine here with me, Chief, because you've got the men too."

Lucy yipped, and Julie said, "Of course, Lucy, and most importantly, you."

Larry leaned close to me after he opened my car door and whispered, "You aren't the only diva in the family, after all."

When he continued to chuckle as he helped me out of the car then put his arm around my shoulders to walk with me to the house, I elbowed him. "Behave."

"I'd like for you to appreciate my high regard for your skills: I didn't say make me." Larry kissed the top my head.

Palace Guard nodded, and Spike held two thumbs up.

Where'd Palace Guard come from?

Larry smiled. "Thank you, guys."

After Larry left, Julie said, "I've got work to do for the Agency. Do you need me for anything before I go heads down?"

"Can't think of a thing." *I still don't have my computer.*

I wandered into Paul's office and sat in the soft chair then put up my feet; Palace Guard stood in the doorway with his back to me.

"Did Larry tell you to stay close?" I grumbled.

When he ignored me, I leaned back. *I'll just rest my eye.*

My phone startled me when it rang. *I must have dozed off.* "Call from Tonya."

When I answered, Tonya said, "Ready for some company?"

"I'd love it; what's the occasion?"

"Mom has an old friend who is not doing well at all; in fact, he was admitted yesterday to the critical care unit at the hospital there. Will doesn't have any family, and no friends to speak of because he's always been antisocial, but for some reason, he and Mom have always been friends. Dad said he tolerated Mom's old friend because he never once judged her as he helped her through more than one rough spot when they were in college, but as far as Dad was concerned, it was like being friends with a scorpion because he thought he was being charming when he was being creepy. She was surprised, though, to learn that she was his emergency contact."

I rolled my shoulders to work out the kinks. "I'm sorry to hear that."

"Mom didn't want to say anything to Julie about us coming there because Julie would feel obligated to host us at the house. Mom is on the phone talking to one of her friends who has a house she rents to tourists that is close to the hospital. We'll be there later this evening. I could pick you up at your house, and we could spend the day together."

"I'm at Julie's right now because Paul and I are working on a case. I'll tell you all about Gray Flanagan Agency and what's going on later."

"That's nice, but tell me now."

I told her about the new business and the investigation.

"I love it," she said. "That makes me your expert research assistant. Can Julie order business cards for me too?"

"I don't know whether Julie's ordering cards or not, but I'll ask her to order some for you too."

Tonya snorted. "We're talking Julie here: she's ordered them."

Palace Guard nodded.

"My list of missing or deceased young women is not very long, but it's fairly complete; I added a few extra details that I thought might be useful. Do you want me to send it to you now, or should I dig deeper to see what else I can find?"

"Now would be excellent."

"Will do; I'll call you tomorrow after I drop off Mom at the hospital."

After we hung up, I went into the kitchen. Julie sat at her breakfast bar with a laptop computer.

"Henry's on the back porch; I'm not sure what he's sketching, but he claimed he focuses better when he isn't cooped up. I told him he's feral. I'm almost caught up on our office email, then I'll tackle a few other odds and ends. Can I get you a glass of sweet tea or a cup of hot tea?"

"Hot tea sounds good."

Julie turned on the burner under the kettle then set a cup with a tea bag in it on the kitchen counter.

"Did I hear you talking to someone?" she asked.

"Tonya called me..."

"I know you must miss her; she's a wonderful person, isn't she?" Julie opened the back door, and Lucy and Spike came inside. "Do you want any sweet tea or coffee, Henry? What about a snack?"

"Whichever's convenient for you," he said.

After Julie gave Lucy a homemade treat, she poured Henry a large glass of iced tea then put a handful of grapes and a slice of cheddar cheese on a plate with a paper napkin on top.

When she went outside, Henry said, "My favorites; thanks, Julie."

After she returned to the kitchen, she poured the not-quite boiling water into my cup. "Have you noticed how dreadfully thin he is? His doctor wants him to put on a little weight; so far, he hasn't refused a snack when I offer him one."

As she set the cup in front of me, she continued, "I absolutely do not understand your affinity for tepid coffee and tea; this might be too hot for you because I forgot to watch the kettle, so it wouldn't boil, but it won't take long to cool."

Does she know how funny that sounded?

When I side-glanced Palace Guard, he rolled his eyes, and I fake-sneezed into my elbow to hide my smile.

"Bless you," Julie said. "How was lunch?"

"It was great."

"I made Reuben sandwiches for the three of us with a side of pasta salad for Henry. I think Paul may have been a little sad, but I told him we needed to watch our weight; after all, we're not getting any younger, and those pounds just leap on and refuse to budge after they settle in."

When Julie's phone rang, she said, "Oh, it's Martha."

I picked up my cup and headed to the living room; Palace Guard, Spike, and Lucy followed me.

"Who can I bribe to take me home so I can get my computer?"

Palace Guard scowled, and Spike raised his hand then did his wacky dance.

I giggled and danced my version; Lucy howled, and Palace Guard crossed his arms and glared.

When I laughed and dropped onto the sofa, Lucy jumped up with me, and Spike gave me his polite golf-clap. I responded with a haughty princess wave, and even Palace Guard smiled.

Julie's eyes were wide as she came into the living room. "What's wrong with Lucy? Do we need to rush her to the emergency veterinarian hospital?"

An opening!

I sighed. "I'm afraid she thinks she's being punished because we left our house so abruptly and didn't bring her favorite blanket. Lucy's never been without her blankie, and poor thing misses the familiar smell of her backyard; if we could take her there for five minutes, she'll be fine until we go home at the end of this week."

Palace Guard and Spike stared at me, and Lucy hung her head. *Well done, Lucy.*

"You're such a good girl; I'm sure we'll go home later this week." I hugged Lucy.

"That's terrible; I'm so sorry, Lucy." Julie lowered her voice to a whisper. "Do you think we could dash over there and get back here before anyone catches us?"

"Well..."

"You're right; let's load up and do it. Paul has no idea how many speeding tickets I have; one more won't make a difference. I have a line item in my household budget called 'Shoes.' It's actually my ticket money, and there's enough left for one more this month."

I rushed to put on my coat and grab my backpack then reached inside my backpack to be sure I had my house key. After I didn't find it in its usual spot, I searched the main compartment thoroughly then narrowed my eyes. *Just as I suspected, that sneak Larry took my keys.* I unzipped the small pouch I kept in the side pocket and pulled out my spare house key.

"I'm ready."

"So am I; let's go." Julie giggled. "Lucy's blocking the front door. Do you think she knows where we're going?"

I smiled. "Are you ready to go too, girl?"

Lucy grinned.

When we reached her car, Julie said, "You should ride in the back, Gray Lady, and stay down."

Palace Guard took the passenger's seat while Lucy, Spike and I climbed into the back seat; Lucy sat in the middle.

"Everybody ready? Hang on." Julie drove slowly through the neighborhood while I kept my face hidden in Lucy's fur.

Julie sped to the highway then accelerated to race to the exit. I peeked at Palace Guard and he was holding onto the dash with both hands.

Julie swerved from the far left lane to exit the highway, and the force threw me against the door. When I glanced at Lucy, Spike was holding onto her.

"Well done," I said quietly.

"Thank you," Julie said. "I'm positive no one is following us. The next exit is five miles away."

She turned left instead of right, which threw me off balance again. "We're going back to your exit."

Spike held up a thumb, and I nodded.

When she accelerated on the ramp to get back onto the highway, I was ready.

After Julie exited, it seemed like she was crawling. *I'll bet she's going the speed limit.*

"There's a gas station up ahead; stay low," Julie said.

When we reached the house, Julie pulled close to the backyard then parked. "We'll be in the backyard. Let us know when you're ready to leave."

After Palace Guard and I were in the house, I said, "I'll put my computer and its charger into my computer bag. Can you find something that could resemble Lucy's blanket?"

Palace Guard rolled his eyes then left while I packed my computer bag; on a whim, I tossed in Larry's laptop.

When he returned, I followed him to the bedroom. He pointed to a box on the floor on my side of my closet. When I opened it, I found a small Christmas quilted tablecloth with the edges bound with red ribbon.

"This looks like a covering for a coffee table; where did it come from? Never mind, must be Jennifer."

Palace Guard blocked my way and pointed to the floor behind me. When I turned, I noticed our small safe on the floor where Palace Guard had pointed. *I should have asked Larry to pick it up. We shouldn't have left it.*

I dropped the quilt on a chair on the front porch then carried my computer bag to the car. *How am I going to do this?*

I left the car door open then returned for the small safe. The box with my eyepatches caught my eye. *Why didn't I pack any extra eyepatches?* I slipped my arm out of the sling then stuffed all the eyepatches into my sling before I lifted the heavy box with both hands. The intense pain in my right arm took away my breath as it shot up to my shoulder like a bolt of lightning, but I kept going.

After I set the safe on the back floorboard, I carefully braced my arm and eased it back into the sling on top of my eyepatches then hurried back to the house, locked the front door, and snatched up the quilt before I rushed to the back yard.

"I've got it, Lucy." I waved the quilt like a flag flapping in a breeze.

"Let's blow this joint," Julie said.

Julie stopped at the end of our driveway then maintained her constant speed at the speed limit as she headed to the highway. She accelerated on the ramp then sped home even faster than she did on the way to the house.

When she parked at her house, Spike patted his hair into place with both hands like the wind had mussed it; I giggled.

"I'm glad to be back too; now, get out as fast as you can, so we don't get caught near the car."

"I like how you think," I said. "Where can I keep the safe and my computer? Paul will be suspicious if he sees either one."

"Safe?" Julie peered in the back seat. "That looks too heavy for you to have brought it to the car with no help. How did you manage that?"

"With great difficulty."

"I've got a garden cart. I'll be right back. Put your computer bag in the closet in the spare bedroom that is next to Henry's. We'll put the safe there too."

CHAPTER ELEVEN

When I returned to the car, Julie had already lifted the safe into the wagon. "This was really heavy to lift. It must have been on a shelf at just the right height for you to be able to carry it out to the car. Did you use your injured arm? Of course you did; you used it as a balance."

I nodded. *Close enough.*

While she pulled, and I pushed the wagon to the house, Julie asked, "What do you have in your safe? Original birth certificates?"

"Shantelle has the originals of all of those types of documents. The items we have in the safe are mostly items that can't be replaced. Larry has a few things from his grandfather, and I have some of my great-grandmother's jewelry that Shantelle thought I should keep."

"Your great-grandmother? You mean Maggie Flanagan? That is totally fantastic. I wonder if she had any jewelry that could inspire a logo for Gray Flanagan Agency? Maybe you can show the pieces to me sometime."

"That's a great idea."

"You need to write some of the stories you heard about her. That would be a wonderful read."

I smiled. *Only if you'd like to read a nonfiction saga about fairies and a society of wealthy women who were also liars and thieves.*

"After I return the garden wagon, I'll need to sweep the floor because these tires are filthy. I'll bring you a glass of sweet tea if you want to set up the computer in your room, but sit on the other side of the bed, so you can slide it under the bed if you don't have time to get it into the closet when Paul comes home. Sometimes he just appears; when I complained I like to know when he's on his way, he claimed he was trying to catch the pool boy in the house." Julie chuckled. "He's so funny sometimes."

I smiled. *I'm not sure what's funny about a pool boy when you don't have a pool. I'll ask Tonya: she'll know.*

I sighed as I relaxed on the soft chair in the bedroom with my computer on my lap. I turned on my computer then put on my earmuff-style headset. Julie tiptoed in and set the glass of ice tea on a coaster on the table next to me then tiptoed out and closed the door.

"I guess she didn't want to disturb me since I must have been listening to something important on my laptop," I whispered.

Palace Guard rolled his eyes.

I opened my email, found Tonya's list, and forwarded it to Paul.

I found an email from Jennifer that she had sent two days earlier and listened to it. It was newsy, and I enjoyed being caught up as she talked about what was going on with the Coyle Detective Agency.

I groaned when she said, "I'm not supposed to say anything, but nobody mentioned typing. Your mother and Sarge are planning to pop in on you this week. I think maybe on Thursday, if they don't run into any bad weather. I tried to encourage her to call you be sure it wouldn't be a bad time for you and Larry, but she wasn't paying attention. Let me know if you need me to divert them, and I will."

I listened to the rest of her email then picked up my phone. "Call Jennifer."

She laughed as she answered. "So, you just now read my email? I was wondering why I didn't hear from you earlier."

"We're in the middle of a case, and we're not even at home."

"It must be a doozy if you're not at home; I'll steer them to our place, but it will cost you. I want to hear all the details after you can go home. Does Larry know you're working on a case?"

I giggled. "As unbelievable as it sounds, he does."

"So, he got himself assigned to the same case, did he? Is Kate involved with that little maneuver?"

"You know us so well."

"How's Lucy doing?"

"She's not moving as fast as she once did but doesn't want to admit it. Spike doesn't mind keeping her company."

"I think that's so sweet that he's always with her. I had to ask because Glenn will ask me. I'll give Sarge a call and let him know that you're working in the field. He'll understand and get through to your mother."

"I appreciate it, and thanks for the heads up; the case is complicated enough as it is."

"Maggie, are you in danger?" The concern in Jennifer's voice made my eyes well up.

"No more than ever," I said.

"Oof. I'd tell you to be safe, but you have no concept of what being safe means; at least, Larry is there with you. Call me if you need us."

After we hung up, I brushed away an errant tear and sighed. "I miss Jennifer and Glenn."

Palace Guard nodded.

I went through the rest of my emails and didn't hear anything else that required immediate action. I searched for Willard Barnes, but my search engine must have been excited because it announced it found over three million results.

I closed my browser window. *I'm not that bored.*

After I logged off the internet and shut down my computer, Palace Guard raised his eyebrows.

"I'm not sure why I was so adamant about having my computer. I guess I wanted it available, in case I thought of something that I'd like to research; as a bonus, it gives me a reason to sit alone in a quiet room with the door closed. I think Julie was feeling obligated to entertain me."

Julie opened the door a crack. "Paul just parked in the driveway. Time to chase out the pool boys."

I giggled. *Maybe I do get it.* "Thanks."

I slipped my laptop and headset under the bed and carried my glass and backpack to the kitchen.

"Henry wanted you to join him on the porch," Julie said.

I left my glass on the counter and put on my warm coat, then Lucy, Spike, and Palace Guard went out with me. "There you are, Gray Lady. Have a seat: I have something I wish I could show you, but I'll have to describe it for you. I sketched a pencil drawing of the man and one of the women he dragged up the fire escape. I'm very visual because I draw from what I see. The man's face is almost completely hidden because he was facing away from me as he went up the steep steps; the woman, however, is very clear. I'll give it to you, so you can give it to your husband; although I don't know how this will help identify the man. Now I can't even tell you why I thought this was Willard Barnes. I'll work on the second time I saw him take a woman up the fire escape next. I don't think it would do me much good to sketch the third scene because it was so near dusk." He folded the paper. "Here you are."

"Thanks." I stuck the drawing into the front pocket of my backpack then rocked in the chair before I shivered and pulled up my hood when the light wind picked up. "It's pleasant out here in the sun, isn't it?"

"I've really been enjoying it; Julie calls the porch my studio, and I don't disagree. I have always loved being outside, but I certainly never felt safe enough to do any sketching when I lived on the street. I think that's why I forgot how satisfying the feel of a pencil in my hand was while I watched the lines turn into a picture."

Paul joined us on the porch. "Julie told me you were in Henry's studio; makes sense now." He sat next to me. "Heather will be here in about fifteen minutes to pick you up, Chief. Do you have everything you need?"

"Is the plan for me to come back here tomorrow?" I asked.

"As far as I know," Paul said. "You might want to ask Heather when she gets here."

Palace Guard nodded.

"That's a good idea."

"Julie pulled out two lemon meringue pies from the oven when I came in," Paul said. "I suspect you'll be taking one with you."

"That's always been my favorite," Henry said. "I didn't realize she'd make one for me; when we were chatting, she asked me what my favorite dessert was. It's been a long time since anyone..." Henry rose and walked slowly around the corner of the house.

"Julie hit a nerve again, in a good way," Paul said. "People think all she does is talk, but she's always thinking about how to make someone happy."

"He seems sad to me."

"He is, but it's a healing sadness. He has missed his wife all these years but never took the time to really grieve her. Julie's helping him through the process, even if she doesn't realize it. Did you grieve for Parker?"

"Yes, I did for a long time."

"Part of grieving is also letting go, and that's where Henry is right now."

"You make it sound like you know this from experience."

"That's a story for another time."

I need to start keeping a list of the stories that Paul owes me.

Henry-blob's shoulders shook.

"It's hitting him hard," I said.

"Yes, it is; let's go inside and give him some privacy."

As we walked inside, I said, "Larry didn't think I was over Parker for quite a while, but I was."

"I can explain that too," Paul said. "That's flat-out man insecurity."

"Larry?" I furrowed my brow.

"Oh, yeah; it happens to the best of us."

"Is this another story?"

"It is, but don't worry, you'll never hear it, if you're keeping a list." Paul chuckled.

I smiled. *Yes, I will.*

Paul's phone buzzed a text; he tapped his reply.

"Heather's on her way. She wanted to know if you could be waiting for her alone by the road; I said yes. She knows I'll be lurking in the woods."

I hurried to the guest room, pulled out my laptop from under the bed, and added it to my computer bag.

"Is that your computer bag?" Paul asked when I hurried to the front door with Palace Guard's help.

"Might be."

"Chief, how did you get that?"

"You're sounding a little suspicious, but we'll swap stories another time," I said. "Is it okay if I say goodbye to Julie and Henry?"

"Make it fast, Chief."

"Julie, I need to leave; thank you for everything."

To my surprise, Julie hugged me tightly. "Be safe, Chief. I'll give your pie to Paul, so you'll have a nice dessert tonight."

I stepped out back; Henry sat on the porch with Lucy at his feet.

"I'm on my way out. Have a good evening." I knelt next to Lucy and hugged her. "See you soon, sweet girl."

"Thank you for finding me, Gray Lady," Henry said. "Lucy will be safe with me."

"Thank you." *Henry's found a purpose with Lucy. He needs a puppy.*

I hurried to the road with Palace Guard's help while Paul followed me as he carried the lemon meringue pie.

Paul caught up with me and asked, "What do I need to know?"

"Henry needs a puppy."

"I know you well enough to know you mean that. What else?"

"I left our fireproof safe in the guest closet."

Paul stopped. "You just made me a part of your conspiracy. There's only one reason you'd do that, Chief; what's going to happen?"

"I don't know; Palace Guard told me to bring it. We need to hurry to the road; if Heather needs me to be there, I have to be waiting."

"You're right."

We stepped up our pace.

When we got near the road, Paul gave me the pie. "Be safe, Chief. Use your jo if you need me; I can still hear you."

"Thank you." I glanced at Palace Guard, and he was scanning the area around us.

"Is something wrong?" I asked.

Palace Guard nodded.

"What did Palace Guard say?" Paul asked.

"There's something wrong."

"I've been feeling the same thing; I'm glad to know I'm in good company." Paul gave me a seashell. "Put this into your jeans pocket. Heather's not the only one who has access to technical solutions. I'll be able to find you as long as you have the seashell."

Paul left me, but I knew he was nearby in the woods.

"Don't let Julie know I told you about going to my house. She was really proud to be included in a conspiracy," I said.

"Your secret's safe, Chief, and thank you for understanding Julie; she's felt like she's a part of the agency."

"She's a hard worker," I said.

A car's headed our way from my left, and it's moving fast.

"Did you hear the car that just now sped past my driveway?" Paul said. "I couldn't tell if it was Heather, but she wouldn't be lost; do you suppose someone is chasing her?"

"It's more likely she wants us to be sure no one is following her."

When a car raced up the road on my right, then slammed to a stop and spun its wheels to back into Paul's driveway, he said, "There she is."

"Paul, the pie."

"Don't worry; I'll give it to Heather."

I nodded. "She won't be surprised to see you."

I wonder if she'll be surprised to see the pie.

When Heather stopped, she jumped out and rushed around to the passenger's door. "Get in fast."

Palace Guard helped me rush to the passenger's seat.

"Chief can hold the pie, Paul."

"How did she know?" I muttered as I climbed in; Paul rushed to my side, handed me the pie, and closed my door before he disappeared into the woods.

"Julie texted me; evidently you and Paul are not as reliable as you'd like to think, according to Julie; she didn't want us to miss dessert tonight." Heather backed out of the driveway then sped away, and I tightly held onto the precious jewel, the lemon meringue pie.

"I'll feel better after we're back in our neighborhood, Calico."

Uh oh. Whatever it is, it's bad: we're racing back to the protection of the neighborhood.

Heather slowed when she arrived at the heavy city traffic but still weaved between the cars and panel trucks.

"It's the advantage of an old car, Chief: other drivers care more about the damage to their vehicles than anyone who drives a junker car like mine would, and they know it." Heather chuckled.

Heather slowed then stopped. "We're here, Chief; hand me the pie then grab your backpack and computer bag and climb out; I'll hand you the pie then park in the garage."

"That is one gorgeous pie y'all have there," Grandma Zee said. "Where'd you find that?"

"We stopped at a grocery store to pick up dessert, and there were church ladies selling pies for a fund raiser for a missionary," Heather said.

"Was it them ladies from the Baptist Church up the road? If it was, that's going to be one good pie."

"I'm not sure," Heather said. "I was too busy lusting over the pies."

Grandma Zee roared with laughter. "Lordy, girl, I know you didn't say nothing like that in front of them because they'd be layin' hands on you for sure."

Heather giggled, so I did too.

I wonder why that's funny.

After we went into the house, Heather put the pie into the refrigerator.

"I didn't understand what was so funny about the church ladies' pie."

"You want a beer now or with dessert?" Heather asked.

"Now, while you explain the joke."

Heather pulled out two beers from the refrigerator. "Let's go into the living room, and I'll tell you while I start a fire."

After Heather had a nice blaze in the fireplace, she sat in her favorite chair with her legs crisscrossed under her.

"If I'd told Grandma Zee the bake sale was the ladies from the Baptist Church, she'd have wanted to know who was there, so she could tell us about our pie baker's misspent youth."

"Do you suppose Julie has a shady past? We'll have to ask her."

Heather snorted. "You go right ahead. You want to hear this or not?"

I pursed my lips and nodded my head.

"When I told her I was lusting over the pies, I created a diversion by getting a big laugh from her."

"What about the laying on hands she mentioned? What does that mean?"

"Her way of saying they'd be praying for me because I was lusting, and she completely forgot to grill me on who was there."

"Ah ha, that would have turned the innocent event of bringing home a pie into a convoluted tale, which is breaking rule number two of the liars' creed," I said.

Heather took a sip of her beer. "What's rule number two?"

"Don't get caught."

Palace Guard rolled his eyes.

"I agree completely, Palace Guard, and I'm definitely not asking what rule number one is; I'm going to put our leftovers into the oven to warm," Heather said.

While she was in the kitchen, Heather asked, "Why did you bring your laptop?"

"I was hoping to do some research, but I suppose it would be too risky for me to use the internet."

"Lucky for you, I've taken care of that. Are you going to work in there or at the kitchen table?"

I rolled my eye. *In here with my feet up in front of the fireplace or sitting on a hard kitchen chair: let me think.*

"Either one, but I'm lusting over the fire."

"Hey, you can't steal my best line; that's plagiarism."

"No, it isn't: you can't have a copyright on a word."

"People have tried it, but not very successfully, unless you count notoriety." Heather joined me next to the fire. "So, does that mean you'd want to work on the internet in here? You don't want to hide whatever you're doing from Larry, do you?"

"I'd like to wait before I say anything because I don't have any idea of why I wanted it."

"Do you see the chest in front of you? It's empty."

I frowned then tried to open the lid, but it seemed to be a solid piece. "What's the trick?"

"Rub your fingers under the lip of the bottom of the chest. When you come to a button, push it, and the top will fly open; keep your face out of the way, or you'll have a nice gash in your chin to explain to Larry."

"Heather decked me," I mumbled.

"I'll back you up on that one, Chief." Heather chuckled. "Let me know when you get to the sign-on screen, and I'll give you your username and password to access the internet."

After I followed her instructions, I listened to the email from Tonya that I had forwarded to Paul. "What if I have a question or two for Tonya? How long do we have to be undercover?"

"Can't you email her?"

"Not really; I need to talk to her."

Heather joined me on the sofa. "Something's rolling around in your head, isn't it, Chief? What is it?"

"I don't know, but it's bothering me."

"Unless we get a cheap, prepaid phone to use, calling her cell or even Martha's is completely out of the question because she's a potential target, and we don't want to draw any attention to her. It would have to be in person, which isn't completely impossible if we change your appearance because you could arrange a rendezvous place and time by email."

"I don't know; let's bring Larry in on the discussion."

"He'll have a different perspective; that's not all bad, Chief."

Larry's old car sputtered as he pulled into the short driveway; I logged off my laptop and put it into the chest in front of us.

"We'll talk more after supper; maybe you'll have a better idea of what you want to ask her, or not. You're a master at winging it, Chief."

Heather grabbed a beer from the refrigerator then unlocked the door, and Larry rushed inside. "Thanks, Pearl."

After she closed the door, I hugged him. "Welcome home, Honey Boy."

Larry kissed me. "You taste good, Calico."

He inhaled deeply. "Leftovers are my favorite, Pearl; I'm starving, and I need my off-duty beer."

"Here's your beer. While you open it, I'll put our food on the table."

While we were eating, Larry asked, "What's going on?"

"We'll talk after dessert," Heather said. "Julie was afraid we'd starve. I thought reheating might ruin everything, but this is delicious."

I ate the last mini-crabcake on my plate. "Could I have a dab more?"

"You want seconds?" Heather asked. "Grandma Zee would definitely approve; she'd say it's about time you put some meat on them skinny bones of yours."

"My mouth needed more."

Heather and Larry patiently waited for me to finish eating my seconds, then Heather served Larry a generous slice of the lemon meringue pie.

"What about you, Calico? Do you want pie now, or do you want to wait?" Heather asked.

"Isn't there a famous saying: there's always room for pie?"

"There is now." Larry took a big bite.

"I'll give you a Calico-sized slice," Heather said.

I took a bite. "Mmm. I never learned to bake anything other than cinnamon rolls; I'll bet I could learn to bake pies."

"We'll get you some pie-baking lessons, Calico, but you need to teach me how to make cinnamon rolls," Heather said.

While Larry washed our few dishes, I asked, "Why did you take my house keys?"

"I didn't take them; that cop, Larry, took them," Larry said.

Heather chuckled. "Honey Boy got you good there, Calico."

"Don't encourage his annoying behavior, Pearl," I growled.

Larry and Palace Guard high-fived, and I stormed toward the living room; Heather grabbed my arm and jerked me to the left. "You almost ran into a wall."

"Might have done my hard head a bit of good," I whispered as we linked arms.

After Larry finished the dishes, we relaxed in front of the fireplace.

While I sipped my hot tea, and Larry and Heather enjoyed their after-dinner beer, Larry said, "Catch me up on today."

"Tonya called me before I left Julie's; Martha has an old friend who is very ill and in the hospital, so they are coming here for a day or two. I need to talk to Tonya."

"I'm sorry you won't be able to see her. Will they be staying at Julie's?" Larry asked.

"No, Tonya said her mom didn't want to impose on Julie, so they found a nice place that is close to the hospital."

Larry nodded. "Tonya will want to give Martha a break now and then, I'm sure. Did Tonya want to get together?"

"No, but I need to talk to her."

"Do a rewind for Larry, Chief, and start from the beginning."

I furrowed my brow while I tried to decide where the beginning was.

Heather sighed, and Palace Guard glared at me.

"The part where you conned Julie into taking you to your house to pick up your computer might be one place to start, Chief."

"Right, so I read the email that Tonya sent me earlier, and I have some questions for Tonya."

"You went to our house and grabbed your computer, so you could read the email here?" Larry asked.

"I set up a secure network," Heather said.

"What about my computer? Didn't it occur to you I might want to check some things too?" Larry raised his voice.

Heather snorted. "What do you think, Larry?"

"You brought mine too? Why didn't you tell me?" Larry narrowed his eyes.

"It's in my computer bag." I bit my lip so I wouldn't smirk. "I was waiting for you to yell at me, so I could be sure you are really you. What do you want to check?"

"I don't know yet," he grumbled. "It was the principal of the thing. What else, Maggie? There's always something else."

"Henry's not as positive as he was originally when he said he saw Willard Barnes dragging women up the fire escape. He's an accomplished sketch artist, and when I asked him to draw what he saw, the man's face was hidden."

"That shatters everything we've been thinking, doesn't it?" Heather asked. "What about all the hospital gossip about Willie and the elevator?"

"I think that rumor was about Martha's friend, Will. Tonya told me her dad didn't like her mom's strange friend because Will thought he was charming, but her dad said the man was creepy. We need to know whether Martha's friend is Willard Barnes."

"I don't understand why..."

Larry interrupted Heather. "Tonya can't come here; we still haven't stopped the killer, and she'd be a prime target."

"I lost track of all the moving pieces there for a minute. Tonya shouldn't go to the hospital at all," Heather said.

I nodded. "There's a possibility that Willard Barnes wasn't the man in the elevator; maybe people assumed he was, based on his lousy social skills, and the killer took advantage of that."

"I need to call Justin," Larry said.

"You can't use your phone here," Heather said. "I have a burner phone."

"What's that?" I asked.

"A phone that can't be traced to anyone; after it's served its purpose, it's thrown away, which is why it's called a burner," Larry said.

"Will he answer a call from an unknown number?" I asked.

"He will; Grandma D told us in one of our classes to never ignore a phone call from a number we didn't recognize because it might be our one chance to talk to a willing informant."

After Heather gave him the phone, Larry tapped in a number. "Hey, it's me." Larry wandered into the kitchen.

"Chief, we need to make some changes before you can go anywhere."

"Like what?" I narrowed my eyes. "The last time anyone told me I needed to change my appearance was when Larry paid a hair stylist to dye my hair red."

"I had almost forgotten about that; pretty bold move for a guy who'd had a crush on you for a couple of years, wasn't it?" Heather chuckled. "I love it, but we'll have to do more. We'll cut your hair, fatten you up, and do away with your eyepatch and your jo."

"Let's just dye my hair red; I'm not ready for all that."

"Too bad. The only optional one is fatten you up because we really don't have time to wait for the form to make you rounder. I probably should order it anyway, so we'll have it available. I'll talk to Grandma Zee about your hair; in spite of the fact you are not the typical demographic for this neighborhood, Grandma Zee will schedule you with a good stylist and make sure there's no chatter about you or your hair."

"What about my eyepatch?"

"No eyepatch, but you'll have a haircut that covers your eye; you'll either be very stylish or retro, depending on the latest whim of the fashionistas. I don't keep up, and I know you don't either, but your hairdresser will know. We'll also leave the color of your hair to your stylist, but I suspect it won't be red. We want you to be plain with no distinguishable characteristics."

"It will be strange to be without my jo, but Palace Guard will be with me, right?"

Palace Guard glared at Heather.

"Absolutely, and while you're getting your hair cut and colored, I'll pick up our new transmitters and drop off Paul's before my appointment."

Larry came into the living room and sat next to me. "Justin's going to come with Tonya and Martha. I told him what we need to know about Martha's friend, so he'll get all the details he can, then he and I will talk."

After Heather gave Larry a quick update on my transformation, she said, "If you need more information after you hear what Larry learned, Chief, you can talk to Tonya yourself in the afternoon after your hair appointment."

"What did you mean when you said your appointment?" I asked.

"I'm going to be you, Chief. I'll have my hair dyed the same color as yours is now, and with your jo and an eyepatch, my transformation will be complete. Paul can shadow me while you talk to Martha, if you need to."

Palace Guard raised his eyebrows, and Larry said, "Palace Guard will go with you. Where are you going?"

"I don't know; I thought we could talk in the morning and come up with a plan," Heather said.

"We need to know who we're looking for; I have an idea that might help, but we'll be fresh in the morning," I said.

Heather yawned. "Cliffhanger at bedtime, but I'm too tired to care." She headed to the stairs. "I can't take it; what's rule number one?"

"Keep it simple."

Heather snorted. "Do you make up stuff like this on the fly? That's brilliant, Calico."

After we were in our bedroom, Larry asked, "What's your idea?"

"Librarian." I unbuttoned his jeans.

He nibbled on my ear then the nape of my neck. "Fine; tell me later."

CHAPTER TWELVE

"Jump in the shower and get dressed; I talked to Grandma Zee then used your jo to catch up Paul on what we're doing," Heather called out from the bottom of the stairs.

"You go first." I kissed Larry's scruffy face. "I'll make up the bed then be right down."

Larry patted my bare bottom then grabbed his clothes and wrapped himself with a towel before he raced downstairs to the shower.

When I hurried downstairs wrapped in my towel, Larry was headed to the kitchen; he stopped and wolf-whistled.

"Leave the hired help alone, fella; your coffee's in here," Heather said.

After my shower, I joined them in the kitchen.

"Your coffee's at your seat, Chief. So what's your idea?"

"It depends. Is our office available yet, Larry?"

"Yes; they cleared it yesterday."

"Heather, can we get a cleaning crew in there this morning, so you as my double can go to the office this afternoon? Martha and Tonya can make sure it's well known at the hospital that I'm going to work this afternoon. I want to call Becky because she'll be happy to hear I'm back on the case."

"Let me guess," Larry said, "We're going to be part of the cleaning crew."

Palace Guard and Heather stared at him, and I laughed.

"You got it, honey."

"You two are scary when you work together, did you know that? Eat your breakfast, Chief. Your appointment is in half an hour."

"I don't have a Plan B." I finished my scrambled egg and rye toast that Heather had over buttered.

After I cleaned the butter off my fingers, I asked, "What's the weather like today?"

"We had a cold front blow in last night, and we may get some rain later today; wear a warm coat and expect to get wet," Heather said. "We'll have our transmitters and earbuds. Call for Plan B, Chief, and it will happen. I'll brief Paul when I give him his transmitter. Honey Boy, what's the best place for us to meet at ten for a handoff of Callie, previously known as Chief?"

"Probably at the grocery store that is close to the office."

"I need a burner," I said.

"Why?" Larry and Heather asked in unison.

Palace Guard rolled his eyes, so I rolled my eye.

"Cut it out you two," Heather grumbled. "We forgot you wanted to call Becky. I'll give you your burner."

Heather opened a kitchen drawer and pulled out an old cell phone then handed it to me. "This phone looks old, but it works by voice. Find the last button at the bottom of the phone. It will send the sound to your transmitter after we pick it up. Don't answer the phone if you get a call, Chief, even if you recognize the number. Tell Becky you've borrowed a phone from one of the

GBI agents because they confiscated your phone. None of us will call you because we'll have transmitters to contact each other. Got it?"

"Yes."

"Let's go; we'll see you at ten, Honey Boy."

When Heather and I walked outside, Grandma Zee said, "Y'all ready? Come on up."

As Heather led the way to Grandma Zee's building, I said, "I thought we were going to a hair salon."

Heather-blob shrugged. "So did I."

The interior stairwell was dark; Heather said, "Give me a second. It's too dark in here to see."

I smiled then saw a small light on the floor in front of her. When we reached the end of the stairs, Heather opened a door, and the light lit up the landing.

"Come on in and meet my girl Trixie."

"I ain't cutting those curls," Trixie said. "Tell me what you got in mind. Undercover, right? What else?"

"She has only her right eye and has always worn a patch over her missing left eye," Heather said. "We thought maybe one of those cuts that would cover that eye would work."

"She's too young to be that much out of style; what about color?"

"Something that won't call attention to her."

"Got it. I'll put some product on her hair to straighten those curls then color her hair dark blond with light blond highlights, which will be perfect with her green eye and pale skin. A low ponytail to pull her hair away from her face will be best."

"What about her missing eye?" Heather asked.

"Take off your patch, Calico."

After I removed the patch, Trixie said, "What do you think, Grandma Zee? A ball cap?"

"That's all she needs. Sunglasses for outside, then put them on top of your head when you go inside, Calico," Grandma Zee said.

"Sit at the kitchen table, and I'll get busy. What's our timeframe, Pearl?" Trixie asked.

"We're meeting Honey Boy at ten."

"What about your hair? What are we doing?"

"How close can you get me to look like Calico looks now?"

"Decoy, huh? I can do that: the color's easy, and I'll give you some curls; the two of you will be out of here by nine," Trixie said.

While she worked, Trixie caught us up on the latest celebrity gossip.

"You got all that, Calico?" Grandma Zee asked.

"All of it, but I don't know who any of those people are," I said.

"Doesn't matter," Heather said. "You'll have the shallow lingo to go with your shallow looks. What about makeup, Trixie?"

"None is best; that's what you're used to, isn't it, Calico?"

I nodded, and Trixie continued with even juicier celebrity gossip.

After Trixie was finished, Grandma Zee gave me a hand mirror. "What do you think, Calico?"

"I cannot believe Kayleigh chose Ishmael over TJ. That girl must be blind."

Heather snorted as she put on my eyepatch. "Don't tell Honey Boy this eyepatch is actually my favorite because I told him the black sparkly patch was my favorite. What color is this one?"

Grandma Zee burst out laughing. "Transformation complete. Good work, Trixie."

Palace Guard held his hand low, palm up, and Heather smacked it.

"If anyone mentions your eye, Calico, glare at them," Grandma Zee said. "You'll look like you're giving them the stink eye."

After we exited the stairwell, Heather said, "No offense, but I'm not going to wear the eyepatch while I drive; it was bad enough going down the stairs. Next on our agenda is to pick up the transmitters then drop off one with Paul. I want to get his opinion on your transformation, and maybe Julie too, if we're feeling brave. Call Becky, Chief."

After I told my phone to call Becky, the phone rang then went to voice mail, so I hung up. "I'll try again later."

Heather pulled into a strip mall parking lot and parked in front of a small shop.

"Give me your jo, so we can activate it with one of the new transmitters."

When she returned, she said, "All set; here's your transmitter."

After I inserted the small earbud, Heather climbed back out of the car and stood in front of the hood.

"You should hear me clearly. Hold up a thumb."

I held up my thumb; she continued, "Tap your ear lightly once to speak and twice to hang up."

I brushed my hair away from my ear and tapped once. "Got it."

I pushed a little hair back into place and tapped twice. "You shouldn't hear this."

Heather climbed into the car. "I heard you say, got it; did you say anything else?"

"Yes, after I tapped twice."

"Good, let's run by Paul's house. He'll be waiting by his driveway because we're running short on time, so we won't be able to get the Julie seal of approval after all."

"Will he have two earbuds?"

"No, even though I thought about it briefly, I decided not to torture him like that; his earbud will work for the team and for jo. The other three will work only for the team. Paul's less likely to be overly involved in one of our clandestine field activities, so he's our best back up for you, whether it's you or me." Heather chuckled. "I've even picked up Gray Lady logic, haven't I?"

"What about a ball cap? I don't have one with me."

"Tell Paul."

I pushed the record button on my jo. "I'll need a ball cap for a day or two. Can you have one with you when we come by?"

When Heather pulled into Paul's driveway, he was waiting for us.

Heather lowered her window, and Paul peered inside. "This is uncanny, Heather; you are a double for Chief, and Chief, I wouldn't know it was you if I passed you on the street. Julie has the cleaning crew lined up for ten thirty at the office; she'll meet them there and unlock, then she'll return at eleven thirty when they are finished and lock the door."

He handed me a sack. "Here's your ball cap, Chief, and there's a spiral notebook with handwritten notes from Becky; Julie said it was mixed in with Vanessa's journals. Bob stopped by earlier and said Becky left the house early this morning and asked him to be sure Julie got Vanessa's journals; he said he forgot because Vanessa never wrote anything worth reading, but he wanted to be sure there wasn't anything of Becky's included with the journals. I told him Julie had glanced through them and said that Vanessa showed exceptional talent in her writing."

"You didn't mention the spiral notebook?"

"He kind of got my back up when he said his daughter never wrote anything worth reading." Paul shrugged. "Call me petty. He asked if Gray Lady was going to be here today, and I told him I wasn't sure, but I could check if he wanted to talk to her. Bob said he was just being curious and had to get back home before Becky returned and caught him out of the house; he seemed really distracted."

Heather held out her hand. "Paul, here's your earbud and the instructions on its use, but basically, tap it once to transmit and twice to stop. You'll be transmitting to the three of us, and you'll hear all three of us, but you'll also hear the jo transmissions, just like always, through the same earbud."

"Good. Who will have the jo today?" Paul asked.

"I will," Heather said. "Callie here and Larry will be part of the cleaning crew. I'll need you to pick me up at the grocery store that's near the office. We're meeting Larry there, but the Gray Lady can't drive away. My plan for the afternoon is to go to the office."

"I'll be there about the same time you meet up with Larry," Paul said. He tapped twice on the top of the car then backed away, and Heather headed toward the grocery store near the office.

"I don't know if it was a coincidence or not, but did you notice Paul tapped twice on the car?" I asked.

Heather nodded. "End of conversation: makes sense to me."

Heather parked her car on the farthest row from the grocery store. "Larry's here. Here's his earbud. Go into the store, and he'll meet you in there. Palace Guard, stay with Chief; Paul will escort me then drop me off at the office later."

I stuck the earbud into my jeans pocket; Palace Guard saluted Heather then guided me to the store with our routine of taps on my shoulder. Once we were inside, Palace Guard guided me to an aisle, then we stopped, and I pretended to inspect the cans in front of me.

"Can I help you find something, Miss?" I smiled at Larry's familiar voice.

"Thank you, but they don't have what I want here; I'll have to go to the other store."

Larry nodded then strolled out of the store. Palace Guard guided me in a different direction, and then to the exit and through the parking lot to Larry's junker car.

"Your chariot awaits, milady." Larry smiled as he helped me into the passenger's seat. I handed him his new earbud.

I love his curls and his smile.

"If I park around the corner from the office, you could wait in the car while I talk to Julie, if you'd rather Julie didn't see you. How are we going to work this?"

"I don't think it matters if Julie sees me. Heather wanted Julie's opinion about my transformation, anyway. Julie can tell the cleaning crew they don't need to clean the meeting room because you are the auditor. You and your assistant are there to examine the records in the meeting room. We can close the door and should probably go through the files."

"I still have the keys to the files," Larry said.

"I have a key to the meeting room if it was locked when the investigators left."

"If we wait a few minutes before we leave, we won't get there before Julie does. I'd rather not be hanging around in front of the office."

"Good; I'd like to make a phone call."

"Who are you calling?"

"A librarian." I recited a phone number to my phone.

"I still don't get it," Larry mumbled. "You're a librarian; why would a librarian call another librarian?"

"You make it sound like a riddle." I giggled as the phone rang.

"Hey, Lily; it's the Gray Lady."

"Do you need bail money or an alibi? I'm ready with either."

I giggled at the sincerity of her tone.

"You're calling the librarian at the campus library in Tennessee?" Larry asked.

I motioned for him to hush.

"Thanks for the offer, but so far, I don't need either one yet. I'm in Savannah, and I need someone with insight about a boy with a particular personality type about forty or so years ago."

"In Savannah? I have an old friend who might have an idea or two for you to pursue. Can I do your legwork? Tell me what you're looking for."

"I'm looking for a boy that was fairly skilled with using a knife, without remorse, to cause pain and suffering in small animals. He probably was a typical bully: afraid of boys who were tough or larger than he was and enjoyed torturing those he deemed to be weak or infirm. He would have had a particular disdain for anyone with a physical or mental deficit. There would probably have been rumors about him, and the girls would have been afraid of him and called him creepy. He may have had a sidekick who did all his dirty work except for the knife work; he would have enjoyed that too much to hand it off to someone else. Adults probably considered him to be a model child."

"One of my old friends is a retired school librarian who has lived just outside of Savannah her entire life. She still keeps in touch with her cohorts, so if she doesn't know of a boy like that, one of her friends will. I'll get back to you as soon as I can. Do I call this number?"

"This is a cheap phone and doesn't take incoming calls. I'll check in with you later, but you can send me an email."

"Gotcha; I'll send you an email as soon as I have something for you and talk to you later. I'm so glad you called; I've been thinking about you quite a bit lately and have been wondering whether your sight has improved."

"Not at all, but I have excellent tools to assist me, so I'm adjusting."

"I'm sorry to hear that, but I'm happy you have access to tools that help you. Anytime you need me to do a little research for you, let me know. I love being on your team."

"Thank you so much; this is so much more than I hoped for."

After we hung up, Larry asked, "Is this what you were thinking when you said librarian last night?"

"Yes, but I didn't expect Lily to jump in and do the research. I was hoping for a contact here. I'm a little embarrassed I didn't think of it sooner, but I immediately jumped to the conclusion that we'd identified the killer."

"We all did, sweetie, and I'm beating myself up because I know better. I guess both of us can just get over it and move on."

"Might as well; we need all our energy focused on stopping the killer."

On the way to the office, Larry said, "I'm glad you're with us, Palace Guard; you're much more practiced than I am with guiding the Gray Lady."

After Larry parked, he opened my door. "We're about a block from the office. Julie's standing in front, and a white van with a cleaning logo just parked. Our timing is perfect."

After I stepped out of the car, I shivered then zipped up my jacket.

As we walked at a brisk pace to the office, Larry said, "I look a little scruffy to be an auditor."

"You were called back from a camping trip unexpectedly."

"Got it."

When we reached Julie, Larry said, "Mrs. Vargas, I'm Henry from your auditor's office. Excuse the beard, but I've been wilderness camping with the boy scouts. My assistant, Callie, and I are here for your audit, but don't let us stop you from doing what you need to do."

Julie extended her hand. "Nice to meet you; the office called me, so I've been expecting you. The files are in our meeting room; I've already told the cleaners to skip cleaning in there. I'll be back in an hour to lock up after the cleaners are finished."

"We won't be that long," Larry said. "You'll receive your full audit report next week."

After we went into the meeting room, Larry unlocked files. "I should have known Heather and Paul would have cleared the way for us, so she wouldn't be surprised. She didn't even give you a glance. What are we looking for?"

"I have no idea." I pulled my reader out of my backpack. "Pick one of the end cabinets, and I'll start at the other end. Heather gave me a text to speech gadget. It works like a scanner, except Heather said it would read the text as I scanned across it; I'll hear it through my earbud, so let me know if I'm missing a conversation."

After Larry opened the top file drawer of a cabinet, I began scanning and reading documents from a cabinet.

"I found something. It's notes Julie took from a conversation with Becky. Becky said she saw a man in the grocery store she thought she'd recognized but assumed he would have gone to prison years ago for some heinous crime because he was so vile." I listened to the rest of the conversation. "Julie didn't say anything about a name."

Larry tapped his earbud. "Callie found a note in Julie's files. Ask Julie if Becky told her the name of the man that Becky had assumed would have been in prison."

Becky's spiral notebook.

I pulled out the notebook and began reading. Larry strode to the door and opened it a crack. "We've got the files we need, Callie. Thanks for your help."

He went out of the room and closed the door with an audible click. After I heard him lock then unlock the door, I listened to his footsteps as he hurried to the front door then opened and closed the door with a controlled slam. The door to the meeting room opened, then Larry quietly closed and locked it.

He tapped his ear and whispered, "We have officially left the office."

Larry sat next to me at the table. "What do you have, sweetie?"

"Becky has two words on this page: high school and cousin."

"High school is underlined and has three exclamation points; cousin is circled with an arrow pointing to it. What's on the previous page?"

"You can read it, but at the end of the page, Becky wrote what do all the mothers have in common? Then on the page after the high school and cousin page she wrote he shouldn't still be around, and why didn't I listen to his cousin."

"High school? Is Becky saying all the mothers went to the same high school?" Larry asked.

"I tried to call her..."

Paul unknowingly interrupted me. "I'm waiting for Noah. Heather and I went to the address where Henry saw the three women being dragged up the fire escape. I know he called them young women, but putting it into perspective, most women would look young to Henry."

"Were you able to see in the apartment?" Larry asked.

"A little more than that: did you know Heather's a whiz with locks? She opened the door, but we didn't go in. The apartment looked and smelled like a slaughterhouse. There is old blood on the floor and walls, but worse, there was fresh blood on the floor. Heather locked the door and is waiting for me at my car two blocks away; I'm around the corner from the fire escape. Gotta go: Noah's here; more later."

The front door opened then closed. "Looks nice; are you finished?" Julie asked.

"Sign here, ma'am," a man said. "Thank you for your business."

"I appreciate how responsive you were. The boss was hoping she would be able to work this afternoon. She's always been..." Julie continued talking as she closed and locked the door behind her.

"I wonder what I've always been," I said.

"Beautiful and absolutely unpredictable." Larry kissed me. "What were you saying?"

"I tried to call Becky earlier, but she didn't pick up; I'm sure it's because she didn't recognize the number. Heather and I thought she could help spread the word that the Gray Lady would be at the office this afternoon."

"Maybe after Paul's released from the apartment, he can check in with Bob," Larry said.

"That's when Heather will be coming here; if it's a quiet afternoon, maybe Julie can call Becky this evening."

"I'm clear and on my way to the Gray Lady," Paul said.

I snorted. "I'm not sure I'll ever get used to..."

A phone in Larry's backpack buzzed a text and interrupted me. He frowned. "I know I wasn't supposed to have this with me, but I have to stay in touch."

Larry pulled out his GBI cell phone from his backpack. "Noah wants me to call him."

Larry tapped in a phone number. "What's up?"

Larry's face became somber as he listened to Noah for the next few minutes. "Let me check a few things, then I'll get back to you."

After he hung up Larry said, "Noah wants to send Sophie Rose to her parents so he can take leave from the state police and join us in our operation."

"Why? What happened?"

"I didn't say anything happened," Larry said.

Palace Guard tilted his head and stared, and I did my best to glare at Larry.

Larry exhaled. "A convenience store owner near the apartment called the police department and was so upset, the dispatcher had trouble understanding what he was saying. When she asked him if someone was sick, the owner said he needed the police then hung up. After the police officer arrived, the store owner told the officer that one of his regulars came into the store and was pale and shaking as he told the owner that someone was in the regular's usual spot. The shopkeeper led the officer outside then pointed to the dumpster behind the store. The police officer discovered the body of a woman behind the dumpster; her throat was sliced so deep that her neck vertebrae were exposed, and her face and chest had been brutally slashed; the number seventeen was carved on her abdomen. It may take dental records to identify her."

"What do you think of Noah joining the team?" I asked.

"Not much," Larry said. "He's in a position to assign his best from the state police to work with GBI, and he has the clout to be sure GBI assigns their best. He's never worked undercover, much less freelance, and we don't have time for him to learn. I thought

I knew undercover, but I've learned I'm a beginner compared to you and Heather, and I know Paul feels the same, but I'm not sure what to tell Noah."

"Tell him exactly what you just said."

Larry nodded. "Thanks for listening; I didn't realize all I needed to do was to talk it out."

He picked up his GBI phone and called Noah. While he and Noah talked, I listened to what Becky had written on the next page while Palace Guard leaned over my shoulder to read.

After Larry returned his GBI phone to his backpack, he said, "Noah asked me if Paul was undercover, and I told him Paul was doing his best; Noah laughed and said that he'd be much worse than Paul. We agreed that Noah's best position on our team is the coach, so he can watch our backs."

I nodded. "I hadn't thought of that; you're really brilliant. What else did he say?"

"He thinks the murdered woman is Becky."

"I was afraid of that." I bit my lip as a tear ran down my cheek; Larry put his arm around me.

I sniffled then inhaled deeply and exhaled. "I read a little farther in Becky's notebook. Martha is on her list of mothers."

Paul broke in. "I got a text from Bob; he found Becky's cell phone on a chair on their back patio. Bob said the last two texts must have been from one of Becky's friends. They must have planned to meet for breakfast this morning because the first of the two asked where Becky was, then the last text apologized for getting the date wrong. Heather and I are going to swing past the diner, so we'll have a better idea of the path Becky might have taken."

CHAPTER THIRTEEN

"Paul, give Noah a call and tell him about the cell phone. He'll make sure someone visits Bob," Larry said.

"That's great," Heather said. "Is Noah on the team now?"

"He's got our back," Larry said.

"Perfect; coaching from the sidelines. I'll call him," Paul said.

"Noah might or might not tell you when you talk to him that the police found a woman's body near the apartment; Noah thinks it is Becky."

"Damn," Paul said.

After no one else said anything else, Larry picked up his GBI phone.

"Sweetie, I need to warn Justin."

Larry called Justin, and I continued going through Becky's notebook. I listened to a story about a young boy who terrorized small animals, then when he was older, a girl in his class suddenly disappeared; her mutilated body was found in a lake. I reread the story several times. At the end the story, Becky had written, "His cousin tried to warn me."

I frowned. *Was this a draft for a middle grade fiction book that Becky was writing?*

After Larry hung up, he said, "Justin said Tonya wants to talk to you."

I picked up my phone from Heather and called Tonya.

"Oh, good; you got my message. Justin talked to Mom, and she finally agreed to go back home today when she learned that one of the nurses knew Doctor Barnes and his family and called a cousin, who will be here tomorrow. Justin's taking off work tomorrow too, so we can get a few things done at home before he has to go back to work on Monday."

"Doctor Barnes? Is your mother's friend Willard Barnes?" I asked.

"Yes, but didn't I already tell you that?"

"I'd forgotten; have a great weekend."

"Will do, and you still owe me details," Tonya said.

"I will the next time..."

Tonya interrupted me. "I'll see you first." She giggled as she quickly hung up.

"I almost had her," I grumbled.

"Did I hear you right? Willard Barnes is Martha's friend who has been in ICU?" Larry asked.

I nodded.

"That confirms what you said earlier."

Larry tapped his ear. "Martha's friend in the hospital is Willard Barnes; doesn't change our plans, but we're back to square one as far as the identity of the killer's concerned."

Larry tapped his ear twice to stop transmitting then continued, "I'll tell Noah about Willard Barnes; I want him to have Becky's notebook, but first, I'll give you enough time to get everything out of it you can because nobody sees things the way you do. The analysts are skilled and smart, but they lack a certain twist that is part of your natural insight."

"Twisted insight?" I rolled my eye.

Palace Guard grinned and nodded, and Larry chuckled.

After a few minutes, I said, "I've listened to the rest of the notes, and the only additional thing I've found is a list Becky titled anti-social."

Larry leaned over my shoulder and read the list on the page. "No empathy, deceptively charming, history of violent behavior, predatory stare."

I shuddered. "I've seen the predatory stare once, and it was terrifying because I had thought Lillian was a friend. Do you remember Lillian? When she came to my house that night to kill me while I slept, her eyes were dark and completely soulless, and I knew she'd murder me on the spot with no regrets. If the killer had a habit of staring at women in the elevator with that fixed gaze, they would feel unsettled and uncomfortable without necessarily understanding why."

"I remember Lillian; she and Mr. Morgan owned a detective agency, and Glenn and Jennifer bought the agency from him when he decided to retire. You were the only one who suspected that Lillian was behind Parker's murder."

"I might not be a fan of my father, but Gary Sloan did too."

"I'm not sure I knew that, but it makes sense in retrospect because he was guarding you at the library. Do I arrange for Noah to have someone pick up the notebook?"

I nodded.

Larry tapped his ear. "We have Becky's spiral notebook and would like Noah to pick it up. Any ideas?"

"Have him send an undercover trooper to the office, and the Gray Lady will hand it over," Heather said. "We'll grab some lunch to eat at the office and bring you something too."

Larry smiled. "Heather always had a reputation for knowing where to get the best local food; Sarge said it was because she frequented all the sketchy places none of us even knew about."

After he sat next to me at the table, Larry called Noah. "We've got a spiral notebook that Becky used to take notes. Can you send someone who is undercover to the Gray Flanagan Agency in about an hour to pick up the notebook from our decoy Gray Lady?"

"What's the support plan for your decoy?" Noah asked.

"Two inside with Gray Lady, and one outside. Gray Lady will probably leave the office in a couple of hours; Paul will pick her up, then we'll return tomorrow morning. We don't want to look like a baited trap."

"Is Paul at the front? We can cover the back from a roof with binoculars and the side with a security camera."

"That would work as long as your spotter doesn't shoot any of us, and our killer doesn't see the security camera being installed."

Noah chuckled. "The security camera was installed yesterday when the traffic light on the next block malfunctioned. It's not easy to stay ahead of y'all, but Sophie Rose told me Gray Lady would probably set up shop at her office as soon as it was available. I've been known to be thick-headed at times, but I'm smart enough to listen to Sophie Rose."

Larry elbowed me then winked.

"You'll see one of my best destitute troopers in about an hour."

After Larry hung up, I picked up my phone. "I need to call Lily."

Lily answered. "Hello, Glenda Lou; I was just thinking about you. I'm at the front desk; just a second, and I'll go into my office. How's my favorite niece?"

Larry furrowed his brow. "Glenda Lou?" he whispered.

"G. L." I mouthed.

"Okay, I'm in my office and have the door closed. I'm glad you called, Gray Lady, because I have some information for you. A retired librarian in a town not far from where you are told me that right after she began working at a local library, she heard about a boy at the school who was completely unmanageable. His mother claimed he was high strung and blamed everyone else when the boy got in trouble at school for being disrespectful to the teachers, not following rules, or hurting other children. One of his teachers had a daughter who had cerebral palsy, and the boy would stab the child with a pencil then laugh when she cried, and there were never any witnesses. His mother claimed the child hurt herself then blamed her son out of spite because her son was so popular. My friend said the teacher quit in the middle of the school year and left town because she feared for the safety of her child. By the time he was in high school, the boy had learned how to manipulate the school administration and the juvenile court system. The librarian couldn't remember the boy's name but will check with one of her friends; I'm supposed to call her back after lunch, so call me back about two."

"I will. Did she happen to mention whether the boy had a follower that did his bidding when he was in high school?"

"No, but I'll call her back right quick and ask her. She may not know, but her friend might. It logically fits the profile, doesn't it?"

"Thank you so much for all you're doing; talk to you later."

After I hung up, Larry said, "I heard; I'll let you know when it's two o'clock."

"I really wish I could run; I keep feeling like I'm missing something, and I need to clear my head."

"I officially hate the idea, but I understand how your mind operates. We're tentatively planning on leaving around three, right? Maybe there's a way we can go to a track where you and

I can run while Heather and Palace Guard watch our backs. I was going to ask if you have your running shoes, but you always do."

Palace Guard and I nodded.

"What about you?" I asked.

"I decided ages ago I wanted to be with you whenever you took off on a run."

I held up my hand and listened as someone unlocked the front door then opened it. "The cleaners did a good job," Paul said. "It smells fresh, doesn't it, Gray Lady?"

"Thanks, Paul; this was much harder than I expected," Heather said.

Larry opened the meeting room door. "We're in here."

"I'll lock the front door so we can eat without being disturbed." Paul said.

Heather brought in a large sack. "I have tacos; it seemed like the thing to do for old times' sake."

Paul came into the meeting room and put a gallon of sweet tea on the table then opened the bottom drawer on the middle file cabinet and pulled out paper cups, plates, and napkins. "I knew Julie wouldn't let us down."

"What all have we missed?" Heather asked as we ate.

"After tacos," Larry said.

"We have one taco left." Heather peered into the sack after everyone ate their fill.

"We have an undercover trooper coming to pick up a notebook. Offer the taco to our trooper, Gray Lady," I said.

Larry filled them in on the additional support from Noah. I told them about Willard Barnes and what I'd learned from Lily.

"I have a few pages in Becky's notebook to show you."

After the two of them read the pages, Heather said, "Becky was profiling the killer, which seems to fit with the page where she says he shouldn't still be around. Did you notice that?"

"Do you think she knew who the killer is? How could Becky be so far ahead of us?" Larry asked.

"She's from here, and she and Bob are recently retired teachers. Maybe the killer was a student in one of her classes," Paul said.

"Did they look old enough to have had a middle aged man as a student, or is our killer younger than we've been thinking?" I asked.

"Either the killer is younger, or he's their age, and Becky knew him in high school," Paul said. "If they became teachers after four or five years of college and retired after twenty-five years, they would be in their fifties. I'll get Julie's opinion because she's seen both of them, but that's how old Bob looks."

"Describe Bob," Larry said.

"He's my height and muscular. He probably works out because he doesn't have the typical middle-aged spread most men his age have."

I frowned. "Because he said they were retired when they came into my office, I assumed they were in their sixties and had a completely different picture of him in my head. That changes everything."

"I fell into the same trap," Heather said.

"I'd like to see the high school yearbooks from Becky's sophomore and junior years," Larry said. "We may find the killer there."

"That would be right up Julie's alley," Paul said.

"Let's wait until after I talk to Lily because I might have a name."

"Did I hear you say wait, Chief?" Heather asked. "That's not your style at all."

I shrugged. "I think we're missing something."

"As soon as we leave here, we're going for a run," Larry said.

"Are you crazy?" Heather asked. "Chief can't go for a run; it's too risky."

"That's the second time she's said we're missing something. Trust me; she has to run," Larry said.

Paul whispered, "Please don't hurt them, Chief."

I sighed loudly and with as much drama as I could without putting the back of my hand on my forehead. "If you insist."

Paul chuckled. "It's almost one o'clock. I need to unlock the door for business."

After he unlocked the door, Paul's phone rang. "It's Bob."

He put his phone on speakerphone.

"Paul, the police were here. Becky's..." Bob sobbed. "They think they found her body. I'm sorry, but I'll have to call back later." Bob hung up.

"I wonder if that's what we're missing," I said. "Did Becky know who the killer was? Does Bob know too? Is that what we've been missing? I've had the feeling that the two of them have been hiding something all along, but what?"

"A relative?" Heather asked.

"If we don't know anything by the time we leave the office, Julie can research Becky's yearbooks, and I can do a genealogy search for Becky and Bob," Paul said. "I need to take my place, so our undercover transient can pick up the notebook and taco, and our killer can show up."

After Paul left, Heather said, "Give me the notebook, and I'll take it and the taco to my Gray Lady office."

"I'll sit at Julie's desk," I said.

"I don't like that," Larry said. "How can I keep you safe?"

"Are you sure you want me to answer that?" I narrowed my eye.

"It didn't come out right; where's the best place for me?"

"In the meeting room, Paul's office, or lurking around Julie's desk."

"Okay, I'll lounge in a visitor's chair and lurk around Julie's desk because I wouldn't want to keep you safe."

I snickered. "Very sensible on your part."

"Thank you, I do my best."

When I sat at Julie's desk, I stared at her dark computer screen. "Better yet, why don't you sit at Julie's desk? You could use her computer to check Becky's and Bob's genealogy. Their application for our services may have all the information you'll need to get started, and Julie would have filed the paper copy."

"I think I saw their signed application when I was going through my first set of files." Larry hurried to the meeting room then soon came out with a file folder in his hand. "Julie's very efficient."

He turned on the computer. "What's Julie's logon?"

"Look in the drawer on your right for an address book. Julie probably put her logon ID and password under M for my computer."

"It's here. How did you know Julie would do that?"

"She'd want it handy, but not terribly obvious."

Larry whistled through his teeth as he tapped on the keyboard and searched for the genealogy software.

"Bob has a brother two years younger than he is. I'll print the page with the brother's information on it."

After Larry printed the page, he tapped on the keyboard. "Oh, fine. Becky had a brother that was two years older. I guess I'll print his information too."

I took the pages into the meeting room and scanned them with my reader wand. "Check deeper into the brothers and Bob; I'm interested in whether any of them served in the military."

While Larry searched on the computer, a man came into the office. Larry and I glanced at Palace Guard at the same time, and Palace Guard held a thumb up.

"Can I help you?" Larry asked.

"You ain't the Gray Lady," the man growled.

"I'll tell her you're here. Was she expecting you?" I asked.

Larry rolled his eyes, and I smiled.

"Maybe."

"Come with me." Palace Guard guided me to my office, and I tapped on the door. "Your appointment is here, Gray Lady."

Heather came out holding my jo, and for a brief moment, I had a clear glimpse of her, except she was me.

"Care for a taco?" she asked as she thrust the sack into the man's hand. "The notebook for the ark is in there too."

"For the Ark." The man snickered then cleared his throat. "Thanks for the taco, ma'am; I don't eat regular these days."

"Tell me about it; sometimes it's days between a decent bite of lunch, isn't it?"

"Gotta go."

After the man rushed out of the office, Larry laughed. "You almost made him break cover, Decoy Chief."

"He needed the practice, and I needed to verify that Noah sent him. How much longer are we going to hang out?"

"Are you serious? It's only been what? like twenty minutes?" I asked.

"What are you doing out of the meeting room?" Heather asked.

"I'm lurking," I said.

"Does that make sense, Larry?"

"No, but I'm going with whatever works right now."

"I'm going into my Chief office and wait for a crazed killer. I won't get a shot at him, though, because the real Chief is lurking."

Larry tapped on his ear. "Our trooper just left."

"What did you all do to him? He came out with a big smile," Paul said.

"Heather made sure he worked for Noah and tried to cause him to break his cover," Larry said.

"She must not have tried very hard because he was able to walk out unassisted. A man is hurrying down the sidewalk toward the office; his jacket is open, and he's wearing a chambray shirt with an embroidered name on the pocket."

Heather returned to my office, Larry sat at Julie's desk, and I went into the meeting room; I considered leaving the door partially open or standing at the window to peek, but I shook my head then sighed as I closed the door.

Palace Guard raised his eyebrows.

"For a second there, I thought I'd take a peek at the man," I whispered.

Palace Guard patted my shoulder.

When the man came into the office, he said, "Are you Paul? I'm Chopra; I own the store down the street. My regulars said the Gray Lady was in the office this afternoon, and they've been pestering me to come make sure she's not alone."

"I'm Sean; Paul hired me to provide security while he's out of the office." Larry put out his hand, and the two men shook.

"Thanks for coming to check on her. Let us know if there's anything we can do to help you."

"Appreciate it. We all know Paul was an excellent detective before he retired; I'm not surprised he brought in someone for extra security. I've been in this neighborhood for almost thirty years; my regulars look out for me, and they've adopted the Gray Lady. Here's my card; text me anytime you need a little extra help."

After Mr. Chopra left, I tapped my ear once. "Paul, I need Henry to do a portrait of the man who went up the fire escape without anyone else in the drawing. I think he saw the man's face more than once and can do that, but he somehow got it in his head that he had to draw the man on the fire escape. Julie can tell him it's urgent, and I need a good enough sketch fast."

I tapped my ear twice.

"Wow; it will sting, but he'll take it as a challenge, won't he?" Paul asked. "I'll call her right now."

Larry and Heather came into the meeting room.

"Where'd you come up with a name so fast, Larry?" Heather asked.

"It's his dad's name," I said. "You're going through names almost as fast as I am, Larry."

"What made you decide Henry could draw a portrait, Chief?" Heather asked.

"He told me that was what he used to draw, but I didn't pick up on it until now."

"After we get the sketch, Paul or I can take it to the man's store, and if we're lucky, we'll get a name," Larry said. "Julie called me back; she must have decided the portrait was important because she told Henry that I was on my way to pick it up. What do you think?"

Heather snorted. "No discussion needed; Paul should go."

I nodded.

Larry tapped his ear. "Go; it was a good move on Julie's part to put extra pressure on Henry. I'll make sure the surveillance team knows you'll be away but back in less than an hour."

"I'm shooting for a half an hour," Paul said.

"Close your eyes, Gray Lady, so you won't be mad at Honey Boy," I said.

"I'll go to my office and fume over whatever I'm angry about." Heather stormed out of the meeting room.

"Thanks, Calico; you're the second best after my sweetie."

Larry sat next to me, so I could listen to both sides of his conversation with Noah. "Paul will be gone from the area for about an hour. Can you let the GBI team know?"

"Do I need to cover for him?" Noah asked.

I giggled.

"That was Maggie, wasn't it?" Noah sighed. "I'll pretend I didn't say anything to embarrass myself and let the team know about Paul."

After Larry returned his phone to his backpack, he smiled. "Noah was stressed, but you reminded him to settle down without saying a word; I can't decide which was more hilarious: your reaction or his."

Larry strode to the door. "It's okay to come back to the meeting room, Gray Lady."

Heather strolled into the meeting room. "Good thing I'm so good natured and get over things quickly, isn't it? You'll tell me later, right, Calico?"

"I'll tell you now because it's too good for you to miss, but you'll have to listen until the end," Larry said.

"Okay, I promise I won't scream or throw a chair until after you're finished."

Larry shrugged. "Fair enough."

He told her about calling Noah, and Noah's response. While he told Heather that I giggled then continued with Noah's reaction, I wandered to the window and pretended I was the lookout, and Palace Guard joined me.

Heather laughed. "That is so funny; poor Noah's having a hard time maintaining his stuffy side, isn't he?"

"I understand how he feels, but I've had years of practice of being Maggie-humiliated, so I'm used to it," Larry said.

I watched as a man casually strolled around the corner of the building where Paul had been. The man stepped into the recessed doorway and blended in with the shadows.

"What's he doing here?" I growled.

"Who?" Larry rushed to my side and peered across the street. "I don't see anyone."

"You saw someone?" Heather crowded in between me and the window. "Is your sight improving?"

"No, I must have caught a glimpse of the shadows and thought someone was across the street."

Larry and Heather turned away, but Palace Guard raised his eyebrows as he pointed to me.

I nodded and muttered, "Yep, Gary Sloan." *The man whose career as a spy was more important than his family when he abandoned Mother and me and who thinks he has any right to make up for twenty years.* I snorted. *Give up, Gary; you lose.*

I turned to sit at the table, but froze at the sound of Paul's frantic voice. "Julie's gone, and her car's gone. Henry said Bob called her and asked her to take him to the morgue to identify Becky's body because he claimed he didn't know who else to ask. She left her phone with Henry, so he could call me or nine-one-one if he felt ill. Henry told me Julie took the sketch with her so she could get it to me. We have to find her; I tried to call Bob, but he didn't answer his phone. I'm going to his house then the morgue."

"Wait, Paul. I'll be right there to go with you." Heather had her jo in her hand as she snatched up her backpack from the floor near the door before she raced out of the room.

Larry asked, "Will you be okay if I go to the morgue? I wouldn't leave if we didn't have the GBI surveillance team; I'll let Noah know what's going on."

"I'll lock up behind you and stay in the meeting room; keep me posted."

"Will do."

Larry tapped his ear. "I'm going straight to the morgue."

After he dashed out of the office, I locked the door with Palace Guard's help then went into the meeting room.

"Doesn't this feel like a setup to you?"

Palace Guard nodded.

I tapped my fingers on the table. "It's too quiet with those two gone."

I picked up my phone and called Lily.

"Glenda Lou," she said. "How nice to hear from you. I'm just rearranging a few shelves, so I'll go into my office, and we can chat."

I listened to the murmur of voices in the background then a click as Lily closed her door.

"You have such good timing, Gray Lady. My friend thinks the last name of the boy who was so cruel was either Clinton or Collins; she wasn't sure which, and she plans to ask her sister who has always been the historian of the family. I just got off the phone with her, so I don't think it will take her long at all. I'm sorry about all these baby steps, but I think we're getting close."

"We're a lot closer than I would be trying to do this solo," I said. "I really appreciate your help."

After we hung up, I said, "Lily called me Gray Lady. The Gray Lady just rushed out of here and as far as anyone would know, disappeared around a corner with her jo."

Palace Guard frowned as he shook his head.

"You haven't even heard what I was thinking, and you're already negative?" I asked.

Palace Guard crossed his arms.

"Fine; you stay here while I go to the apartment by myself; unless you'd like to go along with me, and I'll stay out of sight while you check the apartment."

Palace Guard rolled his eyes then held up his hands in surrender.

"Good, let's go."

Chapter Fourteen

Before we left, Palace Guard pointed to the bottom drawer of Julie's desk.

I opened the drawer and smiled. "I'd forgotten about Julie's sunhat. It's better at hiding my missing eye than a ball cap, and I'll look more like Julie."

I put on the hat and tightened the strap in case a gust of wind tried to take Julie's hat then pulled out the sunglasses that Heather gave me. "I'm ready now."

I glanced across the street as we left the office but didn't see Gary. *He probably followed Gray Lady. Good luck keeping up with her, Mr. Sloan.*

Palace Guard set a brisk pace as he walked alongside me. *Why did I never think of this before? It's like we're running.*

I kept my head up and pumped my arms in my impression of a power-walker. When Palace Guard slowed the pace, I knew we were close to the apartment.

We stopped in a doorway, and Palace Guard showed me where to find the door handle, then he nodded, and we went inside.

I inhaled the sweet smell of gardenias. "Mmm. Smells good."

"Thank you, come in. I'm Irena; is there something I can help you find, or would you rather browse?" A woman with a quiet, restful voice asked as the soft muzzle of a dog nudged my hand.

"Who's my friend?" I asked as I rubbed the sweet canine face that my new companion raised to the height of my waist.

She chuckled. "That's my fierce shop dog, Brutus. He's my watch dog and protector, but he's a softie when it comes to girls. If a female crew of burglars broke into the shop, he'd help them pick out and load up my most expensive, fragrant candles."

"Is that true, Brutus?" I giggled when he gave my fingers a soft nibble. "I'd love to wander around."

"Feel free to try any of them; I have a few more boxes to unpack in the backroom from today's delivery, but give me a shout if you have any questions," the woman said.

"Thank you, I will." Palace Guard guided me to a row then disappeared. I pretended to examine the shelves carefully as I slowly made my way toward the back with my new best friend, Brutus, at my side.

When I was at the back corner, a man came in then pounded on a bell that must have been on a display case near the front and shouted, "Anybody here?"

Brutus growled a low throaty rumble, and I felt his hackles rise on his back.

"Hold your britches, fella," the woman mumbled as she came out of the back room.

When she was close to the front, she said, "How can I help you?"

Brutus left me, and I heard his growl grow louder and more intense as he trotted toward the front.

"I heard my wife's sister came in here; where is she?" the man growled.

I wish I had my jo, so I could snap a photo of him.

"Unless her name is Brutus, she's not here," the woman said.

"Does your dog bite?" I heard the man's voice change from threatening to fearful.

"Actually, he does, but he's only bitten people when I felt nervous, and they all ended up in the hospital." The woman chuckled. "I'm kind of a skittish person, so I'm easily alarmed."

"Oh, well; I guess she's not here." The front door opened then slammed shut.

Brutus trotted to me, and the woman joined us. "Are you okay?"

"Who is that guy? Do you know him?" I asked.

"I've seen him around once or twice, but he's never come in the shop before. What about you? Do you know him? For a minute there, I thought he was looking for you."

I shuddered. "I've never seen him before, but there was something about him that gave me the shivers."

"I know that feeling; I've been warned by more than one of the men who lives on the street near my shop to stay away from the abandoned stores a few blocks from here because that man has claimed one of them as his hideout, and he has a bad temper and a cruel streak."

When Palace Guard joined me, I said, "With all our excitement, I almost forgot my meeting; I'll have to come back."

"Any time," the woman said. "We'll be happy to see you."

When we were outside, I said, "An angry man came into the shop; do you see anyone around?"

Palace Guard shook his head; we power-walked back to the office. When we reached the office, I glanced across the street as Gary rounded the corner. He froze and glowered at me then disappeared into the shadow of the recessed doorway.

After we were inside, I asked, "Did you notice Gary? It's a good thing he's not Glenn because both of us would have been grounded, if I've correctly interpreted that look he gave us."

Palace Guard nodded then helped me lock the door before we went into the meeting room; before I sat down, Palace Guard pointed to my head.

"You're right, I'd better return Julie's sunhat." I removed the sunglasses and put them into my backpack then returned Julie's sunhat to its drawer.

"We're at Bob's house. Two cars here, but no one's home," Heather said.

"I'm at the morgue, but I don't see Julie's car. I'm going inside," Larry said.

"We're on our way to the hospital, then we'll go back to the office, so we can check the apartment," Heather said.

A few minutes later, Larry said, "They were here, but they left. The clerk at the desk said the woman was taking the man home because he was pretty upset."

"Heather's turning around; we'll wait for them at Bob's," Paul said.

"I'll swing by your house, Paul," Larry said.

When no one else said anything, I picked up my phone and called Lily.

Lily took a big breath then her words tumbled out. "I've been waiting for your call in my office; I should have called my sister first. She has the best contacts through her genealogy group. The young boy in the Savannah area with problems was Wiley Collins. His parents lived near her folks in South Carolina, but moved to Savannah before Wiley was born to be near the father's folks who were ill. They had two sons, Robert and Wiley; Robert was six years old when Wiley was born. By the time Wiley was in elementary school, he was a handful. Most of the genealogy people thought the mother must have given up on trying to manage her younger son because she defended his behavior by blaming her husband, her older son, the teachers, the principal, other children, and the police. One of the older women, who actually knew the family but has always taken the opposite side of whatever the consensus is, claimed that it was Robert who was really the problem: the younger boy was only reacting to his older brother, but my sister says to take that with a grain of salt because stirring up controversy is the old woman's favorite hobby. As soon as he graduated, Robert left home to go to college. My sister wanted to make sure you knew she found a few contradictions and holes and filled in with what made sense to her, so you're getting the unscrubbed version with only a few facts because most of it is hearsay. She's going to try to weed through the gossip, but that may take her a while."

"I love a good story with the facts; it's much more interesting that way." I glanced at Palace Guard who nodded vigorously.

"I'm not surprised; every librarian I've ever known has said the same thing. So, while Robert was in college, the mother left her husband because she claimed he was too critical and took her younger son to South Carolina. Wiley was popular at first, especially with the girls. Then there was an incident at the school, and a girl died; no one had any details, so my sister wondered if Wiley might have been involved because the mother abruptly moved with her son to North Carolina. While he was in high school, Wiley had one friend who was a bit of thug, but the boy stuck with Wiley even after his popularity as the new kid wore off. Robert and a sweet girl he knew in high school renewed their friendship during their college years and were married the day after they graduated. Both of them accepted teaching positions in a public school system near Savannah, so they could care for Robert's dad who was very ill; the father died two years later. Wiley bounced from job to job in both Carolinas and Tennessee, and no one's sure why; my sister's looking into it. She heard Wiley moved to Atlanta not long after his father died then moved back here a few years later."

"Wow, your sister gathered more information than I expected."

Lily chuckled. "Can you imagine how much more she'd have dug up if we gave her another day? She still has more people to talk to because she's hoping to get clarification on some of the holes."

"This is definitely quite a bit; thank you so much."

"My sister's calling me; call me back in thirty minutes."

After I hung up, I was startled by a loud, insistent knock at the front door; when the sound changed to a pounding fist, I whispered, "I'll bet that's the man who went into the candle shop."

The man shouted, "Open up! I have to talk to you!"

"Same man," I whispered.

Palace Guard motioned for me to get down, and I sat on the floor with the table and chairs between me and the window. I shuddered at the sharp sound of knuckles knocking on the window that ended with two final slams with the flat of a hand. *Sure am glad we don't have single-paned glass in the windows.*

"Is it okay if I get up now?" I whispered.

Palace Guard nodded.

"I want to see where he goes next." I grabbed my coat, but Palace Guard shook his head then disappeared.

I crossed my arms and pouted as I sat at the table. *He gets to go, and I don't? That's not fair; it was my idea.*

Larry's voice broke into my pity party. "Julie and Bob are at your house, Paul. Julie's fine; Bob's not a threat. Let's meet at the office, so we can all talk."

Palace Guard joined me in the meeting room; he pointed to my coat then the back door.

I smiled as I put on my coat and grabbed my backpack then put on my sunglasses.

"Wait a minute; I almost forgot the tracker seashell that Paul gave me." I pulled it out then placed it on my chair.

I stayed close to the buildings as we walked through the alley together. When we reached the street a block away from the office, we turned left. *We're going away from the apartment.*

Two blocks later, Palace Guard and I stopped in front of a shop, and he pointed to the next block.

"Abandoned stores?" I asked.

He nodded then motioned for me to open the door of the shop. When we went inside, I inhaled the wonderful aroma of fresh bread.

"Welcome, miss. What would you like?" a woman said, and I smiled at the sound of her cheerful voice.

I have no clue.

"What's the special?"

"We just pulled out a nice batch of seedless rye bread."

"That sounds perfect; thank you."

I pulled out my wallet as the woman put a loaf of bread into a sack then tapped my credit card where Palace Guard pointed.

"Do you need a receipt?" the woman asked.

"No, I'm fine."

Palace Guard pointed to the sack on the counter, and I picked it up.

"Enjoy," the woman said as we left.

While Palace Guard and I hurried back to the office, I asked, "Did the man go into one of the stores in the next block?"

Palace Guard nodded.

"What do I do with a loaf of fresh bread? I can't take it to the office."

Palace Guard grinned.

"You're a lot of help," I grumbled.

Before we turned at the alley that was behind the office, Palace Guard stopped next to a vacant bench.

"I get it."

After I sat down for a few minutes, I rose and left the sack on the bench, then we hurried to the office.

"That was a bus stop, wasn't it?"

Palace Guard nodded.

I locked the back door then removed my coat, put my sunglasses inside my backpack then set my backpack on the table.

I put the seashell back into my pocket and sat down with a sigh then called Lily.

"My sister said you need to give her more of a challenge next time. Wiley Collins is an elevator repair and installation tech, and according to my sister's sources, one of the best because he can repair both the mechanical and the electronic components of elevators. That's all she's found so far."

"I'll park two blocks from the office," Larry said. "Everything okay, Calico?"

"I'll call you back later, Lily."

I hung up and tapped my ear. "Awfully quiet."

"That's good," Larry said.

When there was a light tap on the door, Palace Guard blew on his index finger to let me know it was Larry. With Palace Guard's guidance, I unlocked the door.

Larry rushed in and kissed me. "Never gets old, sweetie."

"We're parking a block away," Paul said.

After Paul and Heather came into the office, Paul locked the front door, then all of us went into the meeting room.

Heather pulled off her eyepatch and dropped it on the table. "Does the eyepatch itch when you wear it, Chief?"

"Not really."

"It's probably psychological," Larry said.

"Is not," Heather muttered.

Paul cleared his throat. "We stopped at my house, and Julie met us outside. Bob had asked Julie to go with him into the morgue; she wasn't thrilled about the idea, but she understood. When the morgue attendant took them into the room where the body was, Bob immediately said it wasn't Becky. The woman had on a wedding ring, and Bob said Becky quit wearing her ring several years ago when it became too tight."

Larry and Palace Guard looked as shocked as I felt.

"It wasn't Becky?" I asked.

"That's what Bob said, so Julie asked if it would be possible for her to see the woman's hair but not her face, and the attendant agreed. Julie said the murdered woman had brown hair, and Becky's hair is mostly gray," Paul said.

"I would have been skeptical based on Bob's word alone, but Julie's corroboration sealed it for me," Heather said. "Julie was smart to think of checking the woman's hair."

"We need to find Becky," Larry said.

"Where do we start?" Heather asked.

"I don't have any ideas yet, but I have more information." I told them about Bob's brother, Wiley Collins.

"Do you think Wiley is the murderer, Chief?" Heather asked.

"He seems likely, but I thought we had practically solved the case when Henry told us about Willard Barnes."

"Wiley Collins definitely has ready access to the elevators," Paul said.

"I can see where Wiley could have become Willy as the story grew," Larry said, "but do we care?"

"I guess not, unless Wiley Collins is another dead end," Heather said.

"I'll jump on Julie's computer and see what I can find," Paul said.

"Do you think Bob suspects Wiley?" Heather asked.

"I don't know; I'd rather give him a chance to settle down from the shock. If he says anything, Julie will let me know," Paul said.

"Should I call Lily back and ask her for more information?" I asked.

"As fast as she got us the information about the man with a violent childhood, I'd say yes, but I'd rather know where Becky is. How do we find Becky?" Larry asked.

"There's a possibility that if we find Wiley, we'll find Becky," I said.

"I want to retrace Becky's steps from her house to the diner," Heather said.

"Give me a few minutes, and I'll go with you," Paul said.

"I'll lurk while Paul searches on Julie's computer, so the meeting room will be quiet for you," Larry said.

"I'll keep you company, Chief," Heather said.

I called Lily, and she answered on the second ring.

"I had a feeling you would be calling soon, Gray Lady; everyone's impressed by how dedicated I am to completing my monthly reports." Lily chuckled. "What am I working on now?"

"Any additional information you can get about Wiley Collins, especially if he's been in any type of trouble at work, or if there have been any complaints about him and where he is now."

Lily interrupted. "Just Wiley Collins?"

"Good catch. We'd also be interested in his friend, but give me a few minutes to see if I can get his name for you."

"I'll get my sister busy on Wiley." Lily hung up.

"What did she say?" Heather asked as I put the phone on the table.

"She'll get more about Wiley Collins, but we need to know his friend's name. How do we find out without upsetting Bob?"

"Not our problem, Chief, which is a good thing, because we're too direct. I'll call Julie."

"Really? You're not going to ask Paul to call her?"

Heather closed the meeting room door. "Paul's busy."

Heather pulled out a phone and called Julie.

Heather has a second phone too. She and Larry are twin sneaks.

"Julie, it's Heather. I need your talents to go into overdrive. Bob has a brother, and his brother has had a friend for years. We need the name of that friend."

Heather nodded. "I'll call you in a half hour."

Before she hung up, she said, "Even better."

"What did Julie say?"

"She'll text me the name if she has it before I call her back."

"I'd really like to be there to watch her in action," I said.

"I would too, so what did you do while all of us were gone? The door's closed, so Larry won't know."

"Played cribbage, or more accurately, listened to cribbage," I said.

Heather laughed. "I don't even know what cribbage is."

"It's a card game; I heard some of the residents at the senior center in Columbus talking about it, so I found an online game to listen to."

"Really? Is it easy?"

"Not from what I could tell because I got lost, but I gained a lot of respect for the seniors who played it."

"Sounds boring; I'm sorry you were stuck, Chief, and for the record, I don't believe you."

Palace Guard grinned, and I shrugged.

Heather must know rule number three: if you can't keep it simple, make it boring.

"Do you know how to play bridge?" Heather asked.

I giggled.

"What's so funny?"

"Here's the long answer: when I was a kid, Mother picked me up at school, and we'd walk home together. I asked her to teach me how to play poker as we left one time because I needed a poker face. She told me she'd teach me how to play bridge, and all the other mothers around us who were eavesdropping went from horrified by poker to impressed by bridge. Mother met with her bridge club every week, but I'm convinced they played poker, not bridge. Short answer: no."

Heather chuckled. "Did your mother cheat?"

"Of course, and she was really mad at me when I cheated and won."

"You must have been a handful, Calico."

I stuck up my nose and sniffed. "I was a model child."

Heather's phone buzzed a text. "It's from Julie: Evan Gardner."

I called Lily. "Evan Gardner."

"Got it." Lily hung up.

"That was a short conversation," Heather said.

"Lily's on a mission; I didn't want to get in her way."

"Do we tell Larry and Paul?" Heather asked.

"Sure; when we feel like it."

Palace Guard crossed his arms.

"I'll tell them, so Palace Guard can be mad at you, not me." Heather opened the door. "We have the name of Wiley Collins' friend: Evan Gardner. Chief called Lily, so Lily's sister can research Gardner while she's researching Collins."

"How did you..."

Heather interrupted Larry. "That's for another time; consider yourself lucky I told you the name. Are you ready to go, Paul?"

Paul coughed.

"If I get fired, it's your fault, Palace Guard." Heather put on her eyepatch then grabbed her jacket and backpack.

After they left, Larry said, "Heather asked Julie to get her the friend's name, didn't she? I feel like I missed something not being there to hear Julie in action."

"I don't think Julie got Evan Gardner's name because she came back to us so quickly. I think she asked Henry to talk to Bob. Bob would have joined Henry outside while Julie was busy in the kitchen."

"I think you're right, and for the record: I can see the handprint on the window. Tell me about the man: the whole story, not just little snippets, and don't forget I can see Palace Guard."

Larry and Palace Guard sat across the table from me.

"Okay, I will, but not if this is going to be a panel grilling."

Larry shifted the chair next to me towards me, and Palace Guard stood in the doorway.

I told him about Palace Guard checking the apartment while I waited across the street in the candle shop.

Larry sighed. "Of course, you couldn't let Palace Guard go by himself."

"Right." I told him about Brutus and the man who came into the shop to look for his wife's sister.

"I know you were sorry you didn't have your jo with you."

I nodded.

"Palace Guard returned not long after the man left the shop; I told Palace Guard about the man, and he disappeared."

"Good move, Palace Guard," Larry said.

"Palace Guard followed the man to a block of vacant stores; after Palace Guard returned, we went to the street, so I would be able to tell you the abandoned stores were close to a bakery."

"You just had to do that, didn't you?" Larry sighed. "Never mind; could you show me where it is?"

Palace Guard nodded.

"You have to take me with you, or I'll follow you," I said. "We went out the back door, and I paid attention to the turns."

"We'll see if the bakery has cake or pie while Palace Guard checks to see if any of the stores show signs of being occupied," Larry said.

"That sounds good."

I pulled out Julie's sunhat from the drawer and dropped in the seashell then put on my coat and picked up my backpack.

When Larry headed toward the front door, I said, "It's better if we go out the back door."

"Why? Is someone besides GBI watching the office?" Larry narrowed his eyes.

"You never know," I said.

Palace Guard led the way to the bakery, and I walked alongside Larry as we followed him.

"Are you sure you don't want to take my arm or something, sweetie?"

I shook my head. "When Palace Guard was teaching me to dodge the bad guys after the library explosion, I ran alongside him. I walked alongside him today at a pretty good clip and realized he was checking to see if walking would work just like running. I can walk by your side, but you'll have to adjust where you walk to make sure nothing will trip me, or I'll go flying."

"That makes sense. Do you think you could walk alongside other people too?"

"No, I wouldn't see them clearly like I do you and Palace Guard."

"What did you buy at the bakery while you waited for Palace Guard?"

"A loaf of seedless rye bread. I asked what the special was, and that was what the clerk suggested."

Larry chuckled. "You are so smart; I was trying to figure out how you could have managed. Where's the bread?"

"I left it on a bench by the bus stop. I'm sure it went to a good home."

"I'm sure you're right, sweetie."

When we reached the bakery, Larry glanced at the street sign. "Twenty-third Street," he muttered.

Palace Guard disappeared; we went into the bakery.

"Is that a peach pie?" Larry asked as we stood in front of the bakery display case.

"Yes, sir."

"That would be perfect; that's Sissy's favorite," I said.

"We also have sticky buns if you're looking for something special for breakfast," the clerk said.

"Not this time, honey," I said.

"Are you sure? Okay, then just the pie."

After the clerk slid the pie into a box and rang up the sale, we went outside.

"Where shall we wait for Palace Guard?" Larry asked.

"He would look for us by the alley."

Larry let me set the pace as we hurried to the alley.

CHAPTER FIFTEEN

When we rounded the corner and were in the alley, Larry asked the waiting Palace Guard, "Who was there?"

Palace Guard held up two fingers then pointed at Larry.

"Two men," I said.

Palace nodded then glowered at Larry and shook his finger.

"They're arguing?" Larry asked.

Palace Guard nodded.

"Is there somewhere I can check out the stores without being seen?" Larry asked.

Palace Guard nodded again.

"Stay here." Larry followed Palace Guard around the corner.

They just left me holding the pie; I should put it on the bus bench and leave, except I'd probably fall off the curb and into the street while I was trying to find the bench.

My nose itched. *I need to set down the pies somewhere. Why aren't there benches in alleys?*

I tried to balance the box on a curved trash can lid, but the handle took up too much room, and the pie would have slid off if I hadn't have been ready to catch it. I tried to rub my nose with my upper arm, but the pie was in the way. My left hand cramped, then I had something in my eye. I finally set the pie down on what I hoped were bricks. While I massaged my hand to get rid of the cramp, two blobs appeared in the alley.

"Why'd you drag me over here?" a man growled.

That's the man who came into the candle shop.

"Told you; it's a girl by herself," a second man said.

He was at least twenty feet away, but I could smell his sour breath when he spoke. I unzipped my jacket.

"Hey, girly. Were you waiting for a couple of studs? Here we are," the first man said.

That's a matter of opinion.

The first blob brandished a knife. "That's pretty hair you got there. I might just take a little souvenir with me."

The second blob pulled out a larger knife from its sheath on his waist.

I wish I could tell whether they have guns.

"Those are big knives; you fellas have guns too?"

The first man sneered. "We don't need guns, sweetheart; we're experts with these babies."

As they advanced toward me, I put my right hand on my hip. "Which one of you is the best with the knife?"

"She's not lookin' scared." The second man stopped.

"Probably a mental dee-ficiency." The first man snorted as he continued forward. "I'm the best with a knife and everything else you been wanting."

The second man hesitated then joined him.

"You know what they say about a knife fight, right?" I asked.

"We ain't gonna fight you, girl, we're just gonna have a little fun," the first man said.

The two men rushed me at the same time, and I shot the first man then tossed my knife at the second man. Both men screamed and dropped to the ground, still screaming.

Palace Guard and Larry tore around the corner.

"Are you hurt?" Larry asked.

"I'm fine."

"She shot me; she coulda killed me," the first man screamed.

Larry kicked him in the ribs. "You're wrong, scum; if she wanted to kill you, you wouldn't be laying there squawking."

Larry assumed a shooting stance as he held his gun on the two men. "Go on back; the police are on the way."

"Where's the pie?" I asked.

Palace Guard pointed, and I picked it up.

After we were back at the office, I removed my coat and crossed my arms with my hands under my arms and against my body to warm up. "I'm glad to be out of that cold wind. I must have stuck my gun back into its holster because I still have it, but I don't have my knife."

Palace Guard smiled then blew across his index finger.

I nodded. "You're right; Larry will bring it to me."

Palace Guard patted me on the back.

"Thanks. I tried to warn those two, but they wouldn't pay any attention to me."

When Larry came into the office, he asked, "How are you doing, sweetie?"

"I left my knife."

"I got it for you; are you ready to go back to Pearl's house?"

"I think I am; I need to warm up in front of the fireplace."

Before we left, Larry's GBI phone rang. He listened then snorted. "Do we know their names?"

He raised his eyebrows then glanced at me. "Can we put a tail on the guy who walked into that bullet?"

Larry put his arm around me. "Thanks, I appreciate it."

After he hung up, Larry kissed my forehead. "Sweetie, the two thugs told the police officers that six huge gang members who were from out of town and had guns, chains, and knives jumped them in the alley."

Palace Guard elbowed me and grinned.

"Did you recognize the voices of either one of them?" Larry asked.

"Yes, the man I shot came into the candle shop," I said.

"If the guy in the candle shop and the man you shot were the same man, then he would have left the vacant store before we returned to the bakery. Do you think he met the other man somewhere close?"

"Is there an alley behind the stores?" I asked.

Palace Guard frowned and hung his head, and Larry smacked his forehead with his palm. "I didn't think of checking for back doors."

Larry rubbed his face. "The guy you shot is Evan Gardner; I didn't recognize the name of the other one; I can get it if we need it. Do you think Evan Gardner knows where Becky is?"

"I'm certain he does," I said.

Larry picked up his phone. "Evan Gardner should be released from the hospital tomorrow. I want to put a special tail on Evan Gardner in addition to the GBI agent. Yes, that's exactly who I have in mind. Okay, I'll tell her."

Larry put down his phone then tapped his ear. "Where are you, Heather?"

"On my way to the grocery store to pick up something for supper, then I'll be at Pearl's in forty-five minutes."

"We'll probably beat you there."

On our way to the house, I heard Heather on my earbud. "Paul, I'm keeping your car overnight; is that okay? I'll pick you up tomorrow."

"That's fine; I've got Julie's car if I need anything," Paul said.

As Larry parked at Pearl's house, he said, "I'm not sure I'll ever get used to those two suddenly talking so clearly in my head. I wish there was kind of a squelch break or something to give me a little warning."

"If you mention it to Heather, she'll have it done by morning."

Larry chuckled. "She would, wouldn't she? I don't want to be the one to cause a technical guru to work overnight on a minor inconvenience."

"Welcome home, Honey Boy and Calico," Grandma Zee said. "This afternoon there was a strange white man wandering around the neighborhood; my boys chased him off right quick. Can you imagine white people showing up around here?" She cackled then lowered her voice. "Ya'll be careful wherever you go; my boys told me that man had an evil soul."

After we went into the house, I shivered. "I understand why Heather feels so safe here."

When Heather came in, she pulled off her eyepatch. "I'm exhausted; I don't see how you do this, Chief. Let's go into the kitchen, and I'll put our supper on the table."

While Larry set the table, Heather turned on the oven and pulled out our food from the deli at the grocery store. "It wouldn't hurt to warm the fried chicken a little. What's going on?"

I told her about the men who planned to attack me and how I stopped them.

"Evan Gardner was the man that Maggie shot," Larry said. "He's at the hospital being stitched up and will be released tomorrow."

"We think he knows where Becky is, don't we? Do I get to tail him? Will I have a GBI counterpart?" Heather asked.

"Yep. Here's the number of the team lead; he'll tell you who he has assigned to work with you, and the team lead and I agreed that you call the shots as far as Gardner's concerned. Do you need anything from us?"

"I won't need the jo, Chief. Are you my GBI contact if I need anything, Larry?" Heather asked.

"I sure am."

Heather tapped her ear. "What's your status, Paul?"

"Everybody's settled down; I'm ready anytime."

"I'll pick you up first thing in the morning."

"Are you taking Paul with you?" Larry asked.

"I don't have a choice; I've got his car." Heather cackled as she opened the oven door. "I'm going to warm the fried chicken a little."

"Here's your knife, sweetie; I wiped it off with the guy's shirt."

I furrowed my brow. *What if it still has blood on it?*

"What's wrong?" Larry asked.

Palace Guard pointed to the kitchen sink.

Larry nodded. "I'll wash it thoroughly with soap and hot water."

After he washed, rinsed, and dried my knife, he handed it to me. "I washed it with soap and hot water."

I smiled as I slipped it into its sheath that was inside my left boot.

While we ate, Heather asked, "Am I still the Gray Lady tomorrow?"

"What are your thoughts?" Larry asked.

"It seems like I should be because the main purpose is so I can draw the killer away from Chief."

Palace Guard nodded.

"Thanks, Palace Guard," Heather said. "That makes it unanimous."

I set down my fork. "What about me?"

"You vote in case of a tie, and before you get all huffy, Paul makes the fourth; we're not bothering him because we're unanimous," Heather said.

After we ate, and Larry washed the dishes, Heather opened three beers while Larry started a fire. We drank our beer and relaxed in front of the fire; Heather told us a story about a prank she and one of Grandma Zee's great-granddaughters pulled on Grandma Zee.

"The best part is that the big kids always got in trouble."

We laughed then laughed even harder when Larry said, "The moral of the story is to never be a big kid."

When I yawned, Heather said, "It's time for us little kids to go to bed."

• • • • ● • ● • • •

After I showered and dried, I wrapped a towel around me then put my head down to watch for the stairs when I left the bathroom.

"Don't bump into me, Calico. I'm putting on my coat right in front of you; I'll step past you, then you can continue," Heather said. "Our breakfast burritos are in the oven. I'm taking mine with me to pick up Paul. It's cold out there, and we have thunderstorms headed our way sometime today. Be safe, Calico; watch out for the big kids." She dashed out the door.

"You too, Pearl." I rushed up the stairs and dressed then joined Larry in the kitchen.

"Shall we take our burritos with us too?" Larry asked.

"I wouldn't mind relaxing with a cup of coffee before we tackle the day; why don't we eat here?"

"Works for me; I wasn't sure how I was going to juggle coffee, a burrito, and driving, and for the record, I can't tell you how glad I am that I'm not riding with Pearl to Paul's house."

I sipped my coffee. "This is great; it's not too hot."

"I poured it before you came down for your shower." Larry pulled out our burritos and put them on a plate.

After we ate, I put on my warm coat over my sweatshirt, and we headed to the office.

Larry parked two blocks away from the office, and the cold air took away my breath as we hurried to the office.

"Front door okay?" he asked.

I nodded. "I don't care if Gary sees us showing up; it's all the times we leave that are none of his business."

When we went into the office, Larry bumped up the thermometer a few degrees. "What's our plan for today?"

"We need the profile sketch that Henry did, so we can talk to Mr. Chopra."

"I'll call Julie with my work phone because it shows as 'GBI' on the display; you can talk to her."

I giggled. "Chicken."

"You got it, sweetie." Larry chuckled as he dialed her number then handed me the phone.

"Hello?" Julie answered.

"Hey, Julie; it's Maggie. Larry called you for me on his work phone."

"Oh, good. I thought I was in big trouble for my last speeding ticket, but I was fairly certain I'd paid it."

"Did Henry finish the profile sketch?"

"He kind of did; it looked great to me, but he claimed it wasn't finished yet. I snatched it away from him right before Bob showed up yesterday; Henry's still pouting."

I chuckled. "He's definitely a perfectionist, isn't he? Is it okay if Larry picks it up?"

"Oh, sure. Our mailbox is out by the road; I wouldn't mind taking a fast walk to clear my head. Henry is on the back porch with his sketch pad, as cold as it is; I made him put on one of Paul's old warm coats, and it swallowed him, but at least he's warm. He told me he's drawing me as a dragon; maybe the walk will cool down my dragon breath. What else can I do?"

"Keep a close eye on Henry and keep your phone in your pocket. Call Larry if you need me."

"One of your feelings?"

"Back up."

"It's always good to have back up; thanks, Chief."

After we hung up, I said, "Julie's going to put the sketch in the mailbox for you."

"Aren't you going too?"

"We could, but you could get there and back faster if you go solo."

"Be right back." Larry rushed out the back door.

I tiptoed toward the window but bumped my hip on a chair and knocked it over. When it clattered to the floor, I said, "I was trying to be stealthy, chair, so I could peek out the window, but you jumped in my way."

I glanced at Palace Guard who had raised his eyebrows.

"I have no idea why I thought anyone outside might hear me if I walked like a normal person."

Palace Guard grinned then guided me to the window. He stood behind me while I narrowed my eye to see better. I glanced at Palace Guard, and his eyes were narrowed too as he scanned the building across the street.

"I don't see anything," I whispered then cleared my throat and turned as I spoke in a normal voice. "Do you?"

Palace Guard pointed out the window at the building. I turned in time to see Gary open the door then go inside.

"He's set up camp to watch the office, hasn't he? Do you think he's working for Kate or the GBI, or is he freelancing, as usual? Does this window have blinds? Should I put them down?"

He nodded, shrugged, nodded again, then shook his head.

"I did ask a string of questions, didn't I?"

Palace Guard exaggerated his nod in slow motion.

I tried to hold it back, but my giggle escaped. "Point taken; I'll call Lily, so I won't pester you for at least a few minutes."

When Lily answered, Palace Guard pointed to my phone, so I put it on speakerphone.

"I've got your information, Gray Lady, and it's a doozy. I should take my time and explain all the hoops my sister jumped through, so you'll have the same impatience that I did when she told me every minute detail, but I won't. Evan Gardner was a respiratory therapist, highly regarded by his colleagues. Can you believe that? He worked at a hospital in his hometown in South Carolina, then his wife was killed ten years ago in a head on crash with a teenage driver who had a seizure while driving. The teenager survived the crash but fell in front of a freight train three months later. Her parents took it hard and claimed their daughter was afraid of trains; they refused to believe she had voluntarily gone close to the tracks. After a thorough investigation, the case was closed as an unfortunate accident. After his wife's death, Gardner began drinking heavily and lost his job; he moved near Savannah and has been living off the insurance money."

"Why did he come here? Does he have family here?"

"His old pal Wiley Collins talked him into joining him. Gardner also has a cousin there, and they had been close at one time, but the cousin stopped associating with Evan because of his violent behavior when he was drinking."

"Thank you, Lily; tell your sister she is amazing."

"I'll do no such thing; she would be positively unbearable at family gatherings. Do you have anything else for me?"

"That's all for now."

"Call me anytime; my sister and I loved working for you. She said to tell you if you give me my own business cards, she wants some too, so please don't."

"Okay, I'll cancel the order."

Lily giggled as she hung up.

"Evan Gardner was supposed to be Wiley Collins' witless helper. I'm having trouble nailing down the killer."

I paced around the meeting room table until Palace Guard grabbed onto the back of a chair and moved his head in a slow, clockwise motion.

"Fine; I'm making myself dizzy too." I sat at the table. "I've lost track of how many times I was certain we had found the killer."

Palace Guard held up three fingers then furrowed his brow and changed to four fingers.

"I guess I'm in good company if you aren't sure either."

Larry unlocked the back door and was out of breath when he burst into the meeting room. "What happened?"

I blinked then stared at him. "Nothing."

Larry bent over to catch his breath then sat at the table. "It can't be nothing; there's always something."

"I talked to Lily." I told him what Lily said about Evan Gardner.

He glared. "That's it?"

"Did you get the sketch?" I asked.

"It's a great sketch of Evan Gardner."

Larry took a piece of paper out of his backpack and showed it to Palace Guard, who nodded.

"Let's go talk to Mr. Chopra," I said.

As we hurried to the convenience store, I pulled up my collar to keep the cold off my neck. *I need gloves.*

Larry said, "By the way, I quit. I now officially work for the GBI."

I stopped and tilted my head as I peered at him. "You've worked for the GBI since we left Harperville. What's different?"

"I'm not on the team; I'm here to protect you, and that's it."

I faced him. "We're not discussing this at all? This is what you decided?"

"Yes."

I resumed walking in silence, and he caught up with me in two strides then walked alongside me.

When we reached the convenience store, I asked, "How cold does it get in Alaska?"

He snorted. "Really, really cold."

"Okay, you're off the team; I was starting to crack under the pressure, anyway."

"What does that mean?" he asked as we went into the store.

It means it was hard work to remember not to hide a thing or two from you.

"Hello, my friends," Mr. Chopra said. "Welcome to my store; let me give you a tour, starting with my office."

He quietly said to his assistant who stood next to him behind the counter, "We won't be long. Let me know if you have any problems."

"Yes, Papa," a young girl said.

After we went into his office, he closed the door. "Security business, right, Sean?"

"Yes, sir." Larry pulled out the sketch from his backpack. "This man frequents the neighborhood. Do you happen to know where he stays?"

Mr. Chopra took the paper. "He's not allowed in my store. His name is Evan Gardner, but they call him Butch because he hangs out with Butcher. I've only heard about Butcher, never seen him. Butch stays in an abandoned building a few blocks from here on the same street as the only bakery left in the area. The building is divided into three stores; he's a squatter in the middle store. The drug dealers won't have anything to do with him because he's so unreliable, so I don't know how he makes his money, but he always has enough for booze. He has wildly fluctuating moods from depressed to violent with no warning."

"Thank you," Larry said. "I intend to stop him."

Mr. Chopra chuckled. "I understand he made a mistake and challenged our Gray Lady in an alley."

"She probably ruined his day," Larry said.

"There's a different story going around about a tough gang; isn't that interesting?" Mr. Chopra opened the office door, and he and Larry shook hands.

As we left, the young blob behind the counter waved to Palace Guard. "Nice to see you."

He saluted her, then we left.

"I'm always surprised when someone sees you, Palace Guard, but it does seem to be almost a guarantee with kids, doesn't it?" Larry said.

Palace Guard nodded.

"I can't wait to tell Kate," I said.

"You can't do that, sweetie; Kate sees Spike, but not Palace Guard."

"I know." I giggled.

When we turned at the street that led to the alley behind the office, Paul said through our earbuds, "Larry, there's an elevator repair truck in the back of the hospital. Our plan was for me to meet up with our GBI counterpart while Heather stayed with Evan Gardner. We need help here."

Larry tapped his ear. "I'll be right there as soon as I get Callie back to the office."

"Hurry; if it's Wiley, we don't want to lose him," Paul said.

I put my hand on Larry's arm. "Honey, run to your car, so you can get to the hospital as quickly as you can. Palace Guard will get me back to the office safely; we're not that far away."

"I don't..."

I interrupted him. "Go."

Larry sprinted away, and Palace Guard and I continued to the office. When we reached the back door, Palace Guard guided me to open the door, but the cold door handle didn't turn.

I side-glanced Palace Guard as he stared at the door. "Do you suppose it's frozen or something?"

Palace Guard shook his head.

I sighed. "This is definitely a tactical error on my part: we don't have a key, do we?"

Palace Guard disappeared.

He's checking for a spare key.

Palace Guard reappeared next to me; he shrugged as a low rumble rolled from the darkening sky.

"Maybe it will just blow on past us, but if it doesn't, I don't want to stand out here and get soaked," I said. "I can't call Julie to ask her if there is a hidden key anywhere because she'll realize I locked myself out of the office, and will immediately leave Henry to unlock the door, or worse, make me go home with her."

I blinked in surprise when Larry said, "I'm at the hospital."

"Follow the signs to the loading zone," Paul said.

Palace Guard closed his eyes then deeply breathed in with his nose then quickly blew over his index finger with pursed lips.

"The candle shop?" I asked.

Palace Guard nodded.

"I don't know; I need to think of a reason to hang out at the candle shop."

Palace Guard grinned and held up his index finger.

I furrowed my brow. *One? Higher?*

"Oh, I get it: rule number one. I could keep it simple by telling her I accidentally locked myself out of the office, couldn't I? My coat's warm, so I don't need to take shelter unless it starts raining."

Palace Guard shook his head and pointed at the sky.

"Are the clouds getting darker?"

He nodded then held up his index finger and drew an imaginary zig-zag vertical line.

"Is it..."

I was interrupted by a flash then a crashing boom. "Let's go before we have to make a mad dash through a driving rain and get soaked."

When we rounded the corner from the alley to the side street, fat raindrops slammed onto the sidewalk, and I put down my head to watch Palace Guard's feet as we ran to the candle shop; even with Palace Guard's help, I fumbled with the door in my haste to get inside as a loud crash was accompanied by the roar of wind and torrential rain.

My breathing became ragged as my heart raced in panic. "Is the door locked? What if the shop is closed?"

CHAPTER SIXTEEN

The door flew open. "Hurry, get inside. Oh my goodness, you made it just in time, didn't you, Gray Lady?"

When I raised my head in an effort to see her, she said, "I'm sorry; are you still undercover? I just realized you're not wearing your eyepatch again today."

Palace Guard pushed on the door as she leaned against it to close it against the powerful wind gusts.

I nodded. "How did you know?"

"You and I are the same height; your double is taller, so you must be undercover. I know everything that goes on around here, but I keep things to myself other than what I discuss with Brutus. Would you like some hot tea? I have a tea corner that I set up for my breaks. You won't have to juggle your cup because we'll sit at my small, round table, and I bought chocolate chip cookies from the bakery before I opened this morning in case there was a storm; I love being prepared."

"Hot tea and a cookie sounds wonderful."

As I followed her to her corner with Palace Guard's help, I said, "Having cookies during a storm has to be the best prepper advice I could imagine."

Brutus nudged my hand, and I rubbed his ear. "Hello, Brutus. How's the boy?"

Brutus moaned, and I giggled. "Are you purring?"

"Isn't that funny? He's done that since he was a puppy; sit at the table, and I'll brew our tea."

Brutus flopped down on the floor between us after Irena joined me at the table.

While I nibbled on my cookie and sipped my tea after it cooled, Irena asked, "How can I help?"

"The man who came into the shop yesterday..."

"I heard he had a grievous lapse in judgment and is in the hospital; well done, Gray Lady. The story going around about an out-of-town gang has the men who live on the streets particularly nervous, but I don't think that's all bad; they've gotten a little lax in their awareness of the potential dangers that surround them."

"What do you know about him?"

"There are some who assume he is the killer who has been murdering and mutilating the bodies of young women because years ago a young woman who was high on drugs crashed into his wife's car, and the wife died on the scene. I don't know who the killer is, but it isn't him, but he could be a strong arm for the killer and instrumental in kidnapping the women. It's actually tragic because I understand he was a brilliant, kind man, but the alcohol and drugs fried his brain cells, and his rage has obliterated his impulse control and compassion. Have another cookie."

After a loud, nearby crack and a boom, the room seemed darker.

"Did the lights dim?" I asked.

"We lost electricity; it sounded like a transformer to me, so we may be without power for a while. I know you won't need it, but I'm going to light a candle for me; you'll enjoy the fragrance."

"How do you know so much?"

"Gray Lady, I'm just like the men who live in the street; I've been here a long time because I carry my own burden of despair. I have a small apartment over my shop, and I never have any customers, which suits me just fine." Her chuckle was hollow. "Can you imagine someone from the suburbs coming to our part of the city for a candle they could get at one of the more upscale shops close to them or any of the street dwellers being interested in a sandalwood candle? My saving grace is Brutus."

Brutus raised his head and grinned when she mentioned his name.

"Chopra orders groceries for me; the only time I leave the shop is once a week when I pick them up at his store."

"How do you know about the murders of young women?" I asked. "It's been only recently that the investigators have been able to connect them."

"Street life differs from what you've experienced, Gray Lady. We know and hear everything, but no one wants to call attention to himself, or in my case, herself." Irena-blob sipped her tea.

I glanced at Palace Guard; he put his index finger over his lips.

I stared at my cup. *I need to keep my mouth shut, so Irena can talk.*

Irena sighed. "There is a woman in the middle store. I'd tell you to be careful, but it would be more helpful if I tell you to expect an ambush. More tea? Another cookie?"

I smiled and shook my head.

Irena rose and disappeared, then I listened to footsteps at the rear of the shop as they went up wooden stairs that creaked with each step. While I sat with Palace Guard and Brutus, I listened as the assault of the wind and rain slowed then stopped; birds joyfully sang outside the window. *The storm is over.*

When she returned, Irena said, "You're different, Gray Lady; I don't feel any judgment from you."

She placed a photo on the table in front of me. Palace Guard peered at it then stared at Irena.

"I know you can't see this, Gray Lady; maybe that's why I'm showing this to you. She was my baby, and she was stolen from me a long time ago when she was fifteen months old. I've heard she married a fine man and has two beautiful children. She's been trying to find me, but...I'm too lost."

I stroked the picture I could not see, and Palace Guard smiled.

The room lightened briefly. Irena said, "The lights flickered and the rain's stopped; our power may be restored soon. Shall I go with you to your office?"

I shook my head. "What is her name?"

"Margaret; they call her Peggy."

"Beautiful name." I rose. "Thank you for the tea, cookies, and shelter."

"Anytime, Gray Lady; it's been a long time since I felt useful."

On impulse, I hugged her; she immediately stiffened then relaxed and returned my hug.

As Palace Guard helped me maneuver the puddles on our way back to the office, I heard Larry through my earbud.

"I found Wiley; he's been working on an escalator since early this morning; one of the hospital maintenance workers was assigned to watch him in case he fell down the shaft and broke his fool neck, which is a direct quote from the maintenance guy, who thinks his time is being wasted while he watches someone else work. I'm going back to the office unless there's something else I can do."

"We've got the rest of it covered; thanks for checking on Wiley," Heather said.

I exhaled. "Larry's headed back this way."

I frowned as we reached the alley. "If I'm outside, he'll know I've been out all this time and blame himself for not unlocking the office before he left."

When we reached the back door, I pulled out my phone from a zippered pouch inside my backpack and called Julie.

"Is everything okay, Chief? I'm just asking because you're calling me using your phone, not the GBI one."

"Yes, but you can't tell anyone I've called you; I'm locked out of the office, but I don't want Larry to know."

"I understand completely; there's a tattered piece of cardboard under the large garbage bin in the alley, and under the cardboard is a spare key."

"Can I keep it for a few days, so I can claim I had a spare key?" I asked.

"Absolutely. I have a second spare key hidden too, so if you or I are locked out, we'll still have a way to get inside. Did the bad storm blow through there too? We've got branches down that we'll have to pick up. Henry's sulking in his room because I made him come inside."

"Thank you, Julie; I appreciate you."

"Anytime, Chief."

I rolled away the large bin from its spot, and Palace Guard pointed to the cardboard. After I slid it aside, he pointed to the key. I put the cardboard on the ground and pushed the bin back until Palace Guard held up his hand. He helped me find the lock on the back door, and we went inside.

Paul said through my earbud. "I heard a call for the crash team on Evan Gardner's floor; I'm headed to the lobby."

After a few minutes, Paul continued, "I overheard two nurses talking; there's been a lot of activity on the hallway where Evan

Gardner's room is, and one of them said the police are headed your way, Heather. Do you know what's going on?"

"I will in a second. I know one of the officers who just came out of the one elevator that's been working today."

"I'm almost at the office; do I need to return?" Larry asked.

"I can't imagine why you'd want to leave Chief alone any longer than necessary," Heather said.

Ouch. She went for the throat with that one.

I felt my coat. "It's not wet; that's good, but it's cold. I'll put it in my office, so it can have a chance to warm up a bit. Do we have lights?"

Palace Guard shook his head then guided me to my office. After I draped my coat over my chair, he guided me to the light switch. I flipped it, and he shook his head, so I returned it to its original position.

"Are my boots wet?" I asked as he guided me to the table in the meeting room. Palace Guard peered at my feet then shook his head.

I sat at the table while we waited for Larry. "I should have realized it was strange that there was a candle shop in the area. How well could Irena see into the killer's apartment across the street from hers? I didn't want to ask her."

Palace Guard held his hands over his eyes.

"The windows are covered?" I asked.

Palace Guard nodded.

"That makes sense; I didn't think she would have kept quiet about the murders if she had witnessed them."

When I heard Larry's key in the front door, I jumped up. Palace Guard corrected my path a few times as I rushed to greet him.

Larry flung open the door and grabbed me. "On my way back, I realized I forgot to ask you if you had a key, so I drove like Heather to get back; I'm so glad you did."

He held my face with two hands as he kissed me and kicked the door closed behind him. "Can I fix you a cup of hot tea, sweetie? Are you okay? Have you been sitting in the dark all this time?"

I shrugged and rolled my eye.

He chuckled as we walked together to the meeting room. "I just realized how goofy that question was."

After he guided me to my chair, he strolled to the doorway. "I'll see if the lights work."

He flipped the switch, and the room brightened. "That's good; they do. I don't know how I thought I was going to make you a cup of hot tea with no electricity. I need to slow down and let my brain cells catch up with me."

"Hot tap water would have been fine," I said.

"I would have thought of that, eventually."

I snorted. "Not before I..."

Heather interrupted my potentially witty reply. "The medical crash team is attempting to resuscitate Evan Gardner. A nurse's aide found him not breathing and with no pulse and called for the crash team then started CPR. Details are a little hazy, but I think they've been working on him for at least thirty minutes. I'm trying to find out if he had any visitors."

"I'm in the lobby where I can watch the exit for the stairs and the elevator," Paul said.

"Perfect," Heather said.

"Heather, your GBI agent is at the stairwell and service elevator at the back of the hospital near the delivery dock," Larry said.

"Thank you," she said. "I'll check with the hospital security supervisor to help review the past two hours of recordings from the security cameras."

I waited a few minutes, but no one else spoke. "Honey, isn't it too late to see anyone leaving the hospital?"

Larry set my cup of tea on the table in front of me. "Paul and the GBI agent would have moved into position as soon as they heard the call for the crash team. Heather has never led a team in the field because she's used to working undercover solo, but I'm certain she leads the team that develops her electronic gadgets; she'll be fine."

After my tea cooled, I sipped it.

As I finished my tea, Larry asked, "Do you want any more tea? I'm thinking about making a pot of coffee."

Heather spoke before I could answer. "We've been through all the tapes, and the security supervisor is livid. We discovered that most of the volunteers are using the delivery door to enter and leave the hospital. They've managed to gain parking access to the employee lot in the back of the hospital. The security supervisor wants all of them fired; no one had the nerve to remind him they were volunteers. They'll definitely lose their parking privileges and will have to take their chances in one of the visitors' lots; the security supervisor told me I was welcome to join him at the employee parking lot in the morning because their drama will be entertaining. I told him I'd consider it. Normally, we'd have to wait for the investigator's report for the cause of death, but one of the docs, who is an old friend of mine, told me she'd volunteer to assist the medical officer and give me a call as soon as the exam was completed. Do you want to talk to the GBI agent, Paul? I'll wait for you to pick me up at the entrance."

"Heather, I'll let GBI know you're releasing their agent after he and Paul debrief," Larry said.

"I won't be long, then we can stop somewhere and pick up lunch," Paul said.

While the coffee machine gurgled as it heated up the water, Larry brewed the cup of tea for me then called the GBI leader.

After he hung up, I said, "Paul and Heather are perfect for the Gray Flanagan Agency with you as the overall leader, but not as a full-time, hands-on lead, so you can keep your fulltime GBI job."

"What are you thinking, sweetie?"

"We need Julie back in the office, so I don't have to hang out here all the time and be bored except when the phone system terrorizes me."

"As soon as we find the killer, I don't see why we couldn't do that, but how are you going to get around? Hire a chauffeur?" Larry poured himself a cup of coffee.

I furrowed my brow. "It's an option; do you think Lucy and Spike could get used to riding around in a limo?"

Palace Guard grinned, and Larry laughed. "Sure."

I glared at them. "Was that sarcasm? We might enjoy it; you don't know."

Paul saved Larry from saying something that would have irritated me even more. "I talked to Wiley for a few minutes; he's willing to help us. He expects to be back at his shop around two, so he can clean his equipment in preparation for his Monday client. What do you think about going with me, Larry? Heather said if Chief wants to go back to her house, she'd take your car, and I could drop you off later."

"I'd like to go with you, Paul; Heather's right about my car: it's known in the neighborhood, and so am I. If you drop me off a few blocks away, nobody will bother me."

"We should be at the office in thirty minutes," Paul said.

After they arrived, Heather put the drink caddy that held four large cups with condensation streaming down their sides on the meeting room table, and Paul set the two large, brown grocery sacks and a smaller white sack next to them. When Heather turned the large sacks onto their sides and ripped them open, the tantalizing aromas of warm corn tortillas and chips, green chilies, chili powder, cumin, garlic, and onion, and the heady tang of seared, marinated meat swirled around the room.

"Mmm. I need a napkin," I said.

Paul chuckled. "Can you imagine the will power it took to not pull over and chow down before we got here?"

"I don't know." Larry peered into the white sack. "Seems like there might be fewer tortilla chips in here than I expected for a bag this size."

"Don't worry about it; besides, it's Paul's fault: he drives too slow," Heather growled. "Let's eat."

While we ate, Paul said, "The GBI agent noticed the volunteers and snapped photos of them as they approached the exit door when they looked so furtive. He'll send them to me after his lead reviews them."

"The killer would look arrogant, not furtive," I said.

"Good point." Larry picked up his phone then stepped outside.

When he returned, he said, "It's getting colder out there; I called the team lead, and he will scan through the photos for anyone that doesn't look suspicious then send what they have to me while his team scours the pictures."

Larry refilled his cup with hot coffee. "Want some coffee for the road, Paul?"

When Paul nodded, Larry filled a cup for him while Paul finished eating his taco.

"Those really hit the spot."

"We may get more rain this afternoon," Larry said as they left.

Heather wrapped up the leftovers and put them into the small refrigerator. "If I make some Spanish rice when we get home, we can warm up the tacos for our supper tonight if no one minds warm lettuce."

I smiled. "If we give Larry a beer, sweet tea, or coffee, he'll eat whatever's in front of him."

"Good strategy, Calico."

I jumped when Larry spoke in my ear, and Heather snorted. "Callie, Justin sent me a text. Tonya wants you to call her."

After Heather wiped down the table and hauled out our trash to the dumpster in the back, she said, "I would have thought you'd be used to your earbuds by now."

"I'm used to hearing you and Paul, but for some reason, I'm startled every time Larry speaks. Maybe it's because if he can talk inside my head, he can also hear what I'm thinking."

"I can certainly understand how that would be scary for Larry, but I don't see why it would be scary for you," Heather said. "Call Tonya."

I called Tonya then held my breath as the phone range.

"I hope she picks up," I mumbled.

"Put your phone on speakerphone. I'm certain she will," Heather said.

When Tonya answered, she said, "You have reached a random number with voice mail, beep."

I giggled, and Tonya said, "I don't think robots giggle; you need to up your game, Gray Lady."

"I would have, except I have you on speakerphone, and Heather's with me."

"Do we like Heather?" Tonya asked.

"She's not very normal, so we like her a lot."

"I guess you called because you know I have something to tell you. Do you want the long story or the short story?" Tonya asked.

Heather-blob began pacing.

"Oh, I don't know." I sat at the table. "What do you want, Heather?"

"Short story," Heather growled.

"Everything's okay. Nice to talk to you," Tonya said.

I snickered, Palace Guard smirked, and Heather laughed as she relaxed and sat next to me.

"You two set me up, didn't you?" Heather asked.

I shrugged. "It was almost a shame how easy it was: you were such a willing target."

"You passed the test, Heather; normal people would have walked out," Tonya said.

"Tell," I said.

"Mom's been contacting all the parents she can find with daughters who have physical or mental deficits. A mother called Mom late last night because her daughter, who has a slight limp from a fall a few months ago, went for a walk yesterday morning and didn't come home. The mom didn't want to call the police because she's in the middle of a particularly nasty divorce, and she's afraid her husband would claim her daughter had run away and would convince a judge he should have full custody of the child. Mom was up all night with the mother on the phone until the mother received a call an hour ago from a woman who said she owned a candle shop. The shop owner told the mother the girl was safe in her shop and wanted to come home."

"Candle shop?" I asked.

"Right; after the woman and her daughter were home, the daughter took a shower then promptly went to bed. She told her mother that her special friend, her guide, was going to send his most dependable man to bring her to him so they could talk privately without being overheard. The guide told her to go to a diner and wait for the man, but she shouldn't be afraid if he seemed a little rough because that was just a façade. The man would mention a code word..."

"Eighteen," I said.

"Wow, how'd you know, Gray Lady?" Tonya asked.

"Trade secret," I said automatically.

"Gotcha. Anyway, the girl waited until almost closing at the diner. When she realized the staff was talking about calling the police because they thought she might be a runaway, she left and hid in the parking lot behind a bar that was still open."

"Behind a bar?" Heather asked.

"I forgot to tell you she's only fifteen, which evidently explains why her brain is not fully developed," Tonya said. "She said a nice old man who smelled kind of bad and had trouble standing told her if she had run away, she'd picked the worst possible spot to spend the night. He told her to find the candle shop a few blocks away and hide behind the dumpster because she'd be safe, and the wind wouldn't blow as bad as it did in the almost empty parking lot."

"The kindly drunk must have been an angel in disguise," Heather said. "I can't believe how lucky she was."

"I know; I still shudder at what could have happened," Tonya said. "The girl spent the night behind the dumpster, but I'm sure she was too scared to sleep. Right after lunch, the candle lady came out to throw away trash and found her. She took the girl into her shop and made the girl a bowl of oatmeal before she called the girl's mother. When the mother picked up her daughter, the candle lady told the woman to call the Gray Lady. Of course, the mother had no idea what the candle lady was talking about, so she called Mom."

"Why did she call your mom?" I asked.

"This is a part you can't repeat: Remember that my hearing aids are paired with Mom's phone, and it's easier to not have to fiddle with turning them on and off, so I don't. A little more background for you: Mom has always been proud of her beautiful brown hair, especially when all her friends began turning gray."

"Got it," I said.

"Good, I think Mom has more gray than she realizes because the mother talked about how grateful she was when she heard about the Gray Lady who was trying to find missing girls, so she knew to get in touch with Mom, who had called all the mothers. Mom didn't even blink."

"Oh, no." I snickered. "I hope Martha doesn't realize the mother called her the Gray Lady."

"So do I, at least not for a few years, then she can look back and laugh, or Justin will be transferred somewhere else, and she'll have calmed down before I see her again. Do you know the candle lady, Gray Lady?"

"If I didn't, I guess I do now," I said.

Tonya giggled. "You forget I can interpret what you say; your secret's safe with me as long as Heather isn't a cop, then we'll deny everything."

"Tonya, I hear echoes of déjà vu when I listen to you," Heather said.

"I'm flattered, so Heather's a cop, and we still like her?" Tonya asked.

"She's a retired cop..."

"I'm not retired," Heather grumbled. "I left a promising career with the police force to work for the Gray Flanagan Agency, so I could be irritated every day."

"You're right, Gray Lady; we like her," Tonya said. "I have to go because Kiki's getting restless, and my shoulder is getting pretty warm from dragon breath. Before you ask, I'll text the address of the diner to your real phone, in case you want to check it out. I'll see you first."

"I'll hear you coming." We giggled as we hung up, then my phone that was in my backpack buzzed a text.

Heather laughed. "That's the strangest goodbye I've ever heard, but I do have a question: dragon breath?"

"I must have forgotten to tell you that Kiki is Tonya's tiny, imaginary dragon, and she has a bit of a fiery temper."

"I'll have to meet Tonya sometime; do you think I'll be able to see Kiki?"

I shrugged and pulled out my phone.

After Heather and I listened to the text, she said, "I looked up the diner address on my phone. It's about four blocks north of the bakery."

"Ready for a brisk walk?" I asked. "It will be quicker than driving the car."

"I'm a little worried about the weather. Let's get the car and drive to the diner; you can make friends while I snoop around. Wear your eyepatch and take your jo. I'm out of the Gray Lady understudy business; it's too hard. Do you have an eyepatch in your backpack, or do you want to wear your black one?"

I pulled out an eyepatch from my backpack and put it on. "Ahh, much better."

"I'll put your black sparkly one in your backpack. Are we going out the front or back?"

"Let's go out the front door; I'll give you the key, and you can lock up, so Gary knows we're going home."

As she locked the door, Heather asked, "How can you be so sure Gary's watching you? Wouldn't he just be a blob, just like everyone else?"

"He should be, but he isn't. I have no idea why I can see Gary, but not you or Paul."

As we walked to Larry's clunker of a car, Heather's phone rang.

When I stopped, she said, "Keep walking."

She answered then listened for a few minutes. "Who would know that besides a medical professional?"

Heather listened then said, "You'd be an amazing detective, thanks."

Chapter Seventeen

After we reached the car, Heather started the engine; Palace Guard and I fastened then securely tightened our seatbelts.

"While his assistants moved Gardner's body to the room where the medical examiner was preparing for his investigation of the cause of death, my brilliant doctor friend returned to Evan Gardner's room and snooped around a bit. The room hadn't been touched yet for cleaning. She found two syringes and a vial in the bed. The first syringe was an empty, prefilled paralytic, the second one had a residual fluid in it, and the vial marked potassium chloride was empty. She explained that Evan Gardner's death would have been tortuous. The dose of paralytic would have left him paralyzed but awake; the potassium chloride would have caused a heart attack, and he would have felt the crushing pain and would have been completely helpless and unable to move, breathe, or call out for help as he died. Sounds sloppy, doesn't it? I think the killer did it on purpose to make sure his brutality was not overlooked."

I shuddered; Heather stomped on the accelerator, and my head slammed against the backrest. *This is one of those times when it is a blessing to not be able to see.*

When she spun into the parking lot and slammed on the brakes, I lurched forward. My seatbelt caught me in its viselike grip. *At least I didn't go through the windshield.*

I glanced back at Palace Guard, and his face was pale. He drew his finger across his forehead as he mimed wiping away sweat in relief, and I nodded.

"It's too late for lunch and too early for supper. Why are we going into the diner other than to interrogate the servers?" I asked.

"That's your job, Chief. You tell me."

As we walked along the gravel and dirt path to the door, I said, "Afternoon break; do you suppose they have pie?"

"I would think any diner worth its weight in grease would have pie," Heather said.

When we went inside, the roar of conversation stopped while Heather led me and Palace Guard to a table. After we sat down, the conversations resumed.

Heather said, "I expected it to be empty, but the diner's almost full; most of the customers are construction workers that just got off work, and they're eating meals. I thought we might be obvious because we'd be the only ones here; I think we're the only ones without dirt under our fingernails."

"That makes us sound like sissies," I said.

"No kidding; Paul and Larry would blend right in. We may have to fight our way out, except I'm joking, Chief. After you take down the first guy, the rest of them will back off, so give them a chance to run away."

I snickered. "What are you going to do?"

"I'll stand on the sidelines and taunt them."

A large blob headed toward us. "I brought you girls coffee; it's cold outside," the woman said. "You're the Gray Lady, aren't you?

Pleased to make your acquaintance. Y'all here for cobbler? Peach or blueberry?"

"Nice to meet you too." I smiled.

"We're definitely here for cobbler," Heather said as the woman poured two cups of coffee. "Peach: warmed and with ice cream for me."

"What about you, Gray Lady?"

"Blueberry, and the same."

"It don't come no other way," the woman cackled as she left to place our order.

"How did she know I'm the Gray Lady?" I whispered.

Heather chuckled. "Eyepatch, jo, and what other young woman and her friend would come in here with this crowd of thugs and not be terrified?"

"A fifteen-year-old girl whose brain is not fully developed," we said in unison.

"Do you suppose she had a friend with her, but her friend bailed?" Heather asked.

"We need to know." I pulled out my phone and set it on the table. "Send a text to Tonya: Did the fifteen-year-old go to the diner with a friend?"

When my phone buzzed, Heather said, "I thought your phone read your texts to you."

"It does, but I have it on silent; read it for me."

Heather spun my phone toward her. "She'll check."

When our server brought our cobbler and placed our bowls in front of us, she asked, "Are you here about that girl from yesterday who showed up with a so-called friend?"

"Sure are." I took a bite of hot cobbler and ice cream and burned my tongue and froze the roof of my mouth. "Mmm. This is heavenly."

"It is, isn't it? The friend didn't even sit down; she was what we call mean-spirited and left after she told the girl she wanted to meet the guide not a bunch of low-lifes. The girl told me she was waiting for a friend, but when it was our closing time, and she was still here, the cook asked me to call the police, so we wouldn't be abandoning her. I told her I would call her mom for her, but she said she needed to hurry home and ran out without giving me a chance to stop her. Is she okay?"

"She spent the night behind the candle shop, and the owner called the girl's mom this morning, so she's at home and fine."

"I'll let Cook know; neither one of us slept last night. I almost came back down here at two in the morning to look for her, but I had my grandbabies and couldn't leave them. My daughter-in-law works nights, so I help her out; she and the two babies have been staying with me since my son who is in the military went overseas. I can't tell you how proud I am of my son and his wife."

"What do the grandbabies call you?"

"The older one is three; he calls me Grammie; isn't that cute?"

I smiled. "It really is; sounds like he's a smart boy."

"He is; thanks for listening to me, Gray Lady."

The server growled as she rushed away, "Don't you wave that cup at me again, bud, or you'll be wearing your coffee out on the sidewalk, and that cup will be where the moon don't shine."

My phone buzzed with a text, and Heather read it to me. "It's from Tonya. The girl claims she was alone, but her mom thinks she's not telling the truth."

"Let Tonya know that she isn't, but not to share that with anyone."

"Why not?" Heather asked as she sent the quick text.

"We have enough information for our purposes and don't need to volunteer anything that will embarrass the girl or push her into becoming defensive with her mother."

"Ready to go?"

"Be sure to get a receipt for Julie," I said.

"I'm not used to an expense account, but I'll learn," Heather said as we hurried to Larry's car.

"Do you hear those rumbles? I'm glad we didn't run here after all."

After we were buckled in, Heather asked, "Where to?"

"Let's cruise past the vacant stores to see if we can spot any activity."

Heather circled the block and crept past the abandoned building. "The middle one?"

After I nodded, she said, "I can't even tell what type of store it was; the one on the corner may have taxidermy painted on the window, but the letters have faded. The number over the front door is 25894. I'll look up the address to see if I can find the last owner of the building. Where to now?"

"The office, I suppose; we know more, but I'm not sure how close we're getting to knowing who the killer is."

"You don't think it's Wiley at all, do you?" Heather asked.

I glanced at Palace Guard, and he shook his head.

"No, we don't."

Heather tore through traffic like she was at the wheel of a supersonic jet. When she stopped a block from the office, I sighed with relief.

"What's wrong?" Heather asked.

"It just occurred to me we've missed something basic," I said.

Palace Guard's eyes widened.

I shrugged. *I kind of wonder how I'm going to get out of this too.*

"We can talk at the office."

Palace Guard rolled his eyes, and I bit my lip.

He knows I panicked and said the first thing that popped into my head because I was relieved we'd arrived in one piece.

As we hurried to the alley so we could use the back door to go inside, I furrowed my brow.

Quick: what are the basics?

After I gave Heather the key and we were inside, she said, "I'll make hot tea for us. What did we miss?"

"Where was Becky kidnapped?"

"I don't think we know," Heather said slowly. "I guess somewhere between her house and the diner where she was supposed to meet a friend?"

"We know Bob was home when she left because he said that she'd left early and asked him to get the journals to Julie; so where is her car?"

"Nobody has said anything about finding her car," Heather said. "Where do you suppose Bob is? I'd like to take a peek in their garage to see if her car is there and maybe snoop around the house a bit without having to explain anything."

I pressed the button on my jo. "Call my Maggie phone when no one else is around."

Palace Guard narrowed his eyes and pointed to Heather.

"Palace Guard is right: I'm a little suspicious; why don't you want Larry to know you're talking to Paul, Chief?" Heather asked.

"You were the one who said you didn't want to have to explain anything. Larry is suspicious of everything I do."

"For good reason," Heather muttered as my phone rang.

"What's up, Chief? I stepped out to my car to get something that I'll figure out later what it is."

"You're on speaker phone; Heather's here. She wants to check out Becky's car, which we assume is in their garage, and she'd also like to check the house unaccompanied. We're going back to the basics to see if we missed something."

"I don't think anyone has given Becky's car a thought because Bob didn't report it missing, so how did Becky plan to get to the diner to meet her friend? Am I two steps behind?"

"Maybe one," Heather said.

"I'm improving; my usual is three steps behind Chief. Bob's at Noah's office; they're going over a list of Becky's friends for the investigators to interview. Heather, if you need him out of the way for maybe an hour, you're safe. Any more than that, let me know because I have a few ideas to discuss with Noah and Bob just as soon as I think of them."

"Perfect," Heather said. "Chief will let you know."

"Paul, you might still have your antacid pills in the glove box," I said.

Paul chuckled. "I'll have to check; thanks, Chief."

After he hung up, I asked, "Am I going with you?"

"No, you stay here; I'll text you if I need more time."

"Okay, but text me if you need Palace Guard. He's a great asset when there's trouble."

"Thanks for the reminder." Heather put on her jacket then grabbed her backpack and left.

While I stood at the window and watched for any movement at the building across the street, my phone rang. *Tonya's calling me?*

I smiled as I answered. "Your call is very important to us..."

Tonya giggled. "I wished I'd thought of it before you did; that was absolutely priceless. I've got something for you, but I don't know how useful it is. Fred called me; remember Fred?"

"Vanessa's friend?"

"Yes, he told me that Vanessa was worried about her mother because her mother wasn't sleeping very well and had even put a deadbolt lock on her bedroom door so she could have some privacy. Evidently, Vanessa's parents didn't sleep in the same room. Anyway, Vanessa sneaked into her mother's room and found a hidden diary and gave it to Fred for safekeeping; she told him she'd read it later. Vanessa and Fred had a falling out, and he'd forgotten about the diary until now. I asked him if he would take it to the GBI office, and he said he was afraid to. I told him the Gray Lady's husband, Agent Ewing, could meet him there, and he said he could give the diary to the Gray Lady's husband."

"Cool, can Larry call or text him directly to coordinate meeting him at the office?"

"I asked him if I could give his number to Agent Ewing, and he said it would be okay."

"Excellent; I'll let Larry know what's going on."

"I'll text you the number. See you before you see me."

Tonya hung up while I said, "No you won't..."

She beat me again.

I tapped my ear. "Tonya called me. Vanessa's former boyfriend has a diary that Vanessa took from Becky's bedroom. Fred agreed to give the diary to Agent Ewing at the GBI office. Tonya will text me Fred's number, and I'll get it to you to coordinate with Fred, Larry."

"Do we know what's in the diary?" Larry asked.

"No, Fred said Vanessa hadn't read it, and he didn't either."

"Text me the number after you get it."

I tapped my ear twice to stop transmitting.

"I wonder how long it will be before Larry realizes I just admitted to answering my phone."

Palace Guard smiled.

My phone buzzed with a text, and I changed the setting from silent, so I could hear it.

"Text from Larry: You are so busted, Callie."

I laughed, and Palace Guard grinned.

When I received the text from Tonya, I said, "Forward the text to Larry."

I changed the setting back to silent on my phone and returned to watching the building across the street.

When the office phone rang, I groaned, "Oh, brother, it's my nemesis. I'll just let it ring."

Palace Guard scowled as he pointed to the door to the reception area.

I wrinkled my nose at him. "Fine, but you have to help me."

I sat at Julie's desk, and Palace Guard pointed to the phone; I took in a breath, picked up the receiver, and answered in my best imitation of a bored temporary clerk.

"Gray Flanagan Agency. How can we help you?" I picked up a pen and loudly tapped it on Julie's note pad she kept by the side of the phone.

"Is this Julie?" a man asked. *The voice reminds me of Bob, except it's muffled.*

"Julie? Oh, you mean Mrs. Vargas? She isn't in the office today. Can I take a message?"

"Is Gray Lady there?"

I exhaled to share the irritation that a temp would have at being interrupted from scrolling on her phone. "She's in a staff meeting. Do you want to leave a message or make an appointment?"

"No message; I'll call back later."

"Suit yourself." I hung up.

"I didn't get the feeling he was a prospective client, did you?"

Palace Guard shook his head.

I furrowed my brow. "He asked for Julie and kind of sounded like Bob."

I pushed the button on my jo. "We just got a call at the office. The man kind of sounded like Bob, but he asked if I was Julie then asked to speak to the Gray Lady. Is Bob still with Noah?"

A few minutes after I returned to the meeting room to stare out the window, my phone buzzed a text from Paul.

"Bob's in Noah's office; Noah had a quick conference call to attend but will be back in his office in a few minutes. Do you need me there?"

I pushed on the button. "No, it just seemed odd. I'll check on Julie."

I called Julie.

"Hey, there. How's it going?" Julie asked when she answered.

I smiled. *Julie was careful not to mention a name. Paul was right: we all underestimate her.*

"I'm at the office, and it's a little boring, so I called to check up on you."

"Just a second; let me go into the house. It's getting a little nippy out here."

After I heard the door close, Julie said, "Bob called here earlier and asked me if I was going into work today. I told him Henry had a doctor's appointment, so if I did, it wouldn't be until later, but I was trying to find a temp to cover the phones. Was that okay? It seemed like such an odd question at the time."

"That was perfect. Are you trying to get a temp?" I asked.

"No, but I can if you like."

"No, anyone who calls can leave a message; we might want to think about it, but right now I don't think any of us has the time to train a temp."

Julie continued, "Bob told me he'd thought about dropping by the house to keep Henry company, so he was glad he called first. After we hung up, I asked Henry how well he knew Bob, and he told me he's only met Bob that one time Bob sat with him on my back porch."

After we hung up, I pushed the button on my jo. "All's well with Julie."

Paul texted, "Thanks."

"I'm at the Collins' house; Becky's purse is in the garage next to her car. She was kidnapped before she left her house," Heather's voice echoed in my head, courtesy of the earbud. "I'm headed back to the office."

I sat at the table and finished my cup of tea that was almost cold. "I wonder if Gary's figured out we use the back door these days?"

Palace Guard smirked and nodded.

"I think so too. Mr. Chopra told us Evan Gardner was staying at the middle store of the three vacant ones near the bakery, and Gardner's street name was Butch because his boss was Butcher. I'd like to see if Gardner left anything there that might tell us who the Butcher is. It's not that far away, and we'd be back before anyone missed us, but do we go out the front door or the back door? Seems like we could run if we went out the back door because we'd be less likely to attract any attention from bystanders, but Gary might see us."

I put on my warm coat. "Gary couldn't keep up with us though, could he? Back door?"

Palace Guard nodded.

I frowned. "I don't think Heather returned my door key."

Palace Guard pointed to the table then guided me to the key next to Heather's usual spot; I stuck the key into my jean's small pocket.

"Oh, good; I don't want to be locked out again."

After we were outside, I locked the door, then Palace Guard and I raced to the end of the alley.

I thought I heard a man yell, "Hey!" as we reached the corner; Palace Guard made an abrupt left turn to head toward an alley that would come out close to the diner.

We're not taking any of our usual routes. If that was Gary, he'd have to guess where we were going.

The air was nippy and damp; the wind was brisk, and the alley smelled of rotten garbage and sour urine, but I was exhilarated as I pushed to pass Palace Guard while he stayed a half step in front of me.

When we slowed, then stopped at the street across from the diner, I giggled, and Palace Guard grinned.

"That really felt good; it's been ages since we've had a good run."

We hurried to the alley behind the vacant buildings. Palace Guard pointed to a dumpster, and I stood next to it where I wouldn't be seen from the street; he disappeared.

His face was grave when he returned and pointed at me; after he put his hand over his mouth, he crossed his wrists.

"A woman gagged and tied? Is it Becky?"

He nodded then mashed his face together with his fingers.

"Oh, was she beaten and not recognizable?"

Palace Guard's face saddened as he nodded.

"How do I get in?"

He led me to a window and pointed to my jo.

"Break in? How can I do that?"

He pointed at my jo then clasped his hands together; after I copied him with my hands gripped around my jo, he raised his hands over his head then forcefully brought his hands in front of him.

"Got it." I took my position in front of the window. *He'll help me.*

"I can do this," I growled.

I raised my jo with the tip pointed at the window then gritted my teeth as I carried through hitting the window with my jo with all the strength I could muster. I whooped at the loud crash of breaking glass then covered my mouth. *Rookie move.*

I used my jo to clear the window of shards of glass then took off my coat and put it over the sill. *That was really noisy; maybe the neighborhood is deaf to the sound of breaking glass.*

After I climbed inside the building and pulled in my coat, the rank odor of excrement and the disgustingly sharp smell of roach droppings made my eye water, and I almost gagged. As Palace Guard led me through the room to a dark hallway, I shuddered as squeaks and scratching sounds surrounded us.

Palace Guard led me into a room that was dimly lit from small streams of light from a boarded-up window. He pointed to a woman-blob who lay in the middle of the bare room in a wide pool of blood, and the distinct, potent smell of iron overwhelmed the other nauseating odors. When the woman banged her bound feet on the floor, I hurried to her.

I found the tape across her mouth, then as I slowly peeled it off, she whimpered.

"I'm so sorry; I'm so sorry," I repeated.

I pushed the button on my jo to record, then said as calmly as I could, "I'm in the middle building in the row of vacant buildings. I found a woman gagged and bound; she's been beaten and cut."

The woman gasped for air, and I pulled out my knife to cut the plastic cable ties that bound her ankles together. Palace Guard tapped on my shoulder and pointed to a corner.

"I have to hide in the shadows," I whispered. "Both of us have to be super quiet; someone may be coming in."

The woman became silent then nodded and tucked her head down to hide her face, and I moved away from her as the back door that led to the alley opened.

Palace Guard tapped on my shoulder and showed me the small rock in his hand, and I relaxed and nodded.

The glare of the bare light in the ceiling flooded the room when a blob flipped on the light switch.

"Well, well, if it isn't my lucky day: numbers nineteen and twenty right here together; I've got myself a double: I haven't had a double since I was sixteen. I'll never forget numbers three and four; good times: that high lasted for a full month."

When I stepped out of the shadows, I had my pistol in my right hand and my arm behind my back. "Thank goodness it's you, Bob. I expected Butcher."

He snorted. "You are so dense for someone who is supposed to be a legend. I'll be right with you as soon as I finish off number nineteen, so you can enjoy my technique as much as I do."

I glanced around the room. "The address here is 25896 Twenty-third Street, isn't it? You were Vanessa's guide, and she came here to meet you, didn't she?"

"Every breath she took taunted me."

When Becky moaned, the cruelty of Bob's chuckle startled me, and I bit my tongue; the sharp taste of blood in my mouth kept me from shivering.

"What happened to Evan Gardner?" I asked.

"Not that it's any of your business, but his usefulness ran out, just like Becky's. She became a suspicious snoop and wouldn't take the hint that she was cruising toward the same fate as her meddling daughter."

Bob pulled out a large knife.

"What kind of knife is that?" I asked.

Bob snorted. "You know you're nuts? Who asks a talented genius these kinds of questions while he prepares for the kill? For your information, Miss Nosy Gray Lady, it's a custom-made hunting knife; I asked for a knife with a bone handle that could kill large animals. It's a beauty, isn't it?"

I heard sirens in the distance.

Bob turned his head at the sound then took a step closer to Becky. "Nice try, but the chat's over; I'll be done here and gone by the time they get here. I'll leave your husband a neatly carved nineteen and twenty. Relax and watch an expert at work."

Becky kicked his knee when he got close to her, and he roared; I heard the rock drop and pulled the trigger.

Bob toppled to the ground; Becky pushed his body away from her with her legs then sobbed.

I knelt on the floor next to her. "I'll cut off those ties from your hands."

"It's hard to talk." Becky spoke slowly. "I kicked his bad knee. I hope I broke it; he deserved pain when he died."

Larry and Paul burst through the door.

Larry snatched me up off the floor. "Sweetie, you better be okay."

I nodded. "Bob came to murder Becky."

Paul knelt next to Becky as Gary charged into the room.

"Why didn't you wait for me, Maggie?" Gary grumbled.

Heather pushed past the blobs who had rushed into the building.

"I'm taking you home, sweetie," Larry said. "Let's go, Heather; I'll drive."

Gary strode to Larry and gave him a slip of paper. "The owner of the candle shop gave me a note. It has the name Peggy and a phone number on it; she said Gray Lady would know what to do."

"The ambulance is here, Agent Ewing," a man near the doorway said.

When the paramedic reached Becky, Paul said, "Her face is swollen from being beaten; she's having a hard time seeing or talking, and she may have internal injuries. She has lacerations, but the killer went for pain and slow bleeding."

As Larry, Palace Guard, and I walked toward the door with Heather following us, Gary muttered, "This is absolutely the last time I try to save her."

"Good luck with that, Gary," Larry said.

Gary saluted Palace Guard. "I don't know how you keep up with her."

Palace Guard smiled as he returned the salute.

Heather and Palace Guard jumped into the backseat while Larry helped me into his clunker of a car. "We'll pick up Lucy and Spike at Julie's then tacos and beer on our way home. You owe me one entire weekend off, sweetie; no discussion."

"Oh, really? No discussion? Do you buy that, Heather?"

"He said tacos and beer, Chief; you're on your own."

• • • ● ● • ● ● • •

This is the end of Counted in Blood. If you enjoyed the Maggie series, leave a review with your favorite bookseller!

Are you ready for another series like Maggie? You have more Judith A. Barrett Series to enjoy!

Check Barrett Book Shop to find your next favorite Series!

BarrettBookShop.com

• • • ● ● • ● ● • •

SUBSCRIBE AND SAVE

Join the eNewsletter mailing list and become the first to know about exclusive book specials and read unpublished stories and exciting news!

SUBSCRIBE to her eNewsletter via website

judithabarrett.com/newsletter

ABOUT THE AUTHOR

Judith A. Barrett is a best-selling author of thrillers, mysteries, and romantic suspense novels known for dark twists and unforgettable characters. She lives on a Georgia farm with her husband, two dogs, and a flock of sassy chickens.

When she isn't writing, Judith is chatting with readers at arts and crafts festivals, busy with farm chores, or camping with her husband and dogs.

You keep reading; I'll keep writing!

Find all the Judith A. Barrett Books with exclusive deals at her online book shop: Barrett Book Shop.
BarrettBookShop.com

www.ingramcontent.com/pod-product-compliance
Lightning Source LLC
Chambersburg PA
CBHW050126030726
47505CB00007B/2056